The Crossroads

Of Time

Book One
of the
Orisha Series

by Rhonda Denise Johnson

Cover Art Theophilus Nii Nortey

Acknowledgements

Thanks goes to Jessica McKenzie for helping me understand the use of foreign words.

And more thanks goes to Kelly Branchal of Gatekeeper Press for her tireless editing skills.

Thanks as well to Theophilus Nortey of Ghana for his art work.

Chapter 1

"Go two blocks and turn right," said her GPS.

"Get a good education so you can get a good job," said her mother.

"Never date a man who can't give you his phone number. He might be married," said her best friend.

"Take the core classes first and then the electives," said her academic advisor.

Chloe shook her head. She had no taste for the blue pill, but everyone thought it was their business to try jamming it down her throat—even inanimate talking machines. She went three blocks and turned left. The machine adjusted to her new position. "Go one block and turn left."

"Oh, shut up."

Downtown Los Angeles didn't offer too many scenic routes, but she detected the smell of pizza that boasted of being made with New York City tap water wafting down Sixth Street—a street she wasn't supposed to be on. It wasn't on the itinerary mapped out by the global positioning satellite. Chloe savored the smell and didn't care. She crossed Broadway and hooked a left on Los Angeles. A Greyhound bus nearly sideswiped her on its way to its terminal.

Okay, time to pay attention. Look out for pedestrians. Look out for other cars. Look out for traffic lights, stop signs, and don't miss the turn-off. So much energy expended just to get to school. And the reward, her mother assured her, would be a job working for someone else.

Some ache inside told Chloe she was born for more. None of her advisors had a clue about what was going on inside her. Everyone wanted to play it safe. Whatever happened to the "Give me liberty or give me death" mentality? Chloe didn't know anyone like that. She knew only the common sense folks. She knew only this centrifugal directive away from her center—away from her dreams.

She turned on the radio. Maybe some old school would help her get to that center. Billy Paul startled her.

"This is your life you're living
And it's the only one you've
        got
Don't you think it's time you
        asked yourself for
        what?"

For what? For whom? She maneuvered her car to the turn-off for Cal State University. Chloe mused at all the students scurrying about campus. They were of all kinds. Some were mainstream-looking blacks and whites, Asians and Latinos. Some looked like they came from somewhere with a name she didn't know. And some sported dreadlocks. *Oh my God! They let you wear dreads here?* Maybe there's hope. She saw herself joining the stream, one among thousands in this surging crowd.

Her stomach lurched at the thought of joining any crowd, but she had no time to let it settle before she had to find a place to park. She found the visitors' parking lot, and then consulted a map for directions to the administration building.

This wasn't the tallest building on campus, but it was the most imposing, with its several offices sprawled out helter-skelter around a central courtyard. The offices stood aloof from one another. A strip of grass guarded the front of the building with an ugly iron fence to keep students from walking on it. Chloe wondered if that were why Adam and Eve were thrown out of the Garden of Eden, because they wouldn't stop walking on the grass.

She looked down the walkway at the other buildings in her line of vision. Outside the library, obvious professors approached the automatic doors as if they weren't there, fully expecting them to whisk silently to the side and let them—principal members of the campus elite—in without breaking their stride. But freshmen approached the doors hesitantly, expecting even automatic doors to challenge their entrance into such a hallowed edifice.

Chloe determined that she wouldn't act like a newbie, but would approach the chaos around her as if her presence was a matter of course. If she ever approached the library doors, she'd just keep walking.

She closed her eyes and saw herself in front of the doors. The power of her mind rendered her experience more corporeal than mere imagination could account for. How close did she have to be before the smoky glass panels shuttled apart? She thought each step would be *the* step. But it wasn't, so the next one would be.

Shuddering with dread, Chloe fought against panic. Surely, the doors would move before she bumped into them. She was walking at a pace that required that they not be there when she reached them. She couldn't stop or even slow down, for that would mark her as a freshman, and she was determined not to do that. How embarrassing that would be—a silly freshman crashing into doors.

But she wouldn't crash. She belonged here and the doors would move. Chloe planted her foot eighteen inches from the glass, shifted her weight and lifted her other foot in anticipation of her next step as the doors slid to either side without a sound. Purpose gone and mind without a vision of what lay beyond the doors of the library, Chloe could go no farther. She opened her eyes, surprised to find she was still standing in front of the administration building.

Had it been a dream? But she was awake. And she'd wanted to visualize herself facing the library doors, to enter a mental state of control in this environment where everything tilted out of control. Yet, here she stood in the real world, and she had to deal with it. Deadlines, cancelled classes, and the announcement of new courses droned from a surround sound public announcement system.

She entered the administration area. A tangled crowd of co-eds packed the open courtyard. Many of them were facing a row of windows. Others, like her, were trying to get through the courtyard to other offices and had to bogart their way through the lines facing the windows. If she hadn't known what she was doing there, she wouldn't have known what she was doing there.

After a few *excuse me's* and a couple of dirty looks, Chloe made it to the building where she was to turn in her registration application. The guy in front of her had his application in one hand. He held a sheaf of papers in his arms that was one false move away from spilling to the floor. It was an awkward sight. He looked at Chloe apologetically.

"This is a real paper tiger. They give us so much junk. I'll probably end up throwing most of this away anyhow, so I don't know for the life of me why I'm trying to hold on to it now. All this stuff could be online, but this school is stuck back in the twentieth century. Well, I guess carrying papers does give me a chance to meet people. I must look like a moron. . ."

"You look fine," Chloe lied.

"Oh yeah? Well you're kinda cute yourself. But you know, I like a woman I can have an intelligent conversation with. Can I have an intelligent conversation with you?"

"That depends on how intelligent you are."

"Oh, I'm pretty erudite. Though I guess you couldn't tell behind all these papers. By the way, my name is Ted—Ted Benson. That's short for Theodore. But no one calls me Theodore. Not even my mother. And you are . . ."

Chloe blinked; surprised that he'd actually stopped talking long enough to ask her a question. "Chloe Marshall."

"Chloe Benson."

"Look! I don't know you!"

"Calm down. I'm just teasing. Just being tongue-in-cheek. No need to have a cow. Isn't that what all the girls do anyway—put their first names with some guy's last name to see how it rings?"

"*Girl?* Chloe *Benson* will never ring. Trust me."

"Don't be so quick to rule that out."

"It's your turn at the desk." Chloe gestured with her head for him to turn around and move forward.

When he finished his business and passed her on her way to the desk, he had to say something. "Be seeing you around, Chloe."

She didn't want to say anything. She wanted him to just go away. But she didn't want him to see how easily he'd become a pest, because then he'd take every opportunity to rankle her nerves while he acted like the innocent victim of her preconceived ideas. Smiling, she tossed a "Sure" in his general direction, then strolled to the desk like everything was everything.

The lady behind the desk took Chloe's application and stamped her checklist to show she'd completed that step and was ready to go to the next one. She went through four: financial aid, transcripts, immunizations and student parking. Each one added at least three papers to her package. Fortunately, she'd come prepared with a folder to hold them.

She left student parking and headed for her car. It was raining, so she kept the windows up and turned on the radio. Then she had to stop for a minute because, again, the music startled her. This time, The Dramatics came on.

> "I want to go outside in the
> rain
> It may sound crazy"

It *did* sound crazy. Okay, it had only happened twice now—this thing with the radio. It couldn't mean anything, could it? Some spirit trying to speak to her through the radio? *Oh, come on.* But if it was trying to tell her something, then what was the message? There was no message. Nothing clear that meant anything to her. She could ignore it. What were the rules for the numinous? If it happens once, it's an accident. This was the second time, making it a coincidence. But if it happens a third time . . .

As she swung onto Wesley Avenue, Chloe saw the young kids and teens who thought they owned the sidewalk. Truth was, they owned nothing and didn't know anybody who owned anything. They lived in furnished apartments where their parents didn't even own the beds they slept in. Among the crowd of scantily clad girls, she saw Tonyeesha, her little sister's best friend. Underneath the massive weave, Tonyeesha Jenkins was a beautiful girl. Chloe wanted to stop the car, walk up to Tonyeesha and tell her she didn't need all that fake stuff and near bare body parts to be beautiful. But how could Chloe tell the girl this wasn't attractive when she was, in fact, attracting the boys who called themselves dogs? The boys who'd forgotten—or just didn't want to know—that they were men. To be men in this dystopia they called home would make them conscious of a pain few men could bear. Their lives were more palatable as dogs. Chloe drove on.

At home, she threw the folder full of papers, brochures, flyers and pamphlets from school onto the kitchen table with a promise to go through them. Then she turned on the Windows Media Player, kicked off her shoes, and began to sing and dance in her spacious living room. Spacious might not be the precise word. There wasn't a lot of space. She just hadn't put a couch in yet, so she could throw her hands up in the air, stepping and sliding without a care—as long as she steered clear of knocking her funny bone on the oak particle board computer desk her mother had given her as a high school graduation present. The woman had been so proud of her daughter. She'd just known that Chloe would go on to college and get a high-paying job with some big company. That's all education was about to her mother—not to gain knowledge, not to learn about the world or create something of Chloe's own, but simply to get a job.

Almost as an undercurrent to the music, she could hear her mother's voice chiding her for wasting time dancing. "Look at all those papers you say you're going to read tomorrow. Since when is tomorrow promised? You could die this very night."

Chloe brushed that thought aside with the realization that if she died that night then reading all those papers today wouldn't matter anyway. But the joy of movement and sound would stay with her until she could dance no more.

She paused, slid her bare foot across the rough carpet and made a perfect pivot. Through the open door of her bedroom, she could see her reflection in the mirror. She looked at the girl becoming a woman. It was the epitomic image of the distaff side of her family—mother, aunts, sister, and cousins—staring back at her with the same almond-shaped eyes. The same golden-brown cheeks that tied her to . . . whom? What? What responsibility came with sharing this skin? These bones? This blood?

Chloe shook her head at the thought that this somehow gave her family, or anyone, the right to decide what it meant to waste her time. They thought their dreams for her were so much bigger than her own were. But the dreams she had for herself were so much bigger than they could ever imagine. Only now, she was awake and couldn't recall the slightest image from her dream. It had no clear shape or location. She couldn't have told anyone what she dreamed of. She only knew that she had a dream.

Right on cue, The Montclairs came crooning out of her speakers singing, "Dreaming's out of season . . ."

Did the thought trigger the songs or was this just another coincidence? As the song purred on, Chloe wondered. The second time was the coincidence. This was the third time. This was deliberate. But deliberate by whom? What? Why? She shook her head. If this were a message from someone supernatural, it was unclear.

She didn't know its meaning, so she shook it out of her head and kept dancing. She thought she was dancing, but as the song played on, she felt her body move with a grace it never had before. Fluid like water. Flowing like cream. Her hands flowing. Her feet controlled by the melody of the song and not by her brain. Then she began to sing. But how? She'd never known the words to this song before. Yet, as she danced, the words came, so she danced on. The words came on. When the song ended, she slowed to serene stillness. *What was going on?* Something was going on and she hoped to find out soon.

Chapter 2

"Mama, I want to be an Egun." This Ayodele said to her mother, but really to the Egun themselves—those illustrious ancestors who had done more in life than just die.

In her quiet African village, she watched the Egungun festival swirling around her. Red and purple, yellow and green strips of fine cloth revolved around her brother Bamidele. Deep, hypnotic drums commanded his feet to move at the will of the drummer's hands. Ayodele wanted all this to be for her.

Bamidele made his own costume, adding a new layer of colorful cloth strips each year for the ancestors who had passed and for those about whom he had been told. It was now thick with the memory of five generations of their Egun. And Ayodele wanted to be an ancestor. She wanted her descendants to dance for her.

Dance, Bamidele.
Dance for me.
I am your ancestor.
I am your descendant.
I am all the Egun.

As he and others from their village danced, he moved close to her. Her father's great-uncle Baba Abioye brushed her cheek with the purple and blue hands of Bamidele's memory. Her desire soared. Still, her mother cautioned her.

"Ayodele, not everyone gets to be an ancestor. You must live this life before you worry about the afterlife."

Egungun drums swallowed the voice of caution. Bamidele trembled and began to dance violently. The drums no longer controlled his feet.

"Baba Abioye, is that you?" Ayodele wondered. "Do you want to dance, too?"

Ancestors. They never die. They never stopped whatever they were doing as long as someone living remembered their names.

The whir of Bamidele's black hands shimmered in the moonlight. They were hands. They were strips of cloth. They were ghosts leaving behind a trail of light. If she could see his face behind the Egungun mask, would she see him, or would she see the image of those who never die? Spirits possessed flesh for a moment, but their anode was the Orun Rere where they waited to receive their own bodies.

Ayodele was almost in a trance herself. She saw the *awo* of the Creator in everything around her. The dancers were bright. The essence of the spirits was bright around them. The Creator, Olodumare, commanded the moon to be a witness to the villagers' festival of reverence. It would tell the eternal story generation after generation from its lofty perch over the palm trees.

Ayodele heard a voice calling her name. It came from Bamidele, but that was not his voice.

"Ayodele."

She had never heard him before, but she knew this was Baba Abioye speaking to her.

"I know your desire. It will come with a price. There is much you must learn before joy comes home."

Never had an Egun spoken directly to her before. But then, she had never had such strength of desire before. This night had given energy to all the wistful thoughts in her life. Always she had to brush these thoughts aside to take care of some necessity—water to haul, yams to harvest, money to pay, babies, baskets—everything to think about except what she wanted to think about.

When she was a little girl, Bamidele explained the strips of cloth in his Egungun costume, created with vibrant colors that dazzled the eyes of a curious child.

Since then, she had wondered, wished and mused about the mystery of the Egun. What made them Egun? Could she become one? She knew she had to do more than just die. She had to practice Iwa Pele in life. Practice good character—and what else? What was Baba Abioye telling her? That her desire was to be fulfilled with a price to pay? A lesson to learn? What more was there to learn? In her twenty years of life, she'd never done anything bad—nothing really bad to exclude her from ancestorship. Her father, Kayode, was babalawo of the village. Surely, the opportunity would present itself for her to do something great. She had to be an ancestor. She just had to.

Everyone went to her father when they couldn't resolve their problems. He was second only to the Orisha themselves in wisdom. Ayodele reasoned that maybe she was his daughter so that she could perform some great deed.

Ayodele needed the answer to this mystery Baba Abioye had left her. She whispered to the divine messenger who carried the villagers' requests to the Creator.

"Eshu, I stand at the crossroads. Be the messenger of my prayers and not the trickster."

The sweetest yams grew in the dirt. She had to dig through so much of it to take this present to the babalawo. All her life, he had been her father, and now she hoped that would not interfere with his being her babalawo. Sometimes two people wanted different things, and when those two were actually one person, there was inner conflict. That's why she had never gone to him this way before. But he had to be her babalawo in this situation. He alone could show her what was required of her—what lesson was she supposed to learn, and what price would she pay to become an ancestor.

In his hut, painted eyes stared at her from strange animals some said existed somewhere far away. Ayodele felt them pawing the grass and asking her what she wanted in this place—a dark place with one window and a door facing the stars, not the moon. The eyes questioned her. The darkness engulfed her, but she knew the smell of burning sage would drive out evil spirits, so she relaxed. She was safe. The babalawo would not bite her any more than these painted beasts. Right?

As her eyes adjusted to the darkness, she became aware that what she'd thought was part of that darkness was actually the babalawo himself. She jumped. Her nerves caused not the slightest digression in his purpose.

"Ayodele, place your ebo on the table," Babalawo Kayode's voice whispered from the shadows of his hut. "I have determined that your request is for Osa Meji, and she will love the yams."

Ayodele took note of his tone—as a babalawo, not a father. That was good—she thought. She swallowed the urge to say "Father."

But now she was curious. "Osa Meji? I thought they were for Oya."

"Ha ha! You know the Orisha. You may be correct in thinking some kind of change will enter your life; and therefore, Oya is involved. Welcome to the Odu. We will begin shortly."

The Odu? Was this the lesson Baba Abioye spoke of? Did she have to learn all the intricacies of the Egbado people in order to be an ancestor? A million facts, shrouded in the unknown, danced at the edge of her mind and then sashayed out of her grasp.

Babalawo Kayode cast sixteen kola nuts onto a tray. With one hand behind his back, he began the work of divination with a prayer to Eshu as Laroye, the divine messenger of the river. Ayodele knew this much—she knew everything began with the messenger, Eshu. She held her breath, not wanting even the sound of her breathing to break Kayode's concentration as he recited poems over the nuts.

Finally, he looked at her and said, "Ayodele, your answer is in the wind."

"What? What do you mean?"

"That is all I can tell you. When you meet the wind at the crossroads of your life, you will have your answer."

She had come for answers, but now he was giving her only more mysteries.

"The crossroads? That's where I must make choices."

"Then choose wisely."

He walked to the door to let her know it was time to leave. She thanked him for the "answer" and tried not to look disappointed as she walked out with her head as high as her spirits could muster.

Ayodele had expected the night to be peaceful. She had expected to be resting in the assurance of irrefutable answers. Now, she only sighed at the moon shining through her window. No wind came through her window, and there would be no answers that night.

A shout from outside burst into her thoughts. "Dahomey!"

She crept to the window, hoping to see without being seen. She could not let them see her. She could not let them hear the sweat falling from her body to the ground. The Dahomey looked like her people, but they came with those who did not look like anything produced from Mother Earth. Two-legged, they were, but colorless. The Dahomey men and these strange, grinning creatures kept Ayodele's village as the Egbado kept the chickens. They came when they pleased and took her people to a place she did not know—a place from which no one had ever returned. The streets of Igbogila were quiet and still except for the arrogant trampling of the Dahomey.

Ayodele's people raised no war cries. They'd learned long ago that their weapons were no match for the magic sticks that spat fire. She had seen her men fall dead when no one touched them. Now everyone huddled in fear, not knowing who would be taken.

She heard the steps at her door. No, she could not let them take her. How would she ever be an Egun? How would she ever learn the lesson Baba Abioye gave her in the place they would take her?

She turned to face them. To face the fire. At least here, someone would remember her name. Two tall Dahomeys flanked her door as two white beasts approached her. She could not hope to fight them all. If she escaped one, the others would catch her. But her screams would ring in the village of Igbogila forever. The moon would witness her struggles and the trees would remember her name to the next generation, and the next, and the next . . .

One of the beasts touched her. She screamed, "Eniyan Buburu!"

The coldest blue eyes scraped over her, expressing no feeling but lust, seeing nothing but the promise of a reward. They were the same eyes that scraped over wild game in the forest. She willed her body not to flinch. She was not wild game. There was lust in his scraping eyes and his touch quickly turned into a grasp.

"No!" The horror of such a thing sickened her and she struggled but could not pull away. Where was the strength that accompanied determination? He pulled her toward the door, but she pulled back. She pushed. She bit. He laughed.

One of the Dahomey at the door spat on her floor—*her floor*. He had the nerve to be impatient. He had the nerve to want a quick end to her struggles. "Cooperate or we will beat you. We will remove your rags and drag you through these mud trails you have the audacity to call streets," he growled in the common tongue her people shared with the Dahomey. He then said something to the white beasts in a tongue she did not understand, but the tone of his voice was sycophantic.

Her captor only laughed. She decided to walk. She would not endure the indignity of being dragged. The eyes of her universe would not witness such shame. Nor would she give this brute an unnecessary opportunity to touch her.

But she shuffled her feet so they could carry the stirred-up dust of this place to wherever they must go. She touched everything in her path so she could remember and be remembered. Outside, she reached for the moon, but the Dahomey knew what she was doing and slapped her hand angrily.

"Superstitious abo aja! Keep walking and pick up your feet, lazy trifling."

So she reached out with her mind. The fingers of her spiritual body caressed the edge of the moon disk as a mother's palm cups her child's cheek. She whispered, "Ayodele. Remember me. Remember my name. Ayodele. Joy has come home."

In the moonlight, she saw the frozen grimace of Bamidele's mask lying in the tacit dust and knew he could not help her.

They walked on and on. In time, they converged with other captives, Dahomey men and the strange white beasts. They chained the captives together, one in front of the other. These bound men could not help her. Bamidele could not help her. She wanted Bamidele to kick and scream. Rip the iron fetters that grated the skin of her ankles and let her dance with her brother again. Forgetting that the Dahomey could understand her, she shouted the name of her village and the other captives answered.

"I am Ayodele from Igbogila."

"I am Enitan of Ilaro."

"I am Dayo of Owode."

"I am Olukayode of Oja Odan."

"I am Oluwaseyi of Papa-Alanto."

"I am Yejide of Ibese."

"I am Kayin of Ifo."

"I am Ayotunde of Idogo-Opaja."

Their captors jeered and derided, pushed, slapped and threatened, but they couldn't break the connections these names built among the captives. None of them knew to what death they marched; but they knew where they came from, and they knew they weren't alone.

They walked away from the watching moon. They walked through filth and tears and blood until the sun crept up behind them. Their shadows grew short in front of them, then long behind them; but still, they walked.

"I am sick. I cannot go on." The young girl in front of Ayodele stumbled to the ground.

A Dahomey brute beat the girl with his fire stick. "Get up, abo aja!"

Dayo of Owode lunged for him but the chains did not let him go far enough. Suddenly, there was a loud noise, the smell of smoke and Dayo fell to the ground, never to move again. The weight of his body falling pulled them all. That was the only movement the young girl made. White beasts loosened the two fallen ones from the chains, and tossed their bodies into the anonymous forest. When their bodies hit the ground, Ayodele thought she heard the girl moan. It was a faint sound—a ghostly sound, for that would be her grave.

"Keep moving!" the Dahomey snarled as if nothing unusual had happened.

Ayodele had thought of the Dahomey as men—wicked, ungodly men—but still men. After witnessing such unfeeling brutality, she could not believe even the lowest of human spirits dwelled in their minds. Their skin was black like that of men. The contours of their faces were full like those of men, but inwardly, they were more akin to the white beasts who came with them.

If the Dahomey had been men, she could have talked to them and reasoned with them as the elders of her village reasoned with the elders of other villages. She could think of no argument that would explain the value of life and dignity to those who did not already know of such things. How could she plead her humanity to animals? How could she warn demons to consider the judgment of Olodumare? The animals on Babalawo Kayode's wall were far more real and less frightening than these animated things that stomped through her nightmares.

After many days, the trees that watched, but could do nothing to help, receded. The roots of the trees were deep, but the branches didn't reach to the place the captives were going. If they did, those taken before them would have returned. Ayodele and her fellow captives were the only branches now—branches severed from their roots but still breathing. At least, they tried to breathe the dust-laden wind that blew past their faces and over their bare feet. How could one breathe the wind? It moved where it wanted. Whistling and taunting, it pushed Ayodele's body. She was to find her answer in the wind, but she could hardly coax it into her lungs.

Many moons rose and fell. Many constellations traversed the sky until, at last, their party came upon the biggest hut she had ever seen. This must have been the hut of the greatest elder in Oyo. But they were not in Oyo, and why would their captors take them to their elders? Ayodele's stomach recoiled as black and white beasts cheered and tossed their hats in the air. "Elmina Castle!" they roared.

With half the iron cuffs in their train-dangling empty, their previous occupants dead and gone, the captives and their captors marched toward the huge hut. As they entered, Ayodele found that it was many huts built on top of each other. The people inside looked over the newcomers. In their eyes, Ayodele saw a mixture of disgust and greed. She looked down at herself. She looked like the rest of them—soiled and stained, torn, ripped and ragged. What was left of her clothes barely covered her nakedness.

The white beasts were more naked than she was, for they had no color to cover their bodies, and the sun had baked and burned their unprotected skin to rawhide. Yet, they had washed themselves in lakes and rivers along the way and performed their bodily functions with some decency.

But a noxious stench rose among the captives. It was not possible to distinguish between the smells of feces, urine, blood, vomit and the natural odor of unwashed bodies. How could she defy the looks of disgust these beasts gave her when she appeared before them like this? Even if they were animals, she had never appeared before any animal like this.

Some of them looked at the men the same way they looked at the women, touching and holding their private members as one might hold a hand or a fish.

One of them pointed at Ayodele and a Dahomey removed her chains and took her to more water than she had ever seen in one place. To the right, it stretched. To the left, it stretched. Ahead of her, it met the sky in a thin, curving line. This water was alive. It moved with the rhythm of its life. Thrown to the land and then dragged back by the unseen hand of Olodumare. Who else had so much power? So much majesty? But if he were here, would he not help her? Had he helped those who were taken before her?

The Dahomey pushed her into the water with instructions to wash herself. Brine stung her broken skin. She had never known water like this. She thought it must be the water of the white beasts. This hostile liquid could not be the water of men. She began to whisper, not wanting the Dahomey to hear her prayer.

"Eshu, I asked you not to trick me. Am I here because my question angered you? Is this pain and indignity the only answer I will get?"

In her spirit, she felt him saying "No."

When she was sufficiently clean, the Dahomey beast took her back to the pale demon that had pointed to her before they went to the water. She did not see in his eyes as much disgust as she felt in her whole being. He grabbed her arm and pulled her into a room of the great hut, grinning with something in his eyes that she had never seen in the eyes of any Egbado man. But though he was male, surely he was not a man. Why had she washed only to be touched by this stinking atrocity?

Fear and rage immobilized her. Fear because she remembered hearing whispers that the white beasts ate those they captured. Rage because she was a woman, a human, being treated like an animal by an animal. He threw her on a bed and climbed on top of her. The rags of her clothing posed no barrier. Then he entered that most holy of holy places in her body and some part of her died. She commanded all of her body to die, but her spirit refused to vacate its defiled palace.

She dreaded every day that the sun dipped behind the water, heralding the coming of the Dahomey and the touch of the beast. She used to welcome the night. In her village, it cuddled her in darkness, blending with her as if they were of the same essence. But now, for the first time in her life, the joy of night had shattered.

Seeing that she would not respond to him, the pale demon soon tired of her and yelled at the door in his unintelligible language. As if they'd been standing right outside the door waiting for the beast's summons, the Dahomey entered the room.

From the time they first came to her village, Ayodele had thought the Dahomey brought the white beasts with them; but gradually, she began to suspect the white beasts were in charge and the Dahomey were just servants. She wondered if she served the white beasts, would they treat her better. *No!* She flung the thought away as a despicable thing.

The Dahomey came, dragging another victim by the hair.

"Come on abo aja—he wants you."

With what was left of her strength, the other woman screamed, "My name is Ekundayo. What are you? You are not men. You have no respect for women."

The Dahomey beasts laughed, pushed her through the door, and then turned to grab Ayodele. Ekundayo—sorrow turns to joy. Ayodele was meant to witness this scene. She remembered the teachings of her father—dirt cannot stop the grass from growing.

They took her and the other captives to a place deep under the hut they called Elmina Castle. They went down to a place away from the sun—away from air. A place where she was sure she would die. It was so dark she could not see the faces of those around her. Only screams and prayers, moaning and the stench of death and human waste told her many others were there. They were packed so tightly that she could not move. Day after day, they were taken out to eat and wash in the stinging great water, then shoved back into this hell.

She thought of speaking to the person next to her. Since there was no sliver of space between them, she wondered if maybe she could form some kind of connection. She sighed. What was the point of speaking? She could never know who stood beside her, only that it was not the same person as the day before. She could not raise her arms to comfort those who wept. She could not pull away from the coldness of those who died. In her own delirium, she could not remember the prayer for those who were sick.

One day, she saw Ekundayo retching in the big water. The woman could hardly stand. Ayodele went to her.

"Sister, lean on me."

Ekundayo lifted her eyes but not her head. "I see you."

Ayodele took her away from the water to a rock where they could sit down.

The Dahomey were impatient. "What the hell are you doing?"

Ayodele wanted to tell them that Ekundayo was sick, but doubted they cared, so she said nothing.

One of the brutes stormed over. "Come on, abo aja. You got to get ready for your night of pleasure, anyway."

He grabbed both of them by the arm and dragged Ekundayo while he pushed Ayodele into Elmina Castle.

After many days, their captors put on their chains and pushed them through a door they had never gone through before. A dark tunnel lay on the other side of this door and Ayodele heard the sound of the big water roaring from the other end. She knew in her spirit that this was a door through which they would never return.

Chapter 3

"I don't see why you need to take a class in black history," Chloe's mother said. "If I were you, I'd focus on classes that I could use in a good job."

This prevailed as the main topic of discussion whenever Chloe visited her family. She thought it was some kind of obsession. What would normal life feel like?

"I am taking the required classes," Chloe protested.

"Black history isn't a requirement for a degree in business or for any degree that's going to get you a good job. I don't know how many times I have to tell you. I don't know what it's going to take. It's a shame. What do you need to know about black history? We were savages, swinging from trees and practicing Voodoo. It's a good thing we were brought here where we could learn about Jesus and leave all those satanic religions alone."

Chloe was shocked. "You believe the religions we practiced in Africa were satanic?"

"I don't know what else to call it. Voodoo and Hoodoo and all that stuff."

"But . . ."

"What do you know about African religion?"

"Nothing," Chloe admitted. "That's why I'm taking the class."

"You're taking a class in African religion? Oh Lord, have mercy. Well, don't be trying to cast no hex on me, 'cause I'm protected by the Lord and no weapon formed against me can prosper."

"Cast a hex?" If it had been anyone else, Chloe would've laughed, and they'd have laughed with her. But she knew her mother was serious. She wouldn't even allow Chloe to play anything that didn't support the Christian music industry in her house. Called it devil music. "No, I told you, I'm taking black history. You're the one who brought up African religion. I know nothing of African religion, and until I do, I'm not going to condemn it by calling it satanic."

"You don't need to know nothing about African religion. Any religion that doesn't teach that Jesus is Lord is satanic and that's all you need to know. The apostle Paul told us to know nothing but Christ, and Him crucified."

"Ignorance is bliss."

"What did you say?"

"Nothing."

"As I said before, I really don't see what you need to know about black history. It isn't about anything but slavery, and what do you need to know about that? Slavery is over and we need to get over it and focus on today and tomorrow."

"You didn't say that when I was learning about George Washington and Christopher Columbus. Why do I need to know all about their history but don't need to know my own?"

This sounded so familiar. War is peace. Freedom is slavery. Ignorance is strength. Whose strength? Whose peace? Whose slavery? What was her mother afraid of? From the little that Chloe did know, Voodoo was just a form of magic. If her mother feared magic, what would she say if she knew about the strange things Chloe experienced? Was Chloe evil? Her mother would pray for her. She'd be afraid, and if Chloe didn't share the fear, her mother would be even more afraid. Chloe reasoned that if something is dangerous, it's better to know all about it than to tremble at the unknown.

But then, Chloe had her own unthinkable bogeymen. The mysterious music meant something. Whatever it meant, the same spirits who brought it would also bring the meaning. But her family . . . what would they say? What if the meaning she sought obliged her to be frank with them? There was nothing in her mother's religion that could make room for a different kind of spirituality. Chloe would be alone. Was she ready? She honestly didn't know. And maybe that was why she didn't know the meaning of the music yet—she wasn't ready to know.

"Honey, the Lord knows I just want you to do well in life. We've come so far. They letting us work good jobs, making good money. I'm talking six figures. You could be making that, if you don't throw it all away on some nonsense. You know what I mean?"

"Yes."

"I pray for you, child. Night and day, I do. I don't understand it. You're intelligent. You could be doing so much."

"I have a job. Isn't that what you want?"

"Then why are you still in that little old apartment? You don't even have any furniture. I had to buy you a desk or you'd probably have your computer on the floor. You can do better than that. But you need an education. You won't go anywhere without an education. A good education equals a good job. Are you happy in your job?"

"No."

"Well, there you go. You need more."

Yes. She needed more. But not the kind of more her mother had in mind. The more Chloe needed didn't deal with numbers. Well, there were numbers in music. Numbers involved in dancing. But she didn't focus on the numbers when she danced, just like she could walk across a room without focusing on the number of calories expended or the number of cells that were born and died in her legs with each step.

Her little sister Lisa entered the kitchen and plopped down at the table. Still in her teens, she was more like a niece than a sister. One good thing was their mother didn't let Lisa wear the kind of clothes other kids wore these days. Once she had tried to bring a boy home whose pants hung way below his underwear.

"Girl, I know you've lost your mind. I didn't raise no trash, and don't you bring no trash in my house. The Lord lives here and I won't have it."

Her mother looked like she was about to jump down that boy's throat. The broom in her hand only added to the effect, and he didn't wait around to see what she planned to do with it.

"Mom! You're scaring him." Lisa started after the boy, but her mother intercepted.

"Where do you think you're going?"

"That's my friend."

"You don't have any friends who buy their pants in the plus-sized department. That's nothing but the Devil."

Chloe wondered if she had been like that. It wasn't that long ago. What did the kids used to sing? "Ooh, I see your hiney/It's black and shiny/You'll never know it/ . . ." She forgot the rest.

"Oh, hi, Chloe," Lisa said after a brief glance in Chloe's general direction. "Mom, I need a dollar for the bus."

"I swear, kids think money grows on trees," her mother complained.

"No, I don't. I know money comes out of a machine in the wall."

"If you were as smart with those books as you are with your mouth, you might make good grades in school."

"My grades are okay."

"I said 'good grades.' Okay isn't good. You could make good grades if you tried—much better than you do now."

Lisa turned away, rolled her eyes and walked out. Better grades. Chloe knew this scenario all too well. A better job. Better money. Never any praise for what she was achieving right now. Always something she could be doing better.

She had dreamed one night of being a powerful queen sitting on a golden throne, with a golden scepter in her hand and a crown of diamonds on her head. Her courtiers were decked out in silk, satin and velvet.

Her mother approached her throne on a blood-red carpet of crushed rubies. "Who're you working for?"

"Mother, I am the queen. I work for no one. My queendom works for me."

"Your kingdom? I told you to stay in school. You could have a good job making good money right now. But no, you wanted a kingdom."

"Queendom."

"There are no queens. There are only bosses who'll pay you if you have the right piece of paper."

"Piece of paper?" Chloe laughed.

A knight in shining blue armor approached her with a stream of paper seven miles long and prostrated himself before her feet.

"Your Majesty desired paper. At your service."

Her mother sniffed at the paper disdainfully. "That isn't the paper they want. That isn't the paper that's going to get you a good job."

Chloe awoke wishing that queens still had the power to say, "Off with your head." But it was only a dream. She could do anything she wanted in a dream. Could she please her mother in a dream? Could she be anything more than a civilized savage in the eyes of a woman who thought whites did them a favor when they took them out of Africa?

"A slave master will give you nothing with the intention of setting you free."

In her mother's mind, black people had never known freedom until they were forced into slavery. Somehow, all the brutality, all the humiliation and all the injustice were part of some divine plan to set Africans free. Since whites were already free, they didn't need to be beaten and raped and murdered like blacks did. In the end, Jesus was all that mattered and slavery gave them Jesus.

Chloe couldn't fathom the mindset that made her mother think that way. Why didn't she know what Chloe knew? Chloe considered this question. What did she know? It took courage to embrace knowledge. But how do you embrace that which isn't there? How do you embrace that which is there but isn't valued by those around you?

What were the realities of Chloe's experiences? She was of a different generation than her mother. Chloe was of the post-*Roots* generation. She knew what slavery had really been like. But suppose she had never heard anything else all her life? Then she might believe what her mother said.

Chloe's own knowledge was so scanty. She knew more than a lot of her friends, but there was so much information out there. She couldn't hope to know everything, read every book or listen to every speech. So what was the most important thing she could know? From what she'd read in the online forums, the one commandment her ancestors left her was "*Man, know thyself.*" Then, she figured, she had a long way to go to obey that commandment in the most rudimentary things.

Where could she learn about herself except in Africa—in Soweto, Zaire or Egypt maybe? The thought of telling her mother she wanted a good job so she could make enough money to go to Egypt made Chloe ache.

"Moses took God's people out of Egypt," the woman would say. "Why would you want to go back for?"

Chloe chuckled. Suppose she did? Suppose she danced around the pyramids and dined in Cairo with the pharaohs? What would it be like to be in Africa? What was it like for those who told her to know thyself?

Chapter 4

They took Ekundayo out of Ilaro. Out of the knowledge of kinfolk. Out of her mind. Away from the gentleness of her father Adebayo, who knew the plant for every illness.

"You are not sick," he told her when she came to him.

Ekundayo stared at her father. *Not sick?* With her head and stomach swimming together, her food coming out the way it went in, and such strange foods—yams mashed together with shredded palm leaves. "My sister said I am sick and need something."

Her father smiled. "And does your sister know more than the Odu?"

"I hoped they would tell me what is wrong with me. I hope Eshu is not playing a trick today."

Her father's gentle ways were not without a touch of mischief. "No trick. Not at all, but now you must give an extra prayer and libation to Yemoja."

It took a moment for her father's words to register, and then she sat up with a gasp, staring at him with the widest eyes. "Did I hear you? No. For a minute I thought you said Yemoja."

"That I did."

And so, Ekundayo prayed.

> "Yemoja the Orisha of
>   motherhood.
> Yeye omo eja,
> Mother of the ocean,
> Great waters I have never
>   seen,
> Orisha of her growing womb,
> Keeper of the waters within."

She hoped it would be a girl. Ekundayo danced with joy and peace. *A girl.* She felt blessed to give life to a giver of life.

There would be a celebration to name the baby one week after it was born, with all her family and friends gathered to welcome a new life into the world.

And most of all, to give the new baby a name that would imbue her with strength and character and all the good things she would have been meant to possess.

The Crossroads of Time

But dirty Dahomey snatched away her baby's name before she was born. Ekundayo knew there would be no naming ceremony. She knew she would never see her sisters again. She knew she would not celebrate the Gelede where her family would bestow upon her the great honor of motherhood.

Wrenched away from all that she knew and loved, Ekundayo knew from experience that those left behind would be left to wonder where she had gone. How long was forever? Who? Where? And she would never know who was left and who had been taken as well.

None of those she knew and loved had ever been taken, so she had always wondered what kind of people things like this happened to. She had put those who were taken into a category to which she did not belong—bad people. In that way, she could assure herself that it would never happen to her.

But now, it had happened to her. She had been taken. Did that mean she was bad? Had she not been good—too good for something like this to happen? But what was going to happen? After the blessing of Yemoja, what could possibly happen? She did not know, for none of the taken had ever returned to tell her.

45

Of course, there had been tales told over the fire by the wise and the unwise alike. Dreadful tales of people being cooked and eaten as food. These tales were terrible— too terrible to believe, yet no one ever came back to say otherwise. And here she was, wondering what would befall her in the hands of these dreadful white beasts and Dahomey. All she could go on was the hard, leering faces, the arduous trek, and the unthinkable touch of the colorless manlike creatures. These horrors told her that whatever lay ahead would not be good.

She gazed at the pines as they passed. Her gaze became a trance as if by looking hard enough, she could become the thing she saw, old and rooted, unmoving and immovable. But she did not have roots. She had legs that walked, and could be made to walk whether she wanted them to or not. She had legs that moved and stumbled over the roots of that which she saw but could never become.

"Is she sick?" one of the Dahomey asked.

"She better not be sick. As much trouble as she gave them, she better fetch them a good price for their pains."

Their pains? The colorless one felt pain? She could not imagine it. She had never seen creatures such as these. They walked upright like men, but men they could not be. Men had dignity and respected women. These creatures leered with a hunger akin to beasts. Maybe that is what they were. Yet, they treated her like she was the beast, though no one in her village had treated any animal with such disregard.

They came to a hut made of wood, and the captives were thrust in like so many animals at the market. This was where they were supposed to sleep. Their captors loitered around outside, talking and laughing. Some of them smoked something. Ekundayo had seen the elders in her village smoke when they were together, but the fragrance from their pipes was pleasant. What she smelled coming from these beasts was odious. She did not want to watch them but decided to do so. Perhaps they would betray some means of escape.

After watching them until her eyes ached and she could stay awake no longer, she lay down to sleep. There was not a lot of room to lie down. There was hardly enough room to stand up, but each of the captives found a little space, and they did not mind touching one another.

Ekundayo lay with her back against a wall and her knee against someone's back. That someone was a man. For some strange reason, she felt safe touching him. She slept and dreamed that the man was there to rescue her and her unborn child.

Waking in suffocating darkness, she listened to the talking and weeping, the frustration and rage. Many more captives had joined the group she was in. She did not recognize the language of the Egbado in any of the words.

How could they plan an escape when they could not understand each other? Whatever they did would be without a plan. Each of them would just have to act on whatever opportunity presented itself. But is that not how she was captured to begin with?

Chains constricted her movements and the closeness of the other captives—close enough to constrict one another even without the chains, but too close to help one another.

There would be no opportunity to escape. But maybe there would be an opportunity to die. That might surely be her only means of escape. No chains could hold her spirit. No bodies could constrict the flight of her soul back to her people. She kept her eyes open for that one opportunity.

Soon they left the wooden hut with the new captives and kept walking. Many captives died as they walked. Ekundayo wondered what they did to die. Why could she not do the same? Just take one step too many and have her body refuse to take another. But she kept walking, living, thinking, and doing what she did not want to do. Finally, with bleeding, festering feet their wounded bodies and despondent minds came to a gigantic hut made of the stones of the Earth.

Beyond the hut water stretched from sunrise to sunset. Ekundayo remembered stories told about the sea, which Yemoja owned. She had always thought the sea was a legend or at least something she would never see. Was this it? Was this the sea?

The sun glinted off the water, just as the legends described. She could believe in legends. What was legend? Something someone had seen at some time and tried to describe to those who had not seen it. A thought struck her and she shuddered. If the legend of the sea was true, then maybe the legend that those taken by the Dahomey and colorless ones were eaten was also true. She hoped her opportunity would arrive long before that happened.

The Dahomey cut short her contemplation of the sea by thrusting the captives into a dark room in what must have been the bottom of the great hut. The captives stumbled down many steps before they came to the door of that room. The door was like none in her village. Until then, she had always thought a door was to make it easy to enter a hut. This door was designed to make it hard. There was a heavy bar holding the door fast. With great effort, the Dahomey lifted the bar, and with even more effort, pulled the door open. The door was thick and she thought at first it was to keep them out, but once the captives were pushed inside and the door thundered shut behind them, she realized it was to keep them in.

There had been nothing like this in her village. They did not keep people locked up. Anyone who was not wanted was banished. Like the man who stole the divination tray from the babalawo or the witch who had turned into a goat and brought death to small children. No one wanted the spirits of such people to remain in the village, so they were cast out.

It was not so much the darkness that bothered her. It was the smell of everything that could possibly come out of the human body. And the smell of death. She shuddered.

She longed for death, but not for such a smell to come from her. Yet, the dead do not smell themselves, she mused. It was offensive only to the living, as was everything else in this inescapable hell.

But she was not to stay here. Her captors soon took them out and marched them into the shallows of the sea. The water burned where her skin was cut, but it washed away the filth. The Dahomey singled her out from the other captives. Thinking that she had been chosen to be their first meal, she tried to fight them, but they dragged her by the hair. They came to another door that was not so heavily barred.

The Dahomey only laughed at her struggles.

"That's right, you little abo aja. He likes 'em wild, so give him what he wants." Then the brute wiggled his hips at her. "Straight out of the jungle."

Another Dahomey shot nervous glances up and down the hall. "Don't let Mr. Sanchez catch you doing that."

"You gonna tell him?"

Ekundayo could not stand the indignity of being called out of her name. And to be called an animal by these animals . . .

"My name is Ekundayo. What are you? You are not men. You have no respect for women." She knew her protests were futile—even silly—in the faces of these brutes who cared nothing for dignity and respect. But the words were all she had to declare her humanity when everyone around her denied it.

When the door opened, a dark woman was being pulled out by the Dahomey and Ekundayo was thrust in. This room was unlike any she had ever seen. She had heard of kings living in rooms of such wasteful sumptuousness. The furnishings were made of gold and precious woods. Costly fabrics covered the chair cushions. There were even fine fabrics on the walls. And there was a bed draped in more fine fabrics.

Right in the midst of this splendor was an odious, colorless demon. He leered at her, showing huge, yellow teeth. Ekundayo shuddered. Was she looking at the teeth that would chew her flesh? She pulled her gaze from his teeth and looked into his eyes. What she saw there made her heart all but stop. In his eyes was not the hunger of a carnivorous animal but the lust of a godless man. Then she understood why she had been brought there and what she was expected to do.

For several nights, they brought her there and afterwards she went to the sea to retch in its limitless waters, but her regurgitations did nothing to cleanse her body or her mind from the filth of that demon's touch.

The dark woman Ekundayo had seen on her first night came to her side.

"Sister, lean on me."

The shame of what had been done to her and her own desire for death did not allow Ekundayo to do more than acknowledge her sister.

"I see you."

The woman took Ekundayo's hand and led her to a rock where they could sit. But before they could say a word, the Dahomey came and dragged them back to the odious little hell behind the heavy door. She had no sense of time. How many hours, days, months had she endured the shame and indignity of this place? She had hoped the odors alone would kill her, but her stubborn body refused to succumb to death.

Then the Dahomey came and took them all out of the room. She thought she was going back to the sea to wash in its punishing water. But rather than going straight to the water, the captives were chained and led down a tunnel at the end of which stood a huge door. Something about that door froze the blood in Ekundayo's veins.

They passed through this ominous door and she looked out over the water at the biggest boat she had ever seen. What would happen next? Would they take her on that huge boat? Where did it come from? Where would it go? She did not know the answer to these questions, but she knew that once she was on that boat, she would never see Africa again.

As she and other captives were thrown into smaller boats and taken to the large boat, Ekundayo's desire to die redoubled.

Once on the boat, she, the dark woman and several other women were separated from the men. The men protested. By nature, they wanted to protect their women, but the chains on their bodies restricted their movements and the captors beat them back viciously. One man continued to lunge at the captors, using his chains to bludgeon any of them within his reach. A colorless demon pointed his fire stick at the dark man. There was a loud noise as fire burst out of the stick and the dark man crumpled and fell. Then one of the captors chopped off his head. Ekundayo was stunned, as were all the other captives. They all knew that, even if the body was killed, there was hope for the spirit to return to its place if the head was not cut off. This act of great evil silenced the captives. The demons smirked and laughed, for they knew what they had done.

The women were washed in brine hauled up from the sea. Ekundayo winced as saltwater found every break in her skin. Her body screamed, but the water did not care. Then they were thrown into a room and taken out to be abused each night by the demons. Each time she returned to the room, she collapsed beside the dark woman, whose gentle voice soothed her mind.

"I am Ayodele from Igbogila."

"Will you survive?"

"Yes, I will; and you will also."

Ekundayo shook her head. The power in Ayodele's eyes could have lent sustenance to her words, but surviving was something Ekundayo definitely did not want to do. She had not only to spare herself from the abuse of these colorless demons, but also the baby inside her, if it lived. Would it bear the memory of what she might go through and live in miseries it did not even understand?

When they took her out each night, she noticed that they came very close to the rim of the boat and she could look down at the water. If she could find a way to distract her captors for just a moment, she could make it over the rim. She thought and planned. Then one night she turned to Ayodele.

"You must remember my name."

"I always will, Ekundayo."

"But I mean it, especially now. I am with child. Her name will be Iyabo."

"How can you name a child before it is born?"

"You must remember her name, as well as mine. No one can remember the name of one who has no name. So I have named her Iyabo. I know that she would have been a girl."

"What do you mean 'would have been?' If you wait, in time, the baby will be what it is."

"I cannot wait, so I give her name now. Iyabo means 'mother comes back.' I tell you now so that you may remember."

To Ekundayo's perplexity, Ayodele looked alarmed. They had seen the same horrors. Why did she not understand?

With a trembling voice, Ayodele whispered, "Mother comes back? Where are you going?"

"That is not something that anyone living really knows. But if you remember our names, maybe my baby, too, will remain a part of the living; as are all those who have not yet been born but are destined to do so."

Ayodele shivered and Ekundayo knew she had made her meaning clear. She only hoped that the woman would not try to stop the plan.

"When they take us out tonight, we will dance," Ekundayo said.

"What?"

"Dance. Surely, you know how to dance. The drums will speak in our minds tonight and we will dance the Egungun. I think that will be very appropriate."

Ekundayo felt so happy and content. It was not a happiness brought on by what was going on around them. Not the happiness of one whose future looked bright. It was the happiness of someone who had solved a great personal problem and realized that nothing else really mattered.

When the Dahomey came, Ekundayo lowered her head. She did not want the beasts to see the happiness in her eyes. They'd probably seen it before in the eyes of countless victims. They would see it and would know what she was thinking. Being beasts, they saw only the lowered head—

something they expected to see, something they had always seen; and to them, all was well.

The women were pushed onto the deck of the ship and Ekundayo began to move.

"Dance," she whispered.

Ayodele danced as if retracing Egungun steps she had just seen. Ekundayo had her own choreography in mind.

"What are they doing?" one of the Dahomey asked.

"Who cares what they think they're doing? Let them get hot and ready for the masters."

All the Dahomey laughed and Ekundayo kept dancing. Ayodele and the other women danced, too, but were unsure exactly why—unsure until Ekundayo's dance moved her closer and closer to the edge of the boat.

The Dahomey did not notice. "Will you sing, too? Sing, abo aja," they laughed.

Ekundayo whirled about but let Ayodele's dance draw the Dahomeys' attention away. They were dumb beasts who saw what they expected to see. They saw Ayodele's body dancing in a rhythm suggestive of their desires. They saw a helpless captive trying to make the most of a hopeless situation. They did not see Ekundayo leap over the edge of the boat.

The leap was a part of the dance—a smooth movement in the corner of their eyes. By the time the Dahomey realized that the leap was actually a leap, it was too late. They pushed Ayodele and the other women out of the way and rushed toward the empty air where Ekundayo had been, hoping to grab some part of her to hold her back. But there was no sleeve, no collar, no shirttail or shoe they could grasp in their desperate attempt to save their master's gold.

"Slave overboard!"

Ekundayo turned her face to the waves and opened her lungs to the unbreathable sea. The thing to do now was the exact opposite of whatever her father had taught her to stay afloat. Diving under the waves where the Dahomey could not see her, she continued her dance.

"They wanted me to sing? All right, I will sing."

She breathed in the brine as if it were air and sang the soft songs that used to lull her to sleep in her mother's arms.

Remember my name, Ayodele. Remember my name.

Chapter 5

Chloe settled down in black history class. It was different from high school. The whole university scene was different from high school. There were no lockers in the hallways, so if you brought a bone, you carried a bone. There were no bells. She needed to buy a watch because she was about to get whiplash looking up at the clock every five minutes. But mostly, it was the students who were very different. They didn't pick lint off their book bags whenever the teacher spoke to them. They listened and took notes; and the teacher, Ms. Florida LaMond, insisted they call her Flo. Chloe had been in junior high before she even realized teachers had first names.

Flo had divided them into smaller study groups. "I'm trying to achieve a diversity of viewpoints in each group, so your discussions won't be regurgitations of your own biases. A wide range of ethnic groups is represented in this class and we've all come, hopefully, to learn the history of one particular ethnic group—African Americans."

A white guy sat up. "It's really terrible what we did to them. I mean, I'm really sorry they had to go through that slavery and stuff, really sorry. It was terrible."

Chloe squirmed. *Will he shut up?* She didn't like being cast into the role of the poor victim. She didn't like having people feel sorry for her. Her mother had told her that slavery was all black history was about. That's why Chloe had taken this class—to learn that black people were more than just descendants of slaves still struggling for a piece of the pie.

Flo picked up Chloe's thoughts. "Actually, black history goes beyond slavery and Jim Crow. Yes, we'll discuss Martin Luther King and Harriett Tubman, but we'll also learn about Paul Robeson and Hannibal the Carthaginian. In fact, each group will be responsible for reporting on a particular aspect of black history. But first, you'll want to introduce yourselves to your group members and exchange email addresses so you can stay in contact."

In Chloe's group, there were three women, two men and herself. She listened and wrote down their names as they spoke them.

"Yara Muniz. I am from Salvador, Brazil."

Chloe knew she'd remember that name. Not because it was a foreign name. There were a lot of Latinos and other people in the class with names that clearly weren't American. But she'd remember Yara because of her huge, almond-shaped eyes and decidedly African features. Chloe had heard there were twice as many black people in Brazil as in the United States. That kind of burst her bubble. She had barely heard the song of the African Diaspora; and yet, had been vain enough to think the song was about her and her experience in America. She'd have to talk to this woman and stretch her experience of black history to its global proportions.

"Edna Stone, from right here in California, United States citizen." This woman looked pointedly at Yara when saying the word "citizen."

"Alice Gomez. I am here from Tijuana. Have been in the United States for ten years."

"*In* the United States?" Edna snapped. "Why just *in* the country? Are you an illegal?"

"No, I am a citizen."

"Then say you're a citizen. Don't be talking about you're *in* the United States. Whole lot of folks *in* the United States but don't belong here."

Alice said nothing, but searched her mind for an intelligent answer. Her silence evinced her decision that intelligent words were more suited to intelligent ears.

"I'm Darius Clark from Georgia."

Was Chloe mistaken or did Edna feel more at ease? Chloe could have sworn she saw Edna's body move half a molecule closer to Darius.

"Billy Green. I'm from Fresno, California."

Flo came over to Chloe's group, stooping down to be eye level with them. "Your group will explore the impact of black religion and spirituality."

"Do you want us to focus on any particular religion?" Billy asked.

"You can, but you don't have to. For this assignment, you'll want to get as much of the big picture as possible, so you'll probably want to explore several religions and maybe find a common thread or something. Be creative, and remember your main objective."

Be creative? She squirmed inside at the thought. No, this wasn't high school. She looked at the other members of her group, wondering what they'd decide to do. Would her input count in reaching a consensus, or would her ideas be buried under some majority rule—some common sense decision engineered by the most powerful personality? If only she could work alone.

Then Flo moved on to the next group and Yara began to speak. "Well, there are a lot of different religions that black people practice. In my country, we practice Candomblé and I am a Candomblé priestess."

"But we're not in your country," Edna said. "We're supposed to write about black history. That means America."

Yara's eyes became drills of steel, ready to bore through stony ignorance. She counted to ten to center her spirit before she spoke. "South Americans are as much Americans as North Americans. In fact, there are twice as many blacks in Brazil as there are in the United States."

"Well, I . . ."

"Well you what?"

"South America ain't America. There's a difference."

"What's the difference?"

"America is my country, not yours. You're just visiting and you can go back anytime you want. The sooner the better." Edna managed to keep her voice down so as not to attract the teacher, but her voice grew shriller by the minute.

Yara smiled the knowing smile of victory. "Your rudeness is exceeded only by your ignorance. America isn't a country. America is a continent—two continents, in fact. What makes North Americans any more American than South Americans?"

"You ain't no American. You just ain't and that's all there is to it."

Chloe could see tempers were rising, so she cut in. "We don't have a lot of time. Since we have to do something, why don't we each focus on a different religion?"

Yara chimed in. "There is Candomblé in the United States. It's a form of Ifa, the religion practiced by the Yoruba. Santería is also a form of Ifa, but different."

"Would you like to focus on that?" Chloe asked.

Edna would have none of this. "We not doing no foreign religions. And who made you the boss, anyway?"

Chloe started to open her mouth, and then stopped. What could she say? She wasn't trying to be the boss. Just trying to contribute ideas, and she had to admit, trying to make sure her ideas stayed on the front burner. But that wasn't the same as trying to be the boss. Right? Chloe couldn't answer Edna unless the other group members backed up Chloe's ideas. She waited, looking around surreptitiously to see what they'd say. The other five group members looked at Edna briefly, decided she wasn't contributing anything that would help them make the grade and just carried on.

"Yes," Yara answered. "I will focus on the impact of Yoruba religions on African Americans."

Darius said, "I've always been interested in Noble Drew Ali and the Moors, so I guess I'll report on that."

"I'd like to do something on Ra Un Nefer Amen and the impact of Metu Neter," said Billy.

Edna's eyebrows shot up, as if Billy had pushed her onto a whoopee cushion. "Metu Neter?"

"It's a religion built around the Egyptian pantheon. They have chapters all over the U.S."

"Egyptian! Now I know that ain't American . . ."

But her steam died out when no one fueled it by reacting to it.

Alice cast a pensive gaze at her pencil, and then said, "I guess I could do Elijah Muhammad and the Nation of Islam. I don't know much about it, but it'll be fun to research it and come back with what I've learned."

For some reason Chloe wanted to be last; but Edna was the only one left, and with all the smoke coming out of her nose, Chloe wasn't sure Edna could find the breath to speak. Finally, Edna redirected the smoke into her vocal cords and said, "Since nobody else has a mind to study Christianity, a real American religion, I'll do it. Or is God still unwelcome in the classroom?"

No one cared to take the bait. Without even deigning to roll her eyes, Chloe asked, "Is there a particular figure in Christianity you'd like to focus on?"

"Well, Paul is my favorite apostle, but if this is about Christianity, then I want to focus on Jesus."

"This is about black history," Billy said. "Is there anyone in the Christian religion who contributed to black history?"

"Oh, I'm sure there are a lot of folks. There's Martin Luther King. But we already know all about him. There's T.D. Jakes. But he ain't historical. He's still alive, so he don't count. I can't think of nobody off the top of my head. So let me come back to it."

"You do that," Chloe said. "I'll focus on Adam Powell. I guess you could say he put teeth and claws on the black Church."

They were all taking notes, exchanging email addresses, and discussing what they wanted to focus on to find common threads that might bring it all together. All except Edna. Chloe wondered if she was planning to work alone as Chloe had thought she'd wanted to do at first. Edna's ideas weren't being buried in groupthink. But she wasn't able to bury anyone else's ideas either, and she didn't like that. Chloe was all too familiar with Edna's kind and knew exactly what was going through the woman's little mind. Like Chloe's mother, Edna knew her ideas were right, so everyone else's ideas had to be wrong. Closed up in her own little world, Edna was determined not to move, no matter if she choked on the smoke in her little box.

Chloe breezed through her other classes with barely a thought. Even their names bored her: Introduction to Business Administration. The Logistics of Accounting. The Structure of Corporate America.

The Crossroads of Time

They were classes for someone else. Why was she taking them? Because of someone else's expectations, so she decided to do her best for whatever that was worth. Maybe she'd learn something useful. She certainly wasn't interested in the structure of corporate anything. But it was a requisite for . . . for . . . what? To get a piece of paper that would get her a good job, her family had assured her.

What was a good job? These classes sounded like they'd lead to the kind of job she already had—doing work that made ten dollars for someone else, while she took home a dollar. And the work—it was nothing that meant anything to her. With the money she made, she could pay her rent and her light bill. When she was lucky, she'd have a little left over at the end of the month. Though sometimes, she'd have month left over at the end of the money.

The thirty-day cycle. Take classes so she can continue the same old thirty-day cycle. Chloe didn't want this. She thought of throwing it all out the window, but she did have to pay her light bill. So she continued.

Her job used to be called a secretary, but now she was an administrative assistant. For sure, she did more than push papers or tap on a keyboard. That really would drive her up the wall and across the ceiling. So she was lucky. She was a liaison between her boss, Senator Bill Braxbury, and the outside world. He never checked his email, but left it up to her to put the messages in categories, for or against whatever bill or measure they concerned.

"Senator Bill Braxbury's office. How may I help you today?" Chloe prided herself in using good phone etiquette. Not that anyone could get past her to complain to her boss about her performance. It was just her own desire to look back at the end of the day on a job well done.

"Who are you? I want to speak to the senator."

"I'm his administrative assistant and I'd be happy to assist you, if I may."

"I don't want to speak to no administrative ass-sistant, or whatever you call yourself. Putting on airs. I want to speak to the senator him-goddamn-self."

"I understand that, sir, but the senator is unable to take the call at this time. I'd be happy to pass on any message you'd care to leave."

"I'm a concerned father of five boys and that bill he's talking about passing is going to put my family in the poorhouse."

"Which bill might that be, sir?"

What's the number that bill? S2982 something. The one for truckers. They going to allow companies to outsource hauling and take my job. I got a wife and five boys to feed. You tell him I don't want that bill to pass."

"Yes, sir. I'll certainly let him know. May I help you with anything else, sir?"

"That bill is the most important thing to me. You tell him. I'm his constituent. I voted him in and I'll damn sure vote him out if that bill passes."

"Yes, sir. Thank you for calling the office of Senator Bill Braxbury. Your views are important to us. If that's all, have a wonderful day." Chloe hoped he'd take the hint and that it wouldn't be too obvious. He did and hung up. That one wasn't too bad. Some of them cussed her out, but she still could never be less than professional on the phone.

Just when she hung the phone up, it rang again and Alvin came in with the mail. She gestured for him to put it in the inbox while she took the call.

"These September hauls are murder on my back," he said after she hung up. He set the concerns of half the state on her desk. "If I can make it through the November elections without breaking vertebrae, I'll be all right."

"Oh, you'll make it."

With a bleak smile, he bowed out of the door.

She scanned the letters, placing the most important ones on top and the most irate ones in for and against piles that she'd tally later but not show her boss. The most important ones were from other politicians or Political Action Committees. Some were from ordinary citizens who'd called before and mentioned in their letters how helpful she had been on the phone. These always got her boss' attention at the top of the stack.

After sorting the mail, she carried it into his office.

He was standing by the window, one finger raised in the air, his mouth in the process of forming some word.

"Thanks. Set it right there and listen to this."

Continuing the speech, he said, "This bill will cut fifty thousand dollars in taxes in the coming year."

Chloe saw a discrepancy. Under normal circumstances, criticizing one's boss was second to few on the list of famous last words. But Chloe knew this was why he asked her to listen to his inchoate speeches—

to make sure nothing he planned to say tomorrow contradicted what he had said yesterday. As long as she wasn't too critical, he valued her memory and the way she helped him stay in touch with voter sentiments.

"If you'll recall, Mr. Braxbury, last week you indicated the cut would be thirty-seven thousand dollars."

"So I did. I don't know where fifty thousand dollars came from. I remember it from somewhere. I'll have to check my records and see."

"It happens to the best of us, sir."

He stayed in his office most of the time. Mary from the cafeteria brought his lunch everyday and Kevin took the tray back at the end of the day. Braxbury was such a workaholic Chloe wondered if someone went to the bathroom for him. He really didn't know what was going on unless she told him.

She stepped into her own office, closing his door behind her. The workday was hardly over, but she was already tired of the nine-to-five routine, so she broke it by cutting a little step. She kept her floor clean so she could step and slide all she wanted. Chloe stepped and slid to the side, out of her boss' direct line of vision should he open the door.

Around the office, she pranced. Her soft-leather shoes and the carpeted floor muffled her steps. It also muffled the sound of Braxbury's door opening.

"Uh um."

When she heard her boss clear his throat, Chloe's heart froze. The sound had not come from the other side of a closed door. The door was open, and nothing opaque stood between his eyes and her body.

What had, moments before, been the prelude to a swing, turned into a professionally harried pivot toward her fax machine.

"Is there something you need, Mr. Braxbury?" she asked, seeing him for the first time and shrugging disappointedly at the empty fax tray.

Chloe wasn't ashamed of the things she liked. She could buy a watermelon in the summer without a thought about what people might think. But she knew that when she did those things she was representing herself. Here, at work, she was paid to represent him, so she kept them separate.

"Yes . . ." he paused as if thinking about something other than what he wanted to say. "Have you tallied the pros and cons for the overtime bill? I need to have some figures when I speak to the committee, tomorrow."

Chloe nodded and returned to her desk to pull up the requested information.

"I'll send the figures to your inbox. Won't take but a second."

Had she played it off successfully, or had he seen her acting stereotypically on his time? She represented him well enough. She never shirked her other-imposed responsibilities, but sometimes she needed a break—a little time, a little space where she represented no one but herself. Only when she danced could she enter this time, this space within her own body, observed only by the unseen eyes of the spirits all around. She knew these same spirits brought her music to fit whatever occasion she was in.

Chloe wondered at the unknown message of the music. Would dancing reveal this message? Or was the dance a message all by itself? The message would unfold itself, but not if she worried about it. So she put it out of her mind and just danced.

Chapter 6

Tonyeesha Jenkins ordered a thirty-two ounce strawberry smoothie at the K-Tel store on Jasper Street.

"I can't believe how easy this is," her friend Jaleen said.

They had skipped school three times this week and were exhilarated with the freedom of doing whatever they wanted.

"I told you I know how to do it. If we skip every day, they'll call our parents. But they're so stupid. Show up once in a while, and they won't notice."

Tonyeesha wasn't worried. She was in her senior year and the fastest thing her school had on the track team, so her coach wouldn't let her get in any real trouble. He needed her. The team needed her. The school needed her. She leaned back against the counter and sighed, knowing she didn't have to worry.

She didn't know she was in the perfect mood for trouble to come. The boys at the video-game machines caught her eye. Elbowing Jaleen, Tonyeesha gestured toward the guys.

Jaleen grinned. "The one in the LeBron Eights is mine."

"Kewl. You can have one. I'll take the rest."

The girls sashayed over, the wind in their faces, like natural predators.

Jaleen kept her eyes steady on the LeBron Eights. "Oh look, Ton. He's good. He's not just winning—he's kicking ass." This she said with a suggestive pivot.

The boy, hearing this and seeing that, let out a howl and put one arm around Jaleen's waist, while his other hand steered the joystick.

"Hey dog, what's your game?" Tonyeesha teased a tall boy in a black pleather Columbia jacket and jeans that needed a belt very badly.

"You."

They all laughed. They laughed so merrily they didn't see the truant officers enter the store. Big beefy men you couldn't miss unless you were laughing merrily. But mid-laugh, Tonyeesha saw from the corner of her eye, figures moving toward them that were too big to be other kids, and too united to be other customers. She turned and let out a yelp that made the other kids turn, too. What they saw turned their howls of merriment to gasps of dismay—six overgrown power machines with nightsticks in their hands and service revolvers at their hips. One for each kid and there was nowhere to run.

"Aren't you children supposed to be in school?"

Children. Suddenly, they remembered they were children.

"You can't hit us. We're children," Drooping Jeans said. The other boys ruined the whole effect by snickering. Whatever air of ingenuousness he was aiming for flew right past the officers.

"Oh, of course, we don't like to hurt you. But our job is to ensure that you stay in school and we will do whatever you make it necessary for us to do. It's your choice."

Each officer apprehended a kid and headed out the door. The kids tried to be sullen and defiant, dragging their feet to show their indifference. But the officers' grips forced the kids to keep up with the brisk pace or be dragged.

The officers looked at the kids' school ID cards and punched in some numbers on their car computer to see if they had any kind of records. Seeing that Tonyeesha and Jaleen were clean, the men put the girls in a squad car. Tonyeesha had never been in the back of a squad car before. Then the men put the boys in another car to take to another school, or wherever they were headed. Maybe to jail, she wondered. Were they taking her to jail? This was her senior year. She'd graduate in June. She couldn't go to jail.

"Where are you taking us?" she shrieked through the grille.

The officers said nothing. She asked again, louder. But they were obviously ignoring her. She began to panic. She looked at Jaleen who looked straight ahead in vacant terror. *No help there*. Where were they taking them? Then she saw they were pulling down the street to Washington High. She sighed with relief, but cut it short when she realized she'd still be in trouble. No, not big trouble. Not the star of the track team. But what would her pop say? Worse, what would he do?

When the car stopped, the officers yanked the back door open, pulled the girls out and marched them towards the administration building. To Tonyeesha, it felt like a perp walk.

"May I help you, officers?" Ms. Hathey, the principal asked, not looking at Tonyeesha and Jaleen.

"We picked these girls up at the K-Tel store during school hours in the company of other truants and persons of interest."

"Persons of interest?" Ms. Hathey mused. "My, my, but don't we get ourselves in troubles of which we know nothing. Or, you might know more than I think. Never can tell with this kind. Thank you, officers. They are in my custody now."

When the officers left, Ms. Hathey gestured for Tonyeesha to come into her office. "I'll deal with you one at a time. Jaleen, have a seat until I call for you."

Jaleen sat down on a bench next to the wall, and Tonyeesha followed Ms. Hathey into her office. It could've been a large office, but so many boxes and gadgets cluttered the floor that getting to the chair in front of the desk was like running an obstacle course. Ms. Hathey gestured for Tonyeesha to sit down, and she did.

"What possessed you to be out of school so near to graduation?"

"I don't know."

"You don't know. No, I guess you wouldn't. Drapetomania takes many forms, I suppose."

"What's that?"

"Never mind. I'll have to call your father, you know." She pressed a few buttons on her computer while Tonyeesha looked on in mute distress, unsure what to say in a situation that was clearly out of her hands.

"Oh dear," Ms. Hathey gasped. "Your records show you've been absent without excuse for three entire days this week. Tonyeesha, I'm afraid I'll have to suspend you."

"What! But I'm on the track team."

"You should've thought of that when you decided to play hooky."

"But the team needs me. I'm their star runner. The school needs me. You can't beat Garvey High without me."

"The school needs you to attend classes." She picked up the phone and dialed. After a moment, she pressed the speakerphone button and hung up the receiver.

"Hello?"

"Mr. Jenkins?"

"Yes, this is he."

"Good afternoon, Mr. Jenkins. This is Ms. Hathey. I'm the principal at Washington High and I have your daughter Tonyeesha Jenkins in the office with me."

Rhonda Denise Johnson

"In your office? She's not hurt, is she? Why isn't she in the nurse's office?"

"No, Mr. Jenkins, she isn't hurt. She's in my office because she hasn't been attending classes."

"What? I send her to school every day. What are you talking about?"

"I understand that, Mr. Jenkins. However, a truant officer brought her into my office this afternoon and her records show she's been absent without excuse three entire days this week. I'll have to suspend her."

"Suspend her? I'll be damned."

"Since today is Friday, her three-day suspension will begin on Monday. She'll be responsible for all homework which accrues during her days of suspension, so she'll need to keep in touch with her teachers by email and log into her WCTools account each day."

"We don't have a computer," Tonyeesha said.

"I understand that, but these are the requirements of your suspension and you'll have to find a way to fulfill them."

"Is Tonyeesha listening? I'm going to whip your butt when you get home, girl. I'm going to give you the whipping of your life. *Skipping school?* I'm not raising no hoodlums."

Ms. Hathey put on a look of utter shock. "Mr. Jenkins, you do realize that corporal punishment is considered child abuse in this state and is against the law."

"To hell with the law. She's my daughter. Ain't no law going to tell me what to do with my daughter."

"I'll have to call the police."

"Call 'em. But they not going to tell me what to do with my daughter in my house. I'm not raising no hoodlums. Send that child home so she can get what she got coming." Then he slammed the phone down.

Ms. Hathey looked at Tonyeesha with pity and shared embarrassment. Then she picked up the phone and dialed another number.

"Hello, I've got a case of possible child abuse. Please dispatch police to the principal's office at Washington High."

Police? Tonyeesha jolted in alarm. She can't call the police on her pop. You don't call the police on a black man. But Ms. Hathey was white, so she didn't know that, and Tonyeesha sure wasn't going to say it. What could she do? She had to stop this.

"That won't be necessary. I'll just go home. I'm sure my pop didn't mean what he said."

"It sounded to me like he meant every word and every blow. I hate child abuse. I'll still have to suspend you, but I won't stand by and allow you to be abused."

"My pop doesn't abuse me."

"Man ought to be in jail."

"*Jail?*! That's my pop."

"Yes, I know, you poor dear. It's common for children to defend their abusers. So sad when it's a family member. But these things do happen and I try to put a stop to it when I see it."

"You can't call the cops on my father."

"I already have, and here they come." She gestured toward the window and Tonyeesha saw two officers emerge from the police station across the street and head for the school. She felt the panic rise in her throat.

"Don't be afraid, dear. The officers won't allow your father to hurt you. Has he hit you before?"

Tonyeesha watched television, and she knew everything she said would be used against her and her father, so she muttered, "No." This woman is crazy, Tonyeesha thought as the police entered Ms. Hathey's office.

Tonyeesha looked at the officers and the thought struck her like a balloon full of cold water. *They're going to put pop in jail because of me.*

"Officers, this is Miss Tonyeesha Jenkins. She's been suspended from Washington High for excessive truancy." The officers looked at Tonyeesha like they might eat her alive. "I was about to release her into the custody of her father when the man threatened to beat her when she arrives home. My understanding is that corporal punishment is illegal in California, so I summoned you gentlemen."

"Yes, ma'am. It's illegal, and those found guilty are subject to jail time in addition to having their children removed from their home."

Removed? Tonyeesha's mind tumbled over itself. This was getting deeper and deeper. Why are they making such a big deal? All she did was cut a few classes. They weren't teaching her nothing important anyway, and now the whole world was caving in around her. *No, no, no.*

Ms. Hathey smiled. "Her father's name is . . .," she typed on her computer. "Robert Jenkins."

"My pop didn't do anything."

The officers looked at her like they'd heard it all before and turned to Ms. Hathey.

"I'll have to release her into your custody now." She tapped on her computer and her printer spat out a sheet of paper. "Tonyeesha, when the terms of your suspension are complete, you'll need to return to school and bring this form signed by your father. When we have his signature and the signatures of your teachers confirming that you've completed all assigned homework, you'll be readmitted to your classes. Do you understand?"

"Yes."

Tonyeesha folded the paper, put it in a pocket of her jacket, and then followed the officers to their car. *Another squad car.* She paused, not wanting to just jump in like she was an old pro, but she didn't want them to push her in, either. This wasn't Officer Friendly from elementary school. Officer Friendly hadn't had a service revolver. And he hadn't looked at her like just scratching her nose would be the false move he was waiting for to blow her head off.

They gestured for her to open the back door and get in. She could do that. She had been in a car before. She didn't need any special knowledge of police cars. Like the truant officers, the men said nothing during the ride and she didn't dare ask them anything.

When they approached her house, her dread redoubled. They walked up the path beside her driveway. Funny, she should think of something as hers. The possessive pronoun sounded absurd under the circumstances. Nothing was hers—not even her own steps, which brought her inexorably towards some awful occurrence outside her control. All she could do was keep moving.

One of the officers, the taller one with the mustache, rang her bell. She drew in a breath. When her father came to the door, he was taken aback to see the police.

"Are you Mr. Robert Jenkins?"

"Yes. What's going on? They didn't tell me she was in trouble with the law. They just told me she skipped class. What has she done now?"

"Your daughter hasn't done anything, Mr. Jenkins. We received a report that you intend to administer corporal punishment to your daughter. As you may know, that's against the law."

"What the—you called the cops on me?"

"No, sir," Tonyeesha stammered. "Ms. Hathey called them. I tried to stop her, but . . ."

"And what are you wearing? Those aren't the clothes you walked out of here in this morning. You look like a hooker."

Tonyeesha moaned. She had forgotten about her clothes. Her "school" clothes were in her backpack, and in all the excitement, she'd had neither time nor thought to put them back on before meeting her father.

"Miss Jenkins, will you press charges against this man?"

This man? This man? When did her pop become "this man?" "No! That's my pop. Of course not."

"Then Mr. Jenkins, since there are no charges currently against you and no evidence of crime, we release your daughter into your custody. However, if you carry out the alleged threat of corporal punishment, you'll be prosecuted to the full extent of the law."

"Daughter?" Sheer anger left Mr. Jenkins's eyes glazed. He stared vacantly at some point beyond Tonyeesha, beyond the officers, out into the street and beyond that. "What daughter? No daughter of mine would walk around looking like that. Hell no! If you going to come to my house and tell me how to raise my daughter, then you take her. You buy her food and clothes that she throws away to wear some trash you'd never buy.

You stay up with her half the night when she's sick and you got to go to work in the morning to keep a roof over her empty head. I am through!"

"Pop?"

"Don't bring the police to my door and call me pop. Don't you dare. You're on your own." Then Robert Jenkins slammed his door shut with a finality that recalibrated Tonyeesha's heartbeat.

She stood back, staring at these two strange men who brought her down this inexorable path, and she stared at the unwavering door beyond which seethed a father turned stranger. This had all started with the decision to skip school and talk to some boys. She looked and didn't know what world she had stepped into.

The two officers stared at the closed door as if trying to decide whether slamming a door in a cop's face might be against some law. The mustached officer gave Tonyeesha an exasperated glance and turned to his partner. "We can only release her into the custody of a responsible adult."

Tonyeesha knew he was saying this for her sake to make her feel they had to do whatever they were about to do. They looked at each other.

"We'll have to take her down to the station until a responsible adult comes for her."

Responsible adult? Tonyeesha gulped. Only? Police stations? If her pop wouldn't come for her, Tonyeesha knew of no other responsible adult who would. That meant foster homes.

Before either of them knew what was on her mind, she took off running. She wasn't a criminal. They wouldn't shoot her, but they'd try to catch her; so she ran like the ugliest boy at Garvey High would be her date if she lost the track meet. She dashed around a corner and through someone's side yard. There was a shed with a cracked door swaying in the wind. She ran around it, hoping the cops would stop to look in the shed for her. By the time they realized she wasn't in the shed, she'd have turned so many corners that she'd be out of their line of vision.

She feared they might go back for their squad car and chase her in that. But it was a long block on a one-way street. She saw a bus coming and sprinted to the bus stop. Once she was on the bus, it turned a corner and was out of sight.

Responsible adult? She was safe for now, but if she wanted to stay safe, she had to find a responsible adult to vouch for her. She thought of her friend Lisa's big sister Chloe. She was old enough to be considered responsible but young enough not to do something stupid like turn Tonyeesha in to the police. Would Chloe help? Chloe was always nice whenever she visited Lisa. Tonyeesha knew that friendly didn't equal friend, but she had no other ideas. What else could she do?

She stayed on the bus a few more miles to be sure she wouldn't run into the officers, and then she transferred to one that would take her to Chloe's apartment.

Tonyeesha approached Chloe's building. A million questions slowed her to a stop. Suppose she's not home? *Oh, damn, suppose Chloe's not home?* What will she do if she isn't? She has to come home sometime. Just wait. When she reached the door, Tonyeesha thought, *suppose she has company.* Suppose she has a boyfriend? This is dumb. Tonyeesha almost turned around and ran. But that would be really dumb—a good way to find the nearest cop. She knocked on the door.

Chapter 7

"You want to do what?" Chloe exclaimed.

Tonyeesha's appearance at her door was sudden and the child's story sounded incongruous with what Chloe would've expected in a rational world.

"My pop will whip me if I go home and I have nowhere else to go."

"He's not going to whip a great big seventeen-year-old girl. You're almost a grown woman."

"He don't care if I was seventy-seven. He's still my pop and he'd still whip me."

"I don't understand this at all. Why did you come here? What do you expect me to do? Stop him?"

"The police want me to be in the custody of a responsible adult and you're the most responsible adult I can think of, so I came here. Please let me stay."

"Whoa. There are still some things I don't understand. How did the police get involved? What aren't you telling me?"

Tonyeesha took in a breath. "I told you, the principal at my school called my pop and he threatened to whip me, so she called the police, talking about it was against the law. I tried to stop her, but you know how adults are."

"Excuse me?"

"I mean . . . *old* adults. You know what I mean."

"Why did he threaten to beat you? The principal must have called him for a reason."

Tonyeesha looked like that was the one question she was hoping Chloe wouldn't ask. "Well, I . . . I was with my friend Jaleen at the K-Tel store. We wasn't . . ."

"We weren't," Chloe corrected.

"We weren't doing nothing . . ."

"We weren't doing anything."

Tonyeesha thought better of it and stopped just short of rolling her eyes. "We weren't doing anything bad or nothing. It's just that we was . . . *were* supposed to be in class. We were just in the wrong place at the wrong time and these boys started making a whole lot of noise, so the truant officers came and took us back to school. We didn't do nothing bad. We didn't steal nothing or nothing like that. We were just there and . . ."

"In the wrong place at the wrong time."

"Will you help me?"

"Help you how?"

"Let me stay here. I could crash on the floor."

"No."

"I have nowhere to go. My pop said he didn't want me."

"I'm sure he was just angry. I mean, you show up at his door with the police and whatnot. You should know you don't sic the police on a black man—especially not on your own father. You just don't do that."

"I know, but the principal wouldn't listen when I tried to stop her."

"Well, I'm sure he loves you and will take you back. Just go home."

"He'll whip me. Do you want me to get whipped?"

Chloe thought about that. She didn't want to think of a grown man whipping on an almost-grown woman, but Tonyeesha couldn't stay there with her. There was just no way. "Think about your future. You're about to graduate from high school. I don't know if you plan to go to college or get a job, but you can't do anything if you don't finish high school."

"They won't let me go back to school unless my pop signs the suspension form."

"Then there you are. You have to go home. There's no future for you sleeping on my floor."

"I won't be any trouble."

"Yes, you will. You'll be a world of trouble."

"How? I don't do drugs or steal stuff. I won't have wild parties and bring strange people home. I'm a good kid. And Lisa is my friend."

Chloe sighed. She couldn't be angry with Tonyeesha for not knowing what trouble is. She was a school kid. Never paid a bill a day in her life. "Tonyeesha, you have to eat. You do things that require electricity. That costs money. You need money for carfare. You're going to want new clothes and talk to your friends on the phone. Do you think I'm going to take care of you?"

"No, I can get a job."

"What kind of job can you get with no high school diploma? Will you throw your whole future away because you're scared of one little whipping?" Chloe couldn't believe she'd said that. But what else could she have said? She hadn't gotten Tonyeesha into this mess and didn't know how to get her out of it. The child couldn't go through life thinking she could ooze out of whatever mess she wanted to get in, because one day she'd find herself in serious trouble.

But Chloe examined her own self. Was she being cold? It was beyond her power to help this girl. If Chloe was supposed to help, she'd have the means to do so, but she didn't.

Tonyeesha looked absolutely despondent—a picture of hopelessness worth a thousand words of despair. She was in over her head. *Good.* Then maybe Tonyeesha would swim to the top.

But she was still trying to hold her breath. "I don't see why I have to go to school. I'm seventeen years old. They not teaching us nothing."

"They're not teaching us anything. Education is very important."

"If that's true, then why should I be going to a school where they not educating me? It feels more like jail. I get bored and then I can't even go to the store before they act like I committed a crime. Putting me in the back of a squad car where they had thieves and murderers."

"Learning bores you?"

"I learn stuff, but I can't see what to apply it to. If only there were something I could do. If only I had something to look forward to, then it wouldn't be so bad. But there's nothing and I know when I finish what they tell me to do, there still won't be nothing."

Chloe couldn't make empty promises. She couldn't tell Tonyeesha what her own mother told her—stay in school so you could get a good job. Oh, hell. How do you turn a child around when you have nothing to turn them around to? "Look, you've been crying. Go wash your face and I'll go with you to talk to your dad. I'm sure he won't whip you in front of me."

"But after you leave, he will."

"All I can do is talk to him. I wish you had something else to wear. What you have on isn't going to help your case. I might have something to fit you. Why did your father let you leave the house dressed like that?"

"My school clothes are in my backpack."

"Oh, really? Well, wash your face and put them on."

Chapter 8

Robert Jenkins stood in the doorway of his daughter's bedroom, seething with anger. His eyes fell on her iPad and her iPod, her blackberry and her closet full of clothes.

What made these things *hers?* She always referred to them as hers when her friends came to the house. They sat on *her* couch and watched *her* television. When the little boy from next door came over, she told him not to track dirt on *her* floor.

That was the teenage philosophy: what's yours is mine and what's mine is mine. He could forgive that. He'd been the same way some twenty-five years ago. But bringing the cops to his house? There was a point where it became *his* house, and when she challenged his authority, that was the point.

He fumed, sucked his teeth, fell to his knees, and sobbed.

The Crossroads of Time

She was a little girl, so sweet, his daughter. Going off to Sunday school in her frilly yellow dress—so cute. Was the change gradual or did it start the day she refused to wear patent-leather shoes? That's when he should've seen it, even if it hadn't actually started then. He should've known she wasn't the same little girl.

The day she was born, he knew she'd one day grow up; but he'd envisioned a dutiful daughter who adored her papa, especially after her mother died. He was the only one she had to cling to—the only one who took care of her and made sure she had what she needed and some of what she just wanted. What had come to his door with the police at her side, daring him to discipline her, was the deepest betrayal.

Suppose he hadn't been home? Suppose she'd had to go over her aunt's house, as the girl usually did on days he had to work? There would've been no whipping, no cops and he probably would've never found out what she'd done.

"Oh, she's just an angel. Just a little angel. Never any trouble."

Then Big Mae would pat Tonyeesha on her seventeen-year-old cheek and Tonyeesha would roll her seventeen-year-old eyes, which Big Mae never noticed because she was so sure what she beheld was the angelic remnant of her deceased sister.

No discipline and no wonder Tonyeesha was getting in trouble he didn't even know about. He sighed. She was his daughter, but things couldn't go on this way. Would she come back? He'd been very harsh. No, she'd come back when she got hungry—when she started missing her iPad or iPod or whatever you called them things. But would he take her back? Jenkins sat, staring at the blank television—slippers on, thick brows knit, full lips pursed, thinking. He just didn't know.

The room was so empty. Why? He'd always sat in the same room. On his days off, there was never anyone here but he. But the events of today made it seem empty because it was four o'clock and at this time of day, Tonyeesha would be in her room, blasting music while she pretended to do her homework. She was a smart student who made good grades. So he let her play the music as long as she remembered some of the trash the kids were listening to nowadays wasn't to enter his house. His house. So empty.

No, he couldn't let himself get sentimental. If she came back, it had to be on his terms, and there had to be conditions. He knew he couldn't stick to terms and conditions if he got sentimental. So he brushed feelings aside and waited. What was he waiting for? The phone to ring? A knock on the door?

Speak of the Devil. There was a knock at the door. Jenkins sighed and braced himself—for what, he didn't know. Through the frosted-glass window beside the door, he could see a shape that could only be Tonyeesha.

But there was someone with her. Who? Not more cops? No, she wouldn't dare do that again. He wasn't going to raise no hoodlums, and he sure hadn't raised no dummies. Whoever it was, this was his house and he had a right to tell whoever it was to leave if he didn't want them there. It couldn't be the cops. They had a way of erasing whatever rights he thought he had. But it couldn't be the cops again.

He opened the door and looked into the face of a beautiful young woman.

"May I help you?" He wasn't going to show the ire he felt in front of her.

"Mr. Jenkins, my name is Chloe Marshall. My younger sister Lisa is Tonyeesha's best friend. That's why she came to me. I've come to bring your daughter home."

Beautiful or not, she had to understand whose house this was. "Did you now? Well, there are rules in this house. If Tonyeesha doesn't want to abide by them, then she can't stay here."

"I will abide by your rules, pop."

"Last time I saw you, you had different ideas."

"That wasn't my idea, pop. The principal at my school called the police 'cause you . . ." She glanced at Chloe and caught herself. "Were going to whip me. I tried to stop her, but how can I stop the principal? She was trying to protect me."

"Protect you from your father?"

"That's what she thought she was doing."

Jenkins looked at his daughter. At least she'd changed back into her school clothes and looked decent. He figured he could thank Miss Marshall for that. Tonyeesha was a little too big for a frilly yellow dress, but he could still envision her in one. *No.* He shook his head. No sentiment, or they'd both suffer.

"Come inside. It's too cold to stand in the door. I don't know what fool said it never gets cold in Los Angeles." He stood back while Chloe and Tonyeesha walked into the living room.

Tonyeesha stood in the middle of the floor, unsure if she should make herself at home just yet. Jenkins ushered Chloe to the sofa, but Tonyeesha remained standing. Father and daughter eyed each other, not sure what to expect next.

"Pop, I'm sorry. If you still want to whip me, I guess I deserve it, but please be my pop again."

He was astonished. He certainly hadn't expected this. Or maybe he should have. Tonyeesha wasn't a bad kid, compared to some.

"I'll always be your pop, sugar. What're you talking about? I just want you to do what you're supposed to do."

Chloe sat in silence, watching the drama unfold. She knew it wasn't over. There was a lot this father and daughter had to work out, and they probably wouldn't start in her presence.

"See? I told you things would be okay."

"Thanks, Chloe."

"If there's nothing else, I'll be on my way."

They walked her to the door.

"Thanks, Miss Marshall, for bringing my daughter home."

"Tell Lisa I'll call her." Tonyeesha put all her weight on being good—saying the right things, but Chloe knew it was more than just an act. Yet, she knew this wouldn't last unless Tonyeesha found something to look forward to—a reason to do what she was supposed to do.

Chapter 9

"Hey, Chloe, remember me?"

Chloe looked up and groaned. Did she remember him? Did she have to? For a library, the first floor was so noisy that Ted's outburst fit right in. Still, her memories of their first meeting gave her a particular bias against the mere fact that he had weight and took up space.

"Mind if I sit down?" It was a rhetorical question that barely left his mouth before he pulled up a chair beside her. "I don't know why, but I'm glad to see you. How've you been?"

"Busy. Very busy," she said with her attention riveted on her book, hoping he'd get the hint.

He didn't. "All work and no play, I always say."

"Schoolwork doesn't leave much time for playing."

"I suppose you're right. I finished my work and now I want to . . ."

Disturb me, Chloe wanted to say, but decided she'd only have to spend more time with him, apologizing for her rudeness. She kept reading.

". . . Get ready for the Dance Ensemble. Can you dance?"

Now he had her attention. Like someone who'd been speaking Greek and suddenly started speaking English, he had captured her curiosity.

"Dance Ensemble?"

"Yes. We're a group on campus. We call ourselves the Dance Ensemble because we ensemble dances and perform all over town and in neighboring towns. We do ballet, ethnic, pantomime and modern dance. I'm surprised you don't know about us."

"I'm surprised, too." She wasn't so much surprised that she didn't know about them. She had always thought of dance in a therapeutic way, not as something she'd get together with other people and do in front of an audience. She was surprised to find herself interested in something she had never thought of before and was more surprised that Ted had sparked that interest.

"Can you dance?" he asked again. "You look like a dancer."

"Really? What do dancers look like?"

"Oh, they have strong shapely legs like yours. They're graceful and controlled in their movements like you."

This was flattery. Why was he pouring it on so thick? Like he thought it would get him somewhere. Where did he want it to get him? What difference did it make? She wasn't thinking about him, just about the dancers—a whole ensemble of dancers.

"We meet tonight at seven in King Hall 213."

"I must read this book. It's for an assignment."

"So read the book. It's only two. I'm sure a lady as smart as you are can read a whole book in five hours. What are you reading anyway?"

"*Adam Clayton Powell, Jr.: The Political Biography of an American Dilemma.*"

"Adam Clayton Powell, Jr? Never heard of him. Is he kin to Colin Powell?"

"I don't know." She gave him credit for at least knowing about Colin Powell. "Their ancestors might have come from the same plantation, so they took their master's name."

"Maybe, but we weren't all slaves on plantations. What about the Africans who came here before Columbus? What about the Africans who built the stone heads and pyramids in Mexico?"

"Stone heads?"

"They were here. They left statues of themselves wearing cornrows. Don't you think they may have left some offspring? And some of us looking for our ancestors on plantations may have come from them."

She didn't want to be impressed by this guy who'd been a nerd five minutes ago. But she was impressed by his knowledge. It was knowledge she had been looking for. Okay, it wasn't him. She was impressed by the knowledge. She could take it and run. Could she?

She looked at him. She had never looked into his eyes before. There'd been no need to look past the dork shield. But now, she was hearing what she hadn't expected to hear. So she looked, and when she did, she saw that his knowledge came from deep within. She couldn't take one without the other.

No, it was a trap. Once she looked into those eyes, she found that pulling away was more than a notion. No. How could this previous dork—this paper bound nerd—leave her in a state of cognitive dissonance?

Part of her wanted him to go back to being a nerd and part of her wanted to hear more. "You've given me food for thought, but right now, I really must finish this book."

"All right. See you tonight."

"What makes you so sure you will?"

"I know hunger when I see it."

She feigned hurling the book at him. He laughed, threw his hands up to guard his head and left.

Food for the mind, indeed, Chloe mused. When did Africans begin to migrate from Africa to other parts of the world? When did they come to North and South America? At what point did the ones who migrated to Europe lose their color—before or after they left Africa? Questions she had never seriously asked, but now she wanted to know, as if the knowledge would one day be the difference between wisdom and proactive ignorance.

Man, know thyself. Could the answer to these questions be a key to obeying that commandment? It all came down to that. Even the message in the music. Why would it all be coming together like this if it wasn't connected? Where had she come from and when? She had to know. She would know.

Chapter 10

Not again, Ted thought. *No*, not again. He wouldn't think "not again" again. But he just did. He felt destined—inexorably prone—to toss his heart to physically fit, intelligent, good-looking women like Chloe. Well, he thought, at least he had standards.

But those standards told him nothing about what was going on inside a woman. They told him precious little about where a woman was going in life or whether she had room for him in her life. By the time he discovered those things, his heart and mouth were already committed, so his brain had to be the bad guy to wrench them out of the trouble they longed for.

He approached the gym and stopped. Students passing by looked at him like they thought he'd either just won the lottery or was just a silly guy. Could they do otherwise, with him smiling at his own silly thoughts? This wouldn't do. He had to go in the gym and convince his teachers that he could handle thirty-five nine-year-olds on a playground. That took a certain level of sternness, and he'd never win their respect if he showed up mooning over some chick.

But he wasn't stern by nature. He twisted his facial muscles into how stern people looked and imagined the muscles of his body stiff and erect. No teachers pets in his classes. They'd know not to play with him. Act—action. Something that one did: an expression of knowledge about what was required. It wasn't a lie, he told himself. He'd give them what they wanted—a required action.

"The body needs to warm up before it can perform at its peak, and then it needs to cool down."

Ted took his seat in the physical education class. He was glad he hadn't had to cook up a grand entrance of cultivated sternness. They were doing the academic part of the class where he wasn't required to do anything but sit and take notes. He could put a stern look on his face while he sat there and just be one stern face among many.

He guessed the other students were glad, too. The time would come when they'd all have to prove themselves on their feet, and their teachers would watch for any lapse.

"If your students are running, don't make them stop suddenly. Leave room at the finish line for them to slow down from run to trot, and finally, to walk."

Chloe. Did he need to slow down from run to walk? *Oh hell.* Why was he thinking about her? His face couldn't look stern with such thoughts on his mind. The best he could do was look forlorn. Pay attention to the teacher, Ted reminded himself.

"They're a class of elementary school kids, not a squadron of foot soldiers, so your goal isn't strict obedience and discipline. Your goal is to teach these kids how their bodies work."

The academics went on for an hour. Ted rubbed the sore spot where his pen had pressed a groove in the side of his finger.

The student next to him snickered and typed on his iPad. "Hey, Ted, when are you going to join us in the twenty-first century?"

Ted picked up his pen and pressed it sternly into its customary groove. He didn't want people to think he was an old long tooth, but some things he'd never give up—like paper. It was easier to keep up with the teacher by writing than by poking one letter at a time. Besides, this guy with his iPad could probably sew embroidery into the calluses on their fingertips. Ted liked the solidity of paper. He'd held an iPad before and tried to use it, but it felt like an Etch-A-Sketch in his hands. Once the text scrolled off the screen, he knew it would still be there, but knowing didn't erase the feeling.

"Time breathing with movement," he wrote, and suddenly became conscious of his own breathing. He found it impossible to breathe naturally now, but had to consciously move his diaphragm or he'd stop breathing.

This class was as much for his education as it was for the kids he'd be teaching. *Gee*, he thought, the ancients had it all wrong. The saying should be *when the teacher is ready, the students will appear.*

"Pain is the body's alarm system. It lets you know when something is going on that needs your attention. If there's a fire, ignoring the alarm isn't going to put out the conflagration. There are two kinds of pain: pain from something that should not be happening, like a sprained ankle, and pain from something that's never happened before, like growing pains. Physical education means knowing the difference between a fire drill and a real fire."

The teacher, Mel Jeffries, was tall and muscular. He looked like he'd ignored a lot of fire alarms to obtain his brawn. Ted shifted in his seat, wondering if Chloe preferred that potato sack type to his own smooth dancer's physique. *Pay attention,* he commanded himself.

He realized that as he thought about Chloe, his diaphragm wasn't moving. He breathed deeply and had to make a conscious effort to inhale and exhale. He couldn't make a conscious effort to stop thinking about breathing. He couldn't make a conscious effort to stop thinking about Chloe any more than he could make a conscious effort to stop thinking at all. Concentrate on the teacher, he told himself.

"Your lungs aren't muscles, so when you breathe, your chest shouldn't move. Breathe from your diaphragm."

Ted knew that already. What he didn't know was whether Chloe thought about him as much as he thought about her. He pictured their first meeting in the administration building where he'd looked like a nerd even in his own eyes. He knew he must've looked like one to her, too. He sighed. Maybe their second meeting in the library had been strong enough to erase that god-awful first impression. She had responded more freely today. *Damn. Listen to the teacher.*

It dawned on him that during his musings, something had changed. The drone of the teacher's voice had turned into a murmur interspersed among the students. The teacher was no longer addressing the whole class, but was talking to a cluster of students gathered around his desk. Other students were putting away their iPads. Some seats were empty. Ted looked at his watch. *Damn.* Class was over. What is this woman doing to his mind? Maybe he was a nerd. He didn't know what else to call himself. Certainly, he wasn't the debonair charmer who could rock her biosphere the way he wanted to.

He left the gym and headed towards King Hall, wondering if he'd ever have command of his mind again. Of course, he would—it just didn't look like it.

Focusing his mind, he concentrated on getting where he was going, but the press of so many students headed in fifty million directions slowed his pace, allowing the thought demons to catch up with him, dance around his head and taunt him with images of Chloe. *No good.* He tried to focus on the people around him. Was Chloe somewhere in this throng? He looked around. Was that a yellow blouse he saw? Wasn't Chloe wearing a yellow blouse? *Damn.*

He went around behind the library so he could look out over the valley where the dorms nestled. Not too many students liked to climb the stairs that led up from the valley. He hoped the pristine view would clear his brain. Nature had a way of doing that. He looked down and saw a car cruising along the road that separated the valley from the main campus. Was that Chloe's car? Could she be so near? Ted stretched out his hand, as if he could reach out and touch her. He saw himself flying down the broad, stone stairs to the . . . *Damn. Damn.* This *has* to stop. He turned away and headed for the building.

Once in King Hall 213, Ted opened two windows to let the September breeze dispel the hot stuffy air. Sounds of campus life drifted in with the breeze. The percussion of walking feet mingled with the melody of singing birds to produce songs not found on sheet music. He couldn't write down the notes, but he could choreograph a dance in his mind.

Balancing one hip on the windowsill, Ted tapped his foot to nature's jam session. From his bird's-eye view, he could only look down on the heads of students scurrying along and wonder what it was all about. If he were down there with them, he'd know. Or maybe the thought wouldn't even occur to him that it had to be about something. Like them, he'd just go where he was expected to go and do what he was expected to do when he got there. But as an observer, he could think, so he was glad the practice room was on the second floor, above it all but not so high he couldn't observe the people walking by with their backpacks and briefcases.

What's it all about? He could ask Alfie, but Alfie could only tell him what it was about for Alfie in Alfie's generation. Ted chuckled, remembering how his uncles liked to sing those old school songs. That was the music his generation built on—danced on—like a tabletop where they could move higher, turning what once was into something that had never existed before and yet, had always existed.

He pushed the desks to one end of the room so his dancers could do their routines. Then he rearranged the desks so they could sit and discuss business. He went back to the windowsill to visualize what they'd do. Then he rearranged the desks again to make it a little more suitable to what he had envisioned.

Then he stopped, wondering why he was doing this. Yes, he was a choreographer, moving people to turn their bodies into visual art. But why was he moving furniture? The others would move the desks to their liking anyway. He knew he was running from something—trying to stay busy to stave off some thought lurking around the corners of his mind. Corners were seams and seams had cracks. The desks were okay. But he had to keep busy, or that thought would find the cracks, and he'd think about . . . Chloe. *Damn.*

The breach widened and a torrent of thoughts surged through his mind. Would she come? How would he handle it if she didn't? How would he handle it if she did? Where should he assume he stood with her if she didn't come?

"Hello, Ted. Where's everyone?" Yolanda Perry strode in like a shrouded blessing.

Ted felt instant relief. Safe Yolanda. Around-the-way-girl Yolanda with an around-the-way-girl intelligence, to keep his mind on around-the-way things.

"Oh, they'll be here. It's still early. You know them."

He returned to his perch on the windowsill while Yolanda did some stretches in the middle of the floor. Ted watched her. He couldn't help watching her. After all, she was female and she was safe—easy on the eyes with her soft curves and strong legs. She

118

was safe because she wasn't Chloe. She was wearing a golden-yellow Danskin that blended with her golden-caramel skin. From the waist down, she wore a skirt made of multicolored scarves that moved aside when she kicked up her legs—which she did often. Ted had the Devil's own time reassuring himself that she was safe. The golden slippers on her tiny feet weren't helping him at all. Yet, she was a distraction from what he really didn't—did—didn't—want to think about. He felt like he was snorting cocaine to break a heroin addiction.

Gradually, the other members of the Dance Ensemble trickled in. They were all wearing Danskins of some color. The women wore skirts, shorts or leotards, and the men wore loose pants to ease their movements. Flopping down in the chairs, they dropped their bookbags on the floor and their laptops on the desks attached to the chairs.

"Okay, I set things up at the Greenbaum restaurant. We are scheduled to perform there next month on the eighth," Ted said.

Ann MacArthur extended a long, purple, spandex-sheathed leg. "Kewl. That's an upper middle-class crowd, I assume. Guess we'll be doing ballet." She sighed. She liked ballet and thought of herself as kind of upper middle class as well. It wasn't a matter of money. Her income put her in the lower class. She didn't want to think of herself that way, so she determined class according to refined speech and high aspirations.

"Well, the stage is kind of small, so our performance will have to be very tight ballet with no more than four dancers on stage at a time."

"Only four?" Tommy Duckett repeated. "Which four?"

Ted could hear the sulk in Tommy's voice. The guy was sure that in any competition, he'd be the last one chosen, if at all. He wasn't a bad dancer or Ted wouldn't have allowed him on the team. Tommy just didn't think he was as good as the others and preferred an "everybody included" system.

"Oh, we'll all dance, just not all up there at the same time."

Tommy visibly relaxed and Ted thought he'd do the same, but out of the corner of his eye, he saw movement at the door. He turned his gaze and Chloe stepped into the room. All thoughts of relaxing dissolved into the barely breathable air.

Ted cleared his throat. "Glad you could make it. Everyone, this is Chloe Marshall. She's here to observe, and I hope, to join us."

"You can dance?" Yolanda queried. She cocked an eyebrow and sniffed, as if she were the one to whom Chloe had to prove herself.

With just the right smile, Chloe nodded to each member as Ted introduced them. He liked that she left Yolanda talking to the wall. But he worried that the woman he'd thought of as a safe distraction might prove to be dangerous in the presence of a perceived rival. *Oh damn,* he thought. If Chloe couldn't handle herself around the likes of Yolanda Perry, then what was there to admire? He decided to sit back and see what would happen.

Chloe took a seat and Ted cleared his throat again as he watched the graceful trajectory of her hips sliding into the chair.

"Take five minutes to stretch and then we'll do the routines for *The Silver Swan*. That seems most appropriate for the stage and the patrons at Greenbaum."

Chapter 11

Chloe entered room 213, not knowing what to expect. It's just a room, she told herself. Why should it be any different from entering any other classroom for the first time? She was an old pro now—a veteran at this game. So why was she nervous? Something inside her was shaking like dice, and like a roll of the dice, she didn't know what the outcome would be. *The outcome of what?* Again, she didn't know.

When she stepped into the room, she saw him leaning against the windowsill and knew what it was. *Why?* The nerd whose papers were about to scatter on the floor? The chauvinist who thought all the "girls" wanted to see how their first name sounded with his last name? Him? The guy who knew the truth about Africans in America? The dancer? Yes, him. Well, she hadn't seen him dance yet. She'd see what she'd see.

"Glad you could make it. Everyone, this is Chloe Marshall. She's here to observe, and I hope, to join us."

Chloe smiled. Like a dummy, she smiled. She didn't know why she couldn't help smiling. Then one of the women burst Chloe's bubble.

"You can dance?"

Chloe wanted to say, "Yes, I can dance." But behind the woman's disdainful stare, Chloe saw jealousy. The woman wasn't reacting to Chloe. She was reacting to Ted's unmistakable admiration of Chloe. Chloe wanted to laugh. Fortunately, Ted covered her by introducing her to the other members of the group. Miss Queen's name was Yolanda. Chloe tucked that information away for reference. There were eight dancers in all, plus Ted. Four men and four women. Chloe smiled. With all these dancers to occupy her attention, she needn't give Yolanda any satisfaction. She sat down.

"Take five minutes to stretch and then we'll do the routines for *The Silver Swan*. That seems most appropriate for the stage and the patrons at Greenbaum."

Greenbaum? They were going to dance at Greenbaum restaurant? That crowd barely let blacks eat there. If it weren't for the law. But dance, sing, entertain—oh, yes, always.

The dancers took various positions in the middle of the floor and began their stretch routines. They were graceful. It didn't even look like exercise—more like they were daring their bodies to do what they'd do on a stage. Chloe imagined herself moving that way. She had never lifted her legs so high, never defied gravity or turned on the axis at the center of her body with such fluidity. How would they look when they were actually performing in front of an audience?

Chloe began to doubt herself. Maybe there was substance to Yolanda's disdain. How could Chloe have thought the clumsy slides she did in secret qualified her for a live performance with professionals? She shook such thoughts out of her head. There was a lot she didn't know, but that didn't mean she couldn't learn. There was a lot she had never done before, but that didn't mean she could never do it. She saw herself doing it. Saw her feet float off the floor and her hands flutter like butterflies on the buoyant air around her.

"Freeze!" Ted entered the montage of dancers. "Okay, Bert, Carol and Ann, prepare for *The Silver Swan*. Everyone else, sit down and watch."

This they did. Ted and the three he had called went to their backpacks and donned ballet slippers—those shoes designed to make the feet do what they weren't designed to do. Then the four returned to the middle of the floor and took their positions. If it's possible for living flesh to liquefy and still remain solid flesh, then that's what they did. No music played, but Chloe felt the rhythm and melody simultaneously with each dancer as they moved to some silent composition. Chloe watched Ted. What she had seen in the administration building was a mere caterpillar, and what she had seen in the library was just his cocoon. What she saw moving across the floor of room 213 was a fully developed monarch.

He looked right at her. Each forward step was a step toward her, and each step back was a step away from her. Each movement of his fingers was a caress on some part of her body.

No, she told herself. She wasn't falling in love. She just liked the way he danced. She just liked the strong elegance with which he moved. She just liked that he moved in an atmosphere where no one else existed but her. Even the other dancers were just props in a dance done for her alone. *Stop it,* she commanded herself. She knew she had to stop right then before she went crazy. She had to cut it out before the dance ended and she'd have to face him with this moony-looking smile.

Ted broke her trance by stopping to correct his dancers—lift Carol's leg a little higher, sculpt the curve of Bert's back and tilt Ann's chin just a little more to the left. They kept practicing until they had done it perfectly several times.

"If you don't do it during practice, you're not going to do it in front of an audience." He was a perfectionist, yet none of them complained. "There is no way to excellence. Excellence is the way."

They didn't complain or cut corners, but Chloe thought she saw tension around their mouths and in their eyes whenever they achieved some anatomically complex position.

When Ted was satisfied with that set of dancers, he called the next set to perform the second scene of *The Silver Swan* and put them through the same rigors.

After many hours, he called timeout and they all began peeling off their ballet slippers and packing everything away. Ted moved slower than the others did and Yolanda moved slower still. She shot Ted a furtive glance as if to measure some possibility. Then, she turned her gaze at Chloe, the Devil in the details of Yolanda's plans. The anger in her eyes told Chloe Yolanda knew there was no possibility—not that night anyway. She yanked her pack onto her back and huffed out of the room.

When everyone left, Ted sauntered over to Chloe. "Well, what do you think?"

"Think?" she stammered. "Think, yes. I wasn't really thinking. I was watching. It's hard to believe they were just practicing. But then you're a hard taskmaster. The work you've done with them speaks for itself."

She wanted to sound intelligent, professional, but the feeling wasn't there. She could only hope it came across in her tone anyway. He whiffled on the verge of mooning, too. It was too soon for expressing emotions. She had to get out of there before one of them said something stupid. "It's late and I still have to do some reading tonight for my class tomorrow."

He glanced out the window. "Yes. It is late if you still have stuff to do. Personally, I can't do anything academic after nine. Shall I walk you to your car?"

"Thank you, but I'll be all right. I enjoyed your dancing most of all, but now I really must go." She got up and all but bolted out the door.

She wanted to hurry home, but even though rush hour was long over, there was still a lot of nightlife traffic in Los Angeles. This gave her time to calm down and think about what she had to think about—that book. Adam Clayton Powell. Why had she chosen such a hard person to write about? There was a lot of material about his politics, but she was in the religion and spirituality group and would have to dig for relevant material. *Teeth and claws into the black Church.*

How could she separate that from the struggle against racism and just see him as a spiritual leader? Why did she need to? What's the value of spirituality that doesn't respond to the realities around it?

Her group expected her to have something to say tomorrow. She could see the spiritual focus as a limitation or as a way to structure her thoughts. It was something other writers didn't focus on. *Perfect.* That's what she'd do.

Chloe googled for information about the two hundred-year-old Abyssinian Baptist Church and the National Negro Congress. *Negro?* Chloe hated that word. It was just a slip of the tongue away from the word *nigger.* She realized that in Powell's generation, that's what they called themselves because that's what they were called. They used the word, yet they still thought of themselves as progressive black people.

She read the book, stopping only long enough to pop a chicken potpie in the microwave for a quick dinner. She didn't notice herself drifting off. Fifteen minutes, half an hour, an hour went by and she still kept turning pages, seeing the words, but not registering what she was reading in her brain, which was fast asleep. In the morning, she reread her notes to distinguish what she'd read from what she'd dreamed she'd read. She was ready. She had enough material to give her group a decent progress report.

Sunlight shining through the windows onto her books took on many colors. She looked up and saw the stained-glass windows of Abyssinian Baptist Church. She looked around and all the familiar furnishings in her home were now made of marble. From somewhere, a massive gospel choir resounded, sending a river of serotonin through her mind.

"Keep your hand on the plough."

Yes, she would.

"Hold on! Hold on! Hold on!"

She definitely would. She had to hold onto something because she didn't know where she was or how she'd gotten there. At some point, she had stepped into the Twilight Zone. When she opened the door, a stream of ten thousand ghostly laymen flowed past her into what should've been a magnolia-studded courtyard but was now a street. *But the street?* It wasn't Wesley. The sign at the corner read West 138th Street. Harlem had jumped off the pages of the book she'd been reading last night into her mind. There were no soup kitchens in twenty-first century Los Angeles, but a line of people now waited at the side of the apartment building-turned-church, carrying bowls and looking positively destitute. The electric lights on the street looked new, like they hadn't been there that long. The visible wires betrayed an infrastructure that was still making the transition from gas to electricity.

Keep her hand on the plough? Where was the plough? Where was Cal State? She had to get there—her class. She walked in the direction she'd parked her car last night. Though none of the landmarks was familiar, thankfully, the car was still there. But now it was a low-rider with wings and sideboards. Chloe hesitated. Was this her car? This *was* her car. It had to be. She had a car. She'd parked it here, so this had to be her car.

She got in and stared dumbfounded at the polished cherry wood dashboard. A horse walked past her window. She looked up and saw a cop sitting on the horse, formally dressed with a policeman's cap and a billy club. His gun had a pearl handle. Chloe watched the horse's tail swish from side to side like a hypnotist's watch until it was out of sight.

This had to be a dream. Should she fight against it or let it happen. Then she thought about it and realized this wasn't a dream. She never knew she was dreaming while she dreamt. Only upon waking did her conscious mind take over and categorize what she'd seen and heard as a dream. But if this wasn't a dream, what was it?

As her Mustang-turned-low-rider cruised down unfamiliar yet familiar streets and highways, Chloe wondered how much of what she saw was real. Would the unknown force guiding this vision circumvent real dangers on the roads she wasn't seeing? She sighed. It would have to. When she thought about it, everything she saw was a transformation of what she should be seeing. There were streets where there should be streets and buildings where there should be buildings. This was the Harlem of Adam

Clayton Powell. The Harlem she had sleep-read about last night.

***

"Chloe, are you with us today?"

"Oh, yes. I was just deep in thought."

Yara Muniz peered at Chloe and repeated the question she hadn't heard. "What did you find out?"

Chloe was ready. She knew the man and his world like a scene played before her eyes. "Adam Clayton Powell was a man who did what I'd like to do. He used his knowledge and resources to make a difference in his community."

Edna Stone rolled her eyes. "I heard he was a flamboyant charlatan. Had all kinds of women and was so arrogant that he died a friendless has-been."

"I don't know about all that," Chloe answered. "From what I've read about his accomplishments in the black community, I guess some folks would try to keep the focus on stereotypes about black men."

"Why would people believe a stereotype unless there was some truth to it?"

Chloe sighed. This sounded like something her mother would say. Were they alike? How could people fight oppression if they believed they deserved to be oppressed? "Stereotypes don't represent a people. They only represent what others want to believe about those people. When people have an emotional need to believe something, they'll believe it, despite all evidence."

"The same could be said about your emotional need to believe this Adam Powell was a great guy."

Chloe wanted to slap Edna, but that would prove nothing. Did stupid people deserve to be slapped just because they have magnets in their mouths and hands are made of iron? "No, the same can't be said. I'm looking at the record of what he actually did. He's dead now. His personality and eccentricities died with him. All that remains are the doors he opened for black people. He fought for education, job opportunities, desegregation and economic equality. You can't even say for sure that you would be in school if it weren't for Adam Powell. He almost single-handedly desegregated the facilities in the House of Representatives. How do you know the doors that allowed you to be here today weren't opened by some other representative inspired by Powell?"

Edna smirked. "Our group is supposed to be about spirituality anyway.

What kind of spirituality could he have had with all them women?"

"King David had three hundred wives and seven hundred concubines. He could've given Powell his tip drills, and still David was called the apple of God's eye—a man after God's own heart, even with all those women."

"Well, that was the Old Testament. Things are different now."

"God is the same yesterday, today and forever."

"Well, it's just different. That's all. If you aren't saved and don't have the Holy Spirit . . ."

Yara looked at her watch and Chloe looked up at the clock. She'd let Edna take up enough of her time.

"Like I said yesterday, Adam Clayton Powell put the teeth and claws back into the black Church. After Nat Turner was caught, blacks weren't allowed to congregate for church or any other reason unless there was at least one white person present to monitor what they said."

Billy Green piped in, "You know, they still do that. It's not a law anymore, but they still do it."

"It might still be a law," Darius Clark said. "I mean, it might still be written down somewhere. Why else do they still do it? Black folks can't even meet at a water fountain before somebody white injects himself into their conversation. It has to be written down somewhere 'cause they all know to do it."

Chloe was astonished that the other group members were listening intently and taking notes. By some subtle instinct, she could sense other groups turning their ears toward her. Edna was sighing and rolling her eyes. Chloe decided that that couldn't be helped. There was someone like her in every group. If it wasn't an Edna, it was a Yolanda or someone else.

She continued. "Powell's church, Abyssinian Baptist Church, first began as a protest against the segregation practiced in the white church they attended. In fact, the name Abyssinia refers to Ethiopia in Africa. Under Powell, the black church turned from a besieged institution to a vanguard force in the struggle against racial oppression. The church provided educational and economic support to the Harlem community."

Chloe felt like taking a bow. They each had to present their findings about the person they'd chosen to research, and then write a paper integrating all these leaders.

She looked around at her classmates and an uncomfortable question entered her mind: Was she cheating because she'd had the help of spirits? She dismissed the question. It wasn't her fault if they came to her. She'd done nothing to conjure them. "Was that true?" the little voice inside her nagged. She'd entertained the thought of spirits. She'd pondered what message they were trying to send her through music. Was that the same as conjuration? She didn't know and she reasoned that what she didn't know couldn't be her fault. But would she ever know? What would her responsibility be once she did know?

Truth be told, she did want to know. Would it help if she talked to someone? She thought about Yara, a priestess. Yara might be able to answer some of Chloe's questions. If the spirits were trying to tell her something, Yara might be able to decode what they were saying.

Talking to Yara would take things to a whole new level. She could see her mother's eyes roll up into her head. The woman would fall to her knees, praying and even making the sign of the cross. "Lord, have mercy on my child," she'd say.

Chloe couldn't understand why people claimed to believe in the power of

God, but they gave the Devil credit for any real show of power in the real world. Only the Devil spoke in an audible voice. Only demons brought real visions or songs on the radio. She just couldn't believe this. Talking to the priestess of an African religion would be a bold move—a door of no return.

Chloe sighed. She knew her mother couldn't advise her—could do nothing but regurgitate her fears. But Yara? Chloe didn't know, but there was one way to find out.

"Yara, I'd like to speak to you after class."

"About what, may I ask?"

"About the work you do as a priestess. I may need your help."

Chapter 12

"Candomblé is my dance
In honor of the Gods
Axé, Olodumare Lord of Orixa
Axé, Exu divine messenger at
the crossroads
Axé, Xangô royal one of the
Yoruba
Son of Obatala and Lord of
lightning
Fourth king of the Oyo
Yara, daughter of Salvador
Dances to the rhythm of your
thunder
Dances in the sway of your
storm."

Yara's home was a spacious two-story Tudor cottage—rare in southern California and that's why she fell in love with it. Each morning, she threw open the frosted-glass windows of the gable on her second floor and greeted the sun. That hall was a holy place—the *terreiro* she never profaned with mundane activities.

She entered her *terreiro* dressed in a white chiffon gown with red slippers on her feet and a tiara of alternating red and white wooden beads on her head. At night, with the sun behind her house, she was obliged to light candles on the shrine of Xangô. She placed a wooden bowl of freshly brewed beer on the altar, careful not to spill its contents on the leopard-skin mat.

It wasn't a large shrine. Just room enough for four candles, six thunderstones, the bowl and the figure of a woman carved from pure ebony. Yara stroked the double-headed ax protruding from the statue's head and gazed into its calm face, seeing herself possessed of that same serenity.

She barely heard Enriquo's reverent tap on the door that led directly from the outside to her *terreiro*. That was something else she loved about the house because it meant her initiates didn't have to profane themselves by walking through her home. She, too, left her house and entered the *terreiro* through this door so that her mind could separate her everyday life from her spiritual service. Enriquo and three other initiates entered, carrying the costumes and masks to be used in that night's *toque* feast.

Yara heard them and sensed their movements but didn't interrupt her devotions to Xangô for their sakes. They knew what to do and her spirit would tell her if something were amiss. Nothing was amiss. The soft patter of their slippers betrayed no aberrations.

Then she heard the people purify themselves with water from a bowl of water near the door. She thought she heard the crash of thunder. *Very odd*, since there had been no clouds in the sky earlier. She listened and realized it was Enriquo on the drums. His hands moved with a speed that cracked like lightning, crackled like fire and boomed like clashing atmospheres.

The people donned their costumes and began to dance. Someone placed a wooden mask over Yara's face. She rose to her feet and danced. The flames of the candles caught her eyes and held them. As she watched, the four flames became one living conflagration that grew and moved but never consumed anything beyond the wicks of the candles.

"Xangô Lord of lightning,
Orixa of the flame,

> Move me Xangô,
> Move in me."

She chanted and the flame grew until it reached her and engulfed her—became her—the priestess of fire. She danced, but the fire didn't consume her, for it was the fire of the spirit—not of the candles.

All those around her drew back and fell to their knees. There was nothing special about her. Xangô would possess only one of them each time they gathered, and it was a different individual each time. All saw the flames in and around the Orixa's chosen vessel; sometimes it wasn't fire. Sometimes it was a white glory as Xangô alternated between the passion of his father and the wisdom of his mother.

Behind the rush of the flames and the beat of the drums, Yara heard the voice of Olumide, the babalawo of her *terreiro*, singing the deeds of Xangô in the deepest bass.

> "Let the fire of your father be
>   with us tonight,
> Obatala show us plainly the
>   way of reason and
>   good judgment,

Rhonda Denise Johnson

> But Aganju will fuel with
>> passion all that you
>> advise."

When he finished, all was still. The four candles were candles again. Yara sat on the floor—cool, as if she'd doused the flames with her own sweat. Her eyes panned across the room and fixed on Chloe's stricken face. The woman must have come in sometime during Yara's trance, and the scene had obviously unnerved her. These Westernized people always were. They profaned the temples of their gods by holding business meetings and fundraisers in them. They got emotional and the music made them feel good, but nothing really happened. They never saw anything they wouldn't see in a school auditorium or a circus.

But Chloe looked as if she had seen God himself, and indeed, she had, for Xangô, Lord of Lightning, was beloved of Olodumare, as were all his children.

Yara removed her mask as initiates brought in platters of roast lamb and vegetables for the feast. She had wanted Chloe to see this—wanted her to know the student from Brazil was a real priestess with real power like none other. She hoped it hadn't been too much.

"Axé, Chloe. I see you."

"I see you, too, but I can't believe it. I thought you were cooking. The fire looked so real."

"That's because it was real. But it is fire that cleanses the spirit. It doesn't burn the flesh."

Olumide strode over and smiled. "It is time for the Oro."

"I see you, Olumide. This is my guest, Chloe, from Cal State."

"Axé, Chloe"

"Ashay," Chloe repeated.

Yara mused that the young woman said what was expected without the slightest idea what she was saying. That was one way to learn on the sly.

Chloe looked puzzled. "The Oro?"

"The sacrifice, you'd call it in your tongue." Tension twitched the corners of Olumide's mouth as he answered a question he probably thought Chloe shouldn't need to ask.

"Sacrifice?" Chloe looked aghast. "I didn't know you did that. That's like what my mother and them do in church. So you sacrifice for your sins like they do? I can't get away from this idea that God loves blood."

Olumide frowned. Yara didn't like it when he frowned. He was her babalawo and there were always consequences when he frowned. Yet, she knew he shared her distaste for this particular kind of misunderstanding.

Then he smiled as if he'd found sweet candy within a bitter coating. "On the contrary, Chloe. We do not sacrifice to appease some gore-loving god as the Christians do. Perhaps the term sacrifice is imprecise. It is more of an offering. By offering the Oro, we feed and nourish the Orixa. Then we eat to share enjoyment and communion with that Orixa. It has not a thing to do with sin."

Yara knew better than to trust that smile. Sure enough, it quickly faded into the frown that lay beneath it.

Olumide scoffed. "Doubtless, as a Westerner, you would spell Orixa as it sounds, o-r-i-s-h-a. But we practice Candomblé here. In Brazil, we use the Portuguese spelling with an x rather than s-h."

Chloe opened her mouth, some objection in her eyes, but she thought better of it and remained silent. Yara wondered how she'd undo all the misunderstandings in this woman's mind before giving her the help she wanted. The Orixa would not help Chloe if she displeased tem, which she'd surely do if she approached them with crazy ideas and a closed mind.

The initiates placed great heaps of food on the table before them. Lamb and plantains for Xangô, goat and aguardente for Exu. Everyone began to eat, but Chloe stared at her plate.

"Shouldn't I know something about the Orixa before I eat their food? This is just food to me. I can't pretend I'm eating it to commune with a god I don't know. That fire I saw, couldn't they make it real if my heart isn't right?"

Yara and Olumide smiled, but they didn't reassure Chloe. Instead, he conceded. "Yara, your guest, Chloe, is wise. You do honor to this *terreiro* and to the Orixa by respecting their food offerings."

Beneath his words and smile, Yara could feel ice and steel. "Respect" and "honor" were words that tempted her to feel Chloe had pleased him. She felt no such thing. Yara summoned Enriquo and instructed him to escort Chloe to the living room downstairs. The banquet continued until midnight. When the last guest was gone, Yara sighed and faced the babalawo.

"Come with me." He headed for the door leading to the street.

Yara shuddered. Whatever he had to say couldn't be said in the *terreiro*. She braced herself and followed him outside.

"Unto what purpose did you profane this holy place by bringing in such an ignoramus?"

"I didn't know."

"Correct. You didn't know. Why would you bring someone into the presence of Exu if you weren't sure of her?"

"She asked for my services as a priestess, and I wanted her to see the power of the Orixa. I forgot about the food." That wasn't a good answer. Yara didn't need Olumide's scornful gaze to tell her that. The words were out now and couldn't be taken back for editing. She wanted to go in the house but didn't dare leave her babalawo until he dismissed her.

"You forgot about the food?"

And Yara didn't need his icy voice to tell her she was in trouble. *Damn him.* She loathed herself for damning him—*but damn him.* She did everything she could to keep her *terreiro* holy, but it still wasn't as orthodox as he'd like it. He wanted a big temple like the one in Brazil. There just wasn't anything like that in Los Angeles.

"I must crawl before I can walk, Olumide."

His baleful eyes offered her no pity. As diverse as Brazilian culture was, Yara thought he'd be more open-minded, but he was clearly one of Exu's tricks to keep her at the crossroads.

"Well, crawl into your house and see what your guest wants."

That was the dismissal Yara had been hoping for, and gracious or not, she took it.

There was no television in Yara's house. She couldn't see the point of keeping the *terreiro* holy if she profaned her own mind with what Westerners called entertainment. She had never watched it, but had heard enough about it to not even think of purchasing one. If the mind was contaminated, the fires of Xangô burned hot. Then Olumide would have a case against her and everything she was trying to do. Most importantly, the Orixa would have a case against her and find her unfit to do what she was trying to do.

Enriquo had turned on the music and Yara heard the drums of Babatunde Olatunji as she entered the living room. Chloe sat on the sofa, contemplating a Rubik's Cube. Yara let her feet scuff the carpet so she wouldn't startle Chloe. "You wanted my help?"

Chloe didn't put the Rubik's Cube down, but she raised her eyes to Yara. "There are spirits trying to tell me something. I keep having these episodes—these visions."

"What do you think they're trying to tell you?"

"I don't know. I thought maybe you could decipher their code or whatever it is they're trying to do."

Yara sat down in the armchair across from Chloe. "What are they doing?"

The self-assured Chloe that Yara knew from Cal State was on hiatus. Chloe studied her shoes as she said, "Sometimes when I'm playing music, a song just comes on that matches whatever is happening around me or whatever I'm thinking. I dismissed it the first two times, but when it happened three times, I started paying attention. And I see visions."

"Visions?"

"Well, episodes. When I need information. I suddenly find myself immersed in a scene that shows me what I need to know."

Yara knew some people really did have visions from the spirits, but those who just claimed to see visions were as plentiful as peanuts in the Western world. What passed for spirituality here was often nothing more than emotional frenzy. Until she knew for sure what she was dealing with, she had to take a secular stance. "That could be a spirit or it could be your own mind."

"I'm not crazy."

"No, I don't mean to say that you are," Yara backpedaled. She didn't want to put Chloe on the defensive. "I mean your mind—your superconscious. You have three conscious states. Your subconscious mind, which holds your memories and your emotions, is at the forefront when you dream. Your conscious mind, which governs your awareness when you are awake, contains your reason, your will and the voluntary movements of your body. And then your superconscious mind is the part of your mind that communes with the universe and can give you visions that aren't dreams."

"That's possible," Chloe conceded. "But it doesn't explain the music. I can't control the music that comes on the radio or my Windows Media Player, which has over three hundred songs playing at random. And even if I could, what would be the point if I'm the only person around to hear it? They're spirits—outside forces—and I don't know what they're trying to tell me."

"Maybe they're not trying to tell you anything. Maybe these spirits just want you to know they're there."

"That makes no sense."

"Doesn't it? Haven't you ever just wanted someone to acknowledge you or just wanted someone to know that you were with them for no other reason than just your presence?"

"Of course. But I'm a person."

Yara wondered how spirits could have contacted someone so spiritually obtuse. She tried to respond with patience. Maybe the Chloe she'd seen in class would show herself. "Do you think spirits aren't people?"

"I mean, I'm human. Spirits don't have emotions like people. They're spirits. They're beyond that."

Yara didn't know whether to chuckle or groan at Chloe's total lack of comprehension. She decided to just give her the benefit of the doubt. After all, Chloe had come to her seeking knowledge—she must want it. "Why not? Spirits are people. At some point in their existence, they walk the Earth clothed in flesh and blood. They are born. They live. And then they die just like you and I do. And one day, we too, will be pure spirits and we'll see them as I see you. So maybe these spirits are just trying to let you know they're there and you aren't alone."

"Maybe. Or maybe they have a purpose for wanting me to know they're there. But I came here with maybes. I was hoping you could turn those maybes into knowledge."

"For that, you will need divination."

"Can you do it?"

"Oh yes. That is one of my services as priestess. But we cannot do it here. This place is profane. We'll return to the *terreiro*, use the *jogo de buzios* and see what's what."

Chloe looked around from the embroidered chairs to the onyx mantle with a surprised look on her face. "Profane? This is your home. It's lovely."

"Yes, it is lovely for me, but I won't summon the Orixa in the same place where I eat and sleep."

"I thought God was everywhere, even in the bathroom."

How disgusting can this woman get? Yara schooled herself to hold her tongue, remembering this was the way Chloe had been raised. Yara hoped she wouldn't bite her tongue in two before the night was over. "That's true. Olodumare is everywhere. But our minds are finite. Our surroundings affect the contents of our minds. To have pure thoughts, we must keep our surroundings pure. I don't want to be thinking about my taxes or my lover when I'm supposed to be thinking about Exu."

Yara rose and walked toward the door with Chloe close behind.

Chapter 13

Chloe pondered the sixteen cowrie shells of the *jogo de buzios*. What could they possibly tell her? She had seen Yara immersed in flames right in this room without even the smell of smoke. That left no room for doubt. Yara was a priestess with great power. But could she tell Chloe what she needed to know?

Yara began to chant.

"Orixa, bless these shells,
Imbue them with your divine
        Axé,
Tell sister Chloe what she
        needs to know and do,
Direct the *buzios* that they fall
        in meaningful ways,
Giving us knowledge and
        wisdom as you see
        fit."

Then she addressed Chloe. "The Odu will answer three questions. Think. What are the three most important things you need to know right now?"

Three questions? Chloe had only one question. The other two would depend on the answer she got for the first. Without hesitation, she asked, "What message are the spirits trying to give me?"

Yara threw the shells onto an ornate tabletop and studied them. Then she started as if she'd heard a noise. She gazed wide-eyed at something behind Chloe. Chloe turned to see, but there was nothing there except what had already been there when they'd first entered the *terreiro*.

"What is it?"

"Let her see me. Let her see me." Yara's voice had become deep and ethereal. Not her voice at all.

She took both Chloe's hands, and Chloe gasped at what she saw. At once, she knew Osa Meji. But how, having never seen her before? Chloe had never heard her name, but Chloe recognized the spirit behind her visions as if she were an old friend.

"I see you and you know me." Osa whispered. "Cast not the *buzios* again, for I will answer your questions. To the first you will find your answer in the wind."

154

"The wind?" Chloe gulped.

"What is your second question?"

Chloe thought about it. *Her second question?* She wasn't sure the first one had been answered meaningfully. But she asked, "What should I look for in the wind?"

This question pleased the Odu. "Look for Oya, Exu and Ayodele."

"When will all this happen?"

"When you are ready." Then Osa Meji vanished.

When Chloe was ready? She thought that she was ready now. That's why she'd come to get answers to her questions. Now she knew no more then she'd known when she first came here. Find her answer in the wind? She sighed. The Odu was gone. Chloe could ask no more questions.

"The spirit is gone now," Yara said. "She won't return tonight, so let's leave the *terreiro*."

Chloe followed Yara down to the kitchen. Yara poured hot water into two cups of chamomile. As the tea steeped, Chloe brooded over the rising steam as if it could fill her mind with the answers she needed.

Yara stared into her cup pensively. "There's a lot going on here."

"I hope you can tell me what it means."

"I haven't the slightest idea what it means."

Chloe didn't want to believe that. She didn't want to believe she had come all the way out here with her hopes only to see them crumble.

To her relief, Yara continued. "But I can tell you this. Oya is the Orixa of the wind. She governs change. So there will be some kind of change in your life. Exu is the divine messenger. He stands at the crossroads. So you'll have to make some kind of decision in your life. Ayodele, I don't know. Never heard of her. But she figures in some way that will be revealed to you. Most interesting is Osa Meji. She's associated with witches. Wonder why she came to you."

"*Witches?*" Chloe choked on her tea. She hoped Yara wouldn't think she was a witch now. "I'm not a witch. I wouldn't cast spells to hurt people."

"That's not what witches do." Yara assured her. "Witches represent female power and all power comes from Olodumare. We see witches as evil because men fear female power. On this planet, we don't use female power for its true purpose. Instead, we use it to free women from male oppression. Until women are free, we can't be who we are."

Female power? Chloe smiled. She was in her element now. Regaining the self-possession to which she was accustomed, she replied, "And men can't be who they are either. Oppressing women can't be the true purpose for male power."

"Exactly. So why did Osa visit you? Why has she been giving you visions? I mean, what specific oppression are you fighting against in your personal life?"

Chloe felt less confused now. She felt like she was moving toward answers to questions she hadn't asked but needed to know.

"I don't know. I just feel like I should be doing something with my life, more than is expected of me. White people send their kids to school so they can learn to rule the world. Our parents send us to school so we can get a good job working for white people. Here I am, doing all this studying, taking all this time, spending all this money; and all anyone expects of me is that I get a good job. I feel like whoever is really responsible for my life—whoever put me on this Earth—expects more of me. But what more, I don't know. And how to deal with my family's disappointment if I don't land a six-figure job, I really don't know."

Her cup was empty, so Chloe poured herself some more, as if she were at home. Why did she feel like she was at home? She hardly knew this woman. And why had Chloe disclosed her deepest wishes and fears to a practical stranger? She could only wait to see how Yara responded.

"It's possible you had an ancestor who was a great queen, king or even a priestess. Or perhaps, it was someone who wasn't glamorous but made a profound contribution to the world. Maybe that is why you feel you should be doing more."

"So you think I'm trying to be something I'm not just because I had a big-shot ancestor?"

"On the contrary, why would the Odu urge you to be what you're not supposed to be? And becoming something you're not yet is the goal of all life."

"Huh?"

"Look out the window. Do you see the tree in my backyard?"

Chloe nodded.

"Every tree is a seed that dared to be something it's not. It's called growth. You can't look at an acorn with your physical eyes and see the oak tree it will become. Growth is the confluence of imagination, effort, and time."

The Crossroads of Time

It was well after midnight, but they kept talking until the wee hours of the morning began to get kinda big. Chloe had to go home. She knew she could give up a good night's sleep, but she had to prepare for class. So she said good night and headed for her car.

In class the later that day, Chloe could hardly keep her attention on Billy's report on Ra Un Nefer Amen. She could only approach what was going on around her by slipping through the cracks between thoughts of Ted and Osa Meji.

Edna's ignorant statements didn't encourage Chloe to pay attention. "I don't know any Egyptians. What does Egypt have to do with black history?"

Billy rolled his eyes as if he had been expecting this argument. He defended his choice. "Most Europeans have no direct ancestry in Greece or Rome, yet they still acknowledge Greece and Rome as a central part of their heritage."

Chloe wondered what Ted would say about this. He knew all about ancient black history. He'd know something about Africans and Egyptians.

"Were the ancient Egyptians black?" Yara asked.

"As the ace of spades."

Rhonda Denise Johnson

"And is this man Ra Un Nefer Amen black?"

"Yes."

"Then Egyptian spirituality is part of black history."

Simple as that. Edna opened her mouth to argue, but Chloe tuned her out. She wondered how this fit in with the Orixa. Was there an Odu in Egypt? Did Osa Meji give the Egyptians visions? Or did they know her by another name?

There were answers to questions and questions to answers. And there was only one place she could find answers to her particular questions—in the wind. Autumn leaves didn't seek the wind. They were just blown to and fro by some invisible force. But birds pulled themselves up on thermals when they wanted to rise. Would she be a leaf or a bird?

She'd find her answer in the wind? What kind of wind? The wind that blew debris in circles down Wilshire Boulevard? The winds of time? The Santa Ana winds? There was fire in wind—fire and sand and water. Chloe wondered if she'd find the fifth element, quintessence, in the winds of Candomblé. She didn't know, but she determined to do whatever she had to do, and somewhere she'd find whatever she'd find.

"Long before the Bible there was the Book of Coming Forth by Day," Billy was saying. Chloe could focus now that she had made her decision. Still, the rest of the day went by like a dream.

***

One phone call disrupted her dream. With a yawn, Chloe picked up the phone to find it was her sister Lisa, and she had some bad news. Chloe knew it was bad news as soon as she heard Lisa's voice. Chloe had passed through the teenage world where Lisa now lived, and the two sisters moved like they really were in two different worlds, speaking two different languages. They didn't know how to connect. Caught up in the exigencies of their own respective worlds, they seldom thought of connecting, unless something bad happened.

"Mom is in the hospital with high blood."

"Oh, my God."

"They're running tests to find what's causing it. They said it could be just stress or it could be a virus."

"What hospital?"

"Daniel Freeman."

"I'll be there in a minute."

Chloe picked Lisa up and they drove to the hospital. As they sat in the lobby, Chloe felt more like she was in a hotel or a museum than a hospital. The Catholics had appointed their hospital with soft carpets, plants and art. The colors were more relaxing—designed, Chloe assumed, to banish the sterile atmosphere of a medical institution. She knew what the room was designed to do, but that didn't change the dread she felt.

When she saw all the tubes and wires taped to her mother's body, Chloe caught her breath. Whatever else her mother had been to her, she had always been the epitome of physical strength. When Chloe was a child, her mother had loomed like a tower of power. Even after Chloe had grown up, she could never attain her mother's level of vigor that always dangled twenty years ahead of Chloe. Now, this frail woman tore the fabric of Chloe's world, as if it were some long-held sense of security that finally proved itself false.

A nurse came in to check her mother's vital signs. She positioned her pillow and wrapped a blood pressure cuff around her arm.

"Will she be okay?" Lisa asked.

Chloe could only guess what might be going through her little sister's heart and mind. The child had never faced anything serious—not like this. Lisa's voice was calm, but Chloe saw a tic at the corner of her eye that belied the calm exterior. She might be holding back an avalanche with nothing but her own untried strength.

The nurse didn't look up from her ministrations. "Until the tests come in, we can only hope that she will."

"She's our mother," Chloe said.

Smiling, the nurse said, "Oh, I don't mean to worry you. Everything looks pretty good." Then she looked at the monitor, took some notes and left.

Chloe looked at the monitor. She couldn't decipher it, but she knew from watching television that moving, squiggly lines were good and a flat line was bad—very bad. The lines were squiggly, like a picture of sound waves.

She took a little heart. But she was still nervous about the uncertainty of what might happen. People died from high blood pressure. Her mother's intense personality made things even worse. Her brand of Christianity compelled her to feel like she needed to control so much: the words, beliefs and thoughts of those around her, the level of faith needed to move God's hand this way and that, along with her children's attainment of what she thought of as success.

So much. Chloe couldn't feel guilty for not being what her mother wanted. That may have contributed to her mother's stress; but if she died because Chloe could be nothing but her own self, Chloe knew she'd feel bad—very bad—but not guilty.

She chided herself for thinking the worst. The monitor connected to her mother showed signs of life—and where there was life, there was hope.

Chloe wondered if there was anything she could do to make that hope a reality. *Pray?* She had seen her mother pray a hundred prayers. If five of the things she'd prayed for happened, her mother took it as proof that her god answered prayers. Chloe mused. Those were the same odds people used when they played the lottery. She considered the similarity between the words play and pray. Despite her mother's certitude, Chloe had never seen anything that could inarguably be the result of prayer.

But what about praying to Olodumare? Yara's power was undeniable, but was it anything beyond pyrotechnics? Could she channel it into something useful like healing, Chloe wondered.

***

"My mother is sick in the hospital."

Chloe sat on Yara's couch, taking out her anxiety on the hapless Rubik's Cube. She had meant to return, but not under such dire circumstances. But then, if Candomblé couldn't help, what was the point of coming at all?

"You want the Orixa Omolu," Yara said.

Her answer came so automatically that Chloe wondered how the woman could be so sure. Like it didn't matter what the sickness was. One Orixa for all ailments. "You know a lot more about it than I do."

Yara maintained a somber face. "Omolu is a healing Orixa in Candomblé. Although he is known to bring disease to those who anger him . . ."

"I don't want to fool with something that will bring disease." Chloe couldn't understand why Yara would even suggest such a thing.

Placing a reassuring hand on Chloe's arm, Yara said, "Only to those who have left the path of righteousness far behind."

"Path of righteousness?"

165

"Peace with Mother Nature. There are laws in the universe. Like the law of gravity, we can't break spiritual laws. We can only live in a way that brings unfavorable results. The same law of gravity that keeps you from floating off the floor can kill you if you jump out of a window. Whether you jump intentionally or fall out accidentally, the results are the same."

Chloe pictured herself telling her mother to be at peace with Mother Nature. "Jesus is the only path to righteousness I know," she'd say. Chloe turned the cube again and sighed at the green square floundering in a pool of red squares. She felt like that green square. "My mother won't pray to any Orixa. But maybe I can pray for her. Just pray to Omolu and he will heal my mother?"

Yara looked out the window as if something out there would tell her how to deal with Chloe's naiveté. "Just pray? No, you can't *just* do anything. You Westerners always want a pill to relieve you from the consequences of a bad lifestyle."

"Why do you like to bash Western culture?"

"Call it bashing if you like. That won't change the reality."

"*Reality?*" Chloe realized what this was about. So Yara thought black Brazilians had a monopoly on reality. They used the Portuguese spelling of Orisha, an African word. As if the Portuguese hadn't enslaved Africans in Brazil as brutally as the English had enslaved them in North America. Remembering what she'd come for. Chloe pursed her lips. She couldn't put the woman in her place in her own house and then ask for her help. So she held her peace.

Yara looked away again, as if to compose herself. If this were going to turn into an argument, she'd leave.

But Yara cleared her throat and spoke in a milder tone. "You can't pray against nature. Health is an alignment between the mind and body, our spiritual being and the Divine Cause.

Chloe couldn't help interjecting, "Isn't a god who causes disease acting against nature?"

"Not necessarily," Yara continued. "The air around us is full of disease-causing agents. Every time we breathe, we're breathing in bacteria, viruses, fungi, molds, parasites—even the dead skin cells that shed off people around us. When we live a lifestyle that's contrary to the universal law, we create within our bodies an atmosphere that is conducive to those agents."

"My mother doesn't smoke or drink," Chloe said hopefully. "I can't imagine how her lifestyle could be causing her illness."

"What exactly is her illness?"

Now she asks. Chloe rolled her mind's eye. "She was hospitalized with high blood pressure."

Yara nodded. "The mind and the body work together. Even if a person doesn't abuse substances, the brain releases its own chemicals in response to our thoughts and feelings, and these chemicals have an effect on our bodies."

It was beginning to make sense, but Chloe didn't like what she was hearing, so she wasn't ready to concede. "That makes no sense."

"Really?" Yara raised an eyebrow. "When we're sad, the glands in our eyes release tears. When we are afraid, our bodies shiver. And when we are angry, guess what—our blood pressure goes up."

That was designed to hit home, and because Chloe couldn't deny the truth, it did. "Still, there must be something you can do to help her."

"I can give you herbs and show you the rituals of Omolu, but if your mother

168

doesn't change the lifestyle that raised her blood pressure to begin with, it will continue to rise."

This sounded more like science than spiritual power. Chloe still tried to hold on to this one last argument, although she wasn't sure why she was giving Yara a hard time. Chloe wanted answers and no one would just give her a simple, uncomplicated, straightforward answer. "Then all she needs are the herbs and to change her lifestyle. She doesn't need the Orixa."

Yara matched Chloe's frustration. "Setting out to change one's lifestyle is a wonderful intention, but actually doing it is another matter. From what you've said, your mother probably won't even have the intention."

Chloe wished to god she could argue with that.

Seeming to note this, Yara continued. "How can you embrace an African understanding of well-being and still hold to a Western misunderstanding of the universe? It would be like trying to bake a cake in the same plastic bowl you mixed it in. You can mix the ingredients, but when the heat of reality hits it, the whole cake suffers. The Orixa are teachers and their rituals focus our minds on the principles they teach."

Chloe shook her head. She worried the Rubik's Cube a little more, and then set it on the coffee table. "I just can't see my mother praying to an Orixa. It's not going to happen."

"Then why did you come?"

"I was hoping the fire I saw in you the other day could be channeled towards my mother. Maybe the herbs can take the power to her."

"An herb? A pill." Yara sighed. "There are herbs for your mother and meditations to help you focus on the path of righteousness."

"I'm not sure if I need . . ."

"Do you still want Osa Meji to help you with your original quest?"

When Chloe remembered that, she paused. She had been so caught up in trying to find an answer for her mother that she had forgotten about her own questions. The visions and the power behind them were real enough even if they couldn't help a woman whose mind was stuck on things Chloe knew didn't work. "Yes, of course I do."

"Then you need to focus on getting your own life in line with the universe and the purpose for which you were created."

In a much brighter mood, Yara summoned Enriquo. She whispered into his ear, and he left, returning with a package and a book.

Yara handed Chloe the package. "These herbs are for your mother. They have a calming effect on the nerves and she doesn't have to believe in them for them to work. However, they won't force her to be calm if she's determined not to be." Then Yara handed Chloe the book. "This is for you. It contains meditations and prayers that will teach you a way of life conducive to Orixa power."

Enriquo departed with a bow and Yara stood up. "I must go to the *terreiro* to prepare for the *toque* feast. Enriquo will tell you when it's time for you to come up. Will you stay for the banquet?"

"I don't know." Chloe wished she could've answered with an unqualified affirmative. She still didn't know if mere openness to learn about the Orixa would be enough in the absence of real knowledge. All she could do was go up there and see what happened.

Chapter 14

Chloe found herself dancing to the hypnotic drums, despite not knowing what they meant, and she was sure they meant something. Rhythms of ancient knowledge taught her feet to move. Her feet knew exactly when to rise, where to move and when to fall. They touched the floor at the precise moment the drummer touched his drum and rose with his hands without faltering. Chloe marveled that the rhythms of these drums weren't far from the rhythms that played in her mind when she danced alone. From somewhere, she had known them. In some distant sphere, she had danced to them before.

As she moved, she felt a surge of power not her own. A glow engulfed her body, probing each pore until it gained entry to her mind. It was clean but hot. She saw the people around her move away. They gazed at her in astonishment.

"She's a stranger here. This cannot be," she heard someone say.

"Xangô does as he wills. Who are we to say what he cannot do?" another answered.

Chloe felt the heat burning away a part of her and she trembled in fear. Then she realized that the fire wasn't burning away a part of her at all, but something that outside influences had added to her essence. Burned away were thought drifts and feelings that had disguised themselves as her own because she had forgotten the books, movies and television commercials from which they'd originated. Soon she felt clean. All doubts about her worthiness vanished and she perceived within her mind a new acceptance and overstanding of who she was.

As Chloe continued to dance, she became aware of a man approaching her. The people who'd given her room to dance gave him a wide berth as well. She knew at once who he was and that he wasn't a man, but a god. He bore in his right hand a broom wrapped in leather and encrusted with shells and beads. He held the broom like a dance partner as he danced. Bent over double and trembling, he took three steps and pivoted. His dance turned him this way and that but always toward her.

"Omolu," she whispered. "I'm not sick. Why are you coming to me? I haven't prayed to you or known you."

"But I have known you," the Orixa said. "Did you think you could speak to the Odu Osa Meji and not be known to all of us? You will build a shrine to me and with this broom you will sweep away sickness from your mother's presence."

"A shrine?" Chloe yelped. "My mother won't allow . . ."

"No matter what she allows, you will do it, or she will die." He spoke with such grave finality Chloe couldn't doubt his pronouncement. Yet, what he asked her to do was impossible.

"But she's in the hospital. I can't build a shrine in the hospital."

As if he understood her dilemma, he spoke more softly but still with the same gravity. "On the morrow, you will bring her home. She will still be sick, but you must bring her home. When she is in her bed, you will build my shrine." He placed the broom in her hand and vanished.

"Build a shrine to an Orixa in my mother's house." Chloe gasped. "Or she will die."

Do the impossible or the unthinkable will happen. If this had been some preacher at a fundraiser, she could have laughed it off. She looked at the spot where the Orixa had vanished. Smoke and mirrors couldn't have done that. A mere man could say God made him vanish, but she hadn't just heard about it. She had seen it. She had to do what the Orixa told her or her mother would die.

Chloe was in a daze, hardly aware that the drums had stopped and the people were preparing for the banquet. Enriquo guided her to a seat. Yara and a few others intercepted them with hugs and well wishes. Chloe saw Olumide at the head of the table. His eyes bespoke a grudging acknowledgement of her acceptance by both Xangô and Omolu. He couldn't deny it, but clearly, he didn't like it.

Once seated, Chloe tore her eyes away from the babalawo and focused on her food. Rooster and plantains. She wasn't sure what to do with the broom. Placing it under the table near her feet seemed like sacrilege, so she leaned it against the wall behind her and turned back to her plate. But she couldn't focus. Her heart was too full. The task before her superimposed itself on her vision of the food and the people. What would happen tomorrow? She had to do it tomorrow.

Omolu had not given her a deadline for compliance, but she knew that to delay was to court danger. How would her mother react? How would Lisa react? Lisa went to church with her mother, but Chloe couldn't say for sure if her sister was as closed to new things as their mother was. Most teenagers were easily embarrassed by anything they thought was "weird." But Lisa was old enough to get past that, Chloe hoped. Hope was all she had to her name, because nothing was certain except the inescapable task. She had to do it. Chloe sighed. She had to do it.

The next day, she picked Lisa up and they drove to the hospital.

"What are you going to do?" Lisa asked when Chloe picked her up.

"I'm going to bring Mom home."

"Oh wow. That's great. So the doctors said she will be all right?"

"No, I haven't spoken to the doctors. But she is coming home." Chloe wished she could have just driven along in silence and done what she had to without answering a lot of questions. No one would understand her answers, but she had to make them accept what she was doing whether they understood it or not. And she had to bring Lisa along so she could have at least one ally. Maybe the doctors would relent to a family effort.

"You haven't talked to them?" Lisa looked perplexed. "How you think you can just go in there and demand Mom's release? The doctors have to . . ."

Chloe wanted to scream, "Damn the doctors!" But she needed Lisa to understand, or at least not to interfere. "The nurse said Mom was doing well. Since her vital signs are functioning, she can recuperate better at home with family than in a hospital with the doctors running from sick person to sick person. They can actually spread sickness that way."

"But the doctors know how to protect their patients."

"Lisa, there are people laid up in the hospital right now with stuff they didn't have when they went in there."

"Yeah, right."

Chloe could see that Lisa needed more persuasion. "In fact, it's so common, there's even a name for it. It's called iatrogenesis."

"Really? Naw. You're making that up."

"Look it up."

Lisa took out her smartphone and navigated to Wikipedia. "Wow. 'Originating from a physician.' Then there's a lot of different diseases people can pick up from the hospital. When we were there before, I saw the man in the room next to Mom looked like he had popcorn all over his face."

Chloe froze. Popcorn was one of the foods favored by Omolu because it resembled smallpox, and he was, among other things, a patron of smallpox. "We have to get Mom out of there."

"You got that right," Lisa said with firm resolve.

They needn't have worried. When they arrived, their mother had the same idea. She wanted to go home.

"Mrs. Marshall, you must understand that you're still seriously ill." The doctor stretched his lips into a beneficent smile, as sterile as his long, white coat. For some reason, Chloe had always been averse to men in long, white coats. They were the men who would come if she didn't mind her Ps and Qs.

"I've been here four days. If I'm going to be sick anyway, I might as well be sick at home as be sick here."

"Here we can keep an eye on you."

That's what he thinks, Chloe mused. But Omolu's pronouncement was clear, and she dared not disobey him by putting her trust in the doctor's skills.

Charlotte Marshall turned up her nose. "So can my children."

Chloe hadn't thought about that. They'd have to watch over her mother. But Chloe had to go to work and Lisa had to go to school. The words of Omolu loomed over all practical considerations. *Do it or she will die.* Today was Saturday. Could Omolu make her mother well by Monday? Whether he could or not, they had no other choice.

"Mrs. Marshall." The doctor sighed with exasperation. He was treating her mother like an obdurate old nuisance, and Chloe didn't like it. Admittedly, the family's request was unusual, but as far as Chloe was concerned, that was beside the point. They had to get their mother out of there.

"Am I a prisoner here?"

"Most certainly not."

"Then by Jesus' name, I'm going home." She didn't wait for the doctor to give his okay. She removed the wires taped to her hands and neck and stood up on shaky legs. The monitor flat-lined like a bad omen, but their mother was standing.

Chloe knew it was by Omolu, not Jesus, that her mother was able to stand; but as long as the woman was doing what Chloe wanted, she saw no point in arguing.

"Mrs. Marshall, you must . . ."

But the three women paid him no heed. Lisa took their mother's overnight bag and coat from the closet, and the trio headed out the door. Mrs. Marshall walked slowly and trembled slightly, but she was determined to go and no one could stop her. The doctor, as much as he'd have liked to, had no authority to stop her. Their mother went into the dressing room and changed her clothes. Then the three of them went to the front desk to check out. By the time they got to the car, Mrs. Marshall was leaning heavily on her daughters for support. Lisa swayed from the weight but was determined to carry her if she had to.

They put their mother in the back seat and Chloe thought she would lie down, but Charlotte Marshall looked her daughter in the eyes, saw something there she didn't like, and straightened her back. She maintained that stoic posture all the way home.

"I'm not helpless," their mother assured them, reaching to hang her coat on the coat tree in the foyer.

"We know, mom. But you still need to take it easy." Lisa led her into her bedroom.

Chloe called her uncle Charlie to care for their mother on weekdays when she and Lisa were at work and at school. But when he heard they had taken his sister out of the hospital, he rushed right over.

"Are y'all plum crazy?" The lines on Uncle Charlie's face twisted with rage. He threw his hat on the table and marched into the bedroom where his sister sat propped up by pillows.

"I'm all right, Charlie. Those doctors like to keep me prisoner."

"Now I know you crazy as your daughters. That's where they got it from."

"She's okay. We had to. She's better here at home where people who care about her can take care of her."

"You can't take care of her. You have to go to work and to school."

"That's why we called you."

He opened his mouth to argue more, but Chloe didn't have time to listen. She had to make the herbal tea, build Omolu's shrine and retrieve the broom he had given her. She put water on to boil and took a bag of popcorn from on top of the refrigerator. Then she tried to think of where she could build the shrine so it wouldn't be disturbed. It must be a shrine that only Omolu would recognize as such. She went into her old bedroom and knelt down on the closet floor. There she lined an old shoebox with brown felt and placed seventeen kernels of popcorn inside. She thought she should say some kind of prayer to consecrate the shrine. Chloe wasn't sure how to go about praying to an Orixa. She'd heard her mother pray, but beyond "Now I lay me down to sleep," she'd never prayed to any god herself. But no god had ever spoken to her before. The least she could do was speak to him.

"Omolu, this is for you. It probably isn't according to your book, but it's according to my heart, willing yet woefully ignorant. I hope you'll accept it."

Then she replaced the lid on the box and pushed it into the back corner of the closet. In the kitchen, the water for the tea was almost boiled out. She grabbed a potholder and poured it over the herbs to steep. Smiling like everything was everything, she entered her mother's room laden with a tray of tea things and set it on the nightstand by the bed.

"What's that?" Mrs. Marshall asked.

"This is tea. It will calm your nerves. Let it steep and cool a little."

"I don't need that stuff."

"Yes you do, Mom. You're shaking. This will make you well." Chloe hoped that last bit was true. Yara had said the herbs would calm her mother's nerves, but hadn't said it would heal her. Omolu vouched for the broom, but would he heal someone who thought the healing was coming from Jesus?

Chloe reassured herself by remembering that she hadn't told Omolu about her mother. He had told her and had said the broom would sweep away sickness. He must already know what her mother would do.

Uncle Charlie growled. "Yes, I guess she is shaking. She's sick. If y'all had left her in the hospital and let them doctors deal with her, 'stead of fooling with some tea. What y'all think tea is going to do? I never heard of no tea curing high blood. I bound I'm going to call the doctor."

"No, Uncle Charlie," Chloe and Lisa said in unison.

"Maybe the tea will help you too," Chloe said. "It calms the nerves."

"I ain't drinking no fool tea."

Chloe sighed and went to retrieve the broom from her car. She wondered what her uncle would say when she started sweeping the floor. She couldn't tell him why she was sweeping it. Well, why did anybody sweep a floor? Hadn't they ever seen anybody sweep the floor before? It was just a broom. She'd just be sweeping the floor with a broom. People did it all the time. She looked at the leather, shells and beads encrusted on the handle and knew it was more than just a broom and she'd be doing more than just sweeping the floor. In his intractable mood, would Uncle Charlie assume she was doing the obvious? *Do it or she will die.* Let Uncle Charlie think what he liked. She had to do it. Trying to look as ordinary as possible, Chloe entered the room and started sweeping around her mother's bed.

"Damn fool, what are you doing?" Uncle Charlie roared.

"What are you doing?" Mrs. Marshall and Lisa asked in unison.

"Just sweeping the floor. Don't you have eyes to see?"

"I see that ain't no flipping broom for sweeping floors with," Uncle Charlie said.

"It sure ain't," his sister agreed.

"Look like something come straight out of Africa."

"Actually, it did," Chloe said, hoping to inoculate the obvious truth from their preconceptions.

"Africa!" her mother screamed. "You get away from me with that Devil broom. Oh Jesus! Oh Jesus! Get behind me, Satan!"

"Charlotte, don't you touch that tea. It's probably got some witch-doctor spell on it like that damn broom."

"Get outta my house, Satan! I didn't invite you in and you can't stay." Her voice didn't tremor or crack as it had before.

Chloe noticed her mother's body no longer trembled with weakness. Pure righteous wrath shook her body now. Chloe tried to keep sweeping. She had to sweep the floor or her mother would die.

But Chloe's uncle grabbed her arm and pulled her toward the front door. "You get out of here. You going to make my sister have a stroke. Taking her out of the hospital where she belongs, and then bringing the Devil himself in this holy house. You get out." And he threw Chloe out the door.

She lost her balance and almost tumbled down the porch steps. She let her leg twist so she'd land on the porch instead of the steps, but that still hurt. Her uncle slammed the door, cutting her off from the light with a bang. She looked around in a daze at the darkening sky. While she'd known her task wouldn't be easy. Still, she'd expected some kind of miraculous transformation—anything but this darkness and pain.

"Omolu, I did what you told me."

"Yes, you did."

Chloe started. Her mother often spoke to Jesus, but he never answered in an audible voice. This was new. She looked up and saw him standing before her. His body was bent and trembling with what looked like fever, but the power emanating from him was palpable. She wanted to go to her car and get out of the chill air, but he held her gaze so that her shivering wasn't from the cold and she couldn't move.

"I tried to sweep the floor like you told me, but she won't accept your help. Please don't punish me."

"Why would I punish you? You have done what I told you to do."

"But she won't accept your help. I don't know how to make her accept it."

The Orixa sighed. "I didn't tell you to make her accept my help. All I told you to do is sweep the floor, and that you did."

"But you said if I swept the floor it would drive away the sickness."

"And indeed, it has driven away the infection that was making her sick. That's what I do. But the spiritual delusion and self-hatred is something she must deal with on her own."

With some effort, Chloe tore her eyes away from him, rose to her feet and inched her way down the porch steps. Still, she was puzzled. "Why did you do this? Why did you instruct me to sweep around her bed if you knew she wouldn't accept you?"

Omolu strode beside her as they made their way to her car. When they reached it, he stopped. She was about to open the car door, but he held her gaze again as if to say that he'd go no farther. "It wasn't so much for her as for you."

"For me?"

"For the lessons you have learned watching your mother struggle with herself."

"Is my mother struggling with herself?"

"Oh yes. She fights an incessant battle with the part of herself that's black—the part of herself that is Africa. I wanted you to see how she rejected the broom simply because it looked like it came from Africa."

"For no other reason," Chloe agreed. "But she is still my mother. Please don't hate her. There's good in her deep down."

Omolu's eyes churned with sorrow far deeper than Chloe could imagine. "I do not hate her, precious child. I feel sorrowful, for she is a precious child as well, and I know the good that is deep within her. I know what is buried beneath all the trash Western society has heaped on her."

Chloe beamed with hope. "Then you can help her?"

"Let the god that she has chosen to serve help her. I will not intrude upon another's territory."

"But her god has no power to help anyone do anything but feel good. When she prays it's like she's praying for traffic lights, and when they turn green, she praises the Lord."

"That is her choice. If I could, I'd make her love Africa. She knows that."

Make her love Africa? There were a lot of things this god couldn't do. Chloe pondered the difference between Omolu and the god her mother served. The Orixa didn't claim to be all-powerful. Yet her mother wasn't trembling with sickness when she threw Chloe out of the house. Red-faced, perhaps; but it was the red of rage, not fever. What remained of her troubles was her own doing, not some infection. Unlike her mother's god, the Orixa didn't promise the world then deliver explanations. Yet still, Chloe continued to have questions.

"I was looking for answers. Osa Meji told me I'd find them in the wind. She said I'd find Oya and Exu and someone named Ayodele. She didn't say I'd find you."

"Indeed, you'll find the answers to your questions in the wind, but I will not be in the wind, for I am not part of the answers you seek. I am the prelude to a vision."

Chloe must've blinked. It took that long; for when she opened her eyes, he was gone. With trembling fingers, she opened her car door and sat behind the wheel. She sat there for a while, not trusting herself to drive safely until she had calmed down. But how could she calm down? These dreams or visions were becoming more and more corporeal. If her mother could believe in a god whom she'd never seen or heard, then Chloe had to believe in a god whose face she had seen and whose voice was more than a thought in her own mind. How could she calm down? *The prelude to a vision.* How could she calm down after that?

Chapter 15

Chloe's visions were corporeal. They had lives of their own. They had wills of their own and could take her in the midst of some mundane task, like going to the mailbox. It was but a short walk from her apartment door to the bank of mailboxes across the courtyard, but today, she didn't make it.

She'd always appreciated the sound of the wind chimes that hung near her door. Such natural music reminded Chloe she was alive even after the birds were gone for the winter. Yet, as much as she appreciated the sound, she never broke her stride to listen to it, but let it follow her as she went about her daily errands.

This morning was different. This morning, the chimes had a measured rhythm. Chloe could actually predict when the next chord would strike. She wanted to stop and dance, but the wind blew stronger and caught at her breath, pummeling her nostrils as she tried to draw it into her lungs. She gasped and tried to turn around when a funnel of wind descended on the courtyard and bore her up into the sky. She realized that she was still holding her mailbox key and gripped it tightly as the only solid object she had to her name.

Buildings and trees receded under her feet and she shivered, but she wasn't cold. She wasn't being thrown about but rested in the eye of the storm where the pit of her stomach was the center of gravity. She still heard the chimes urging her to dance. *Dance on what?* There was nothing under her feet. No platform to define the rise and fall of her steps. No surface to form the friction needed to pivot and slide. Still, the rhythm bade her to dance.

"Jalaiye, Ajalorun, fun mi ire." She heard this song. She heard this prayer and realized it was coming from her own lips. She was singing to Oya and dancing in the winds of change.

Presently, the rhythm of the chimes slowed and the wind died down. Then Chloe heard another sound. At first, she couldn't place it, but when she looked around, she realized her feet were on solid ground and the sound she heard was the squeak of wagon wheels. Where there had been a courtyard with magnolia trees scattered here and there and a statue of the water bearer pouring water into a stone fountain, a marketplace now bustled with oddly dressed people , and the fountain was now an auction block. On it was a sweaty-looking white man in clothes much too hot for the weather. Next to him stood a very dark and very naked woman trembling in fear.

"Ladies and gentlemen, I've got a fine specimen for you today. The prime of African wenches. Old enough to cook and shoot out a litter of pickaninnies. Young enough to train to whatever service you want—and I do mean whatEVER service."

A crowd of equally sweaty white men and women clamored around the auction block. The men ogled the dark woman's private parts. She couldn't have been much more than twenty.

"Hundred fifty," yelled one man.

"One hundred and fifty?" The auctioneer was incredulous. "She's worth far more than that. Look at these fine teeth."

The dark woman cringed as he tried to pry open her mouth. When she realized what he was trying to do, she snapped her mouth shut and locked her jaws. Chloe cheered, but the man dug his stubby nails into the woman's arm.

"Bitch," he hissed. "Don't you embarrass me front my customers. I got to get a good price off you, so open your damn mouth and smile when you do it."

She looked at him incomprehensively.

"Damn Africans don't know a drop of English." He sneered at the woman as if it were her part in the bargain to make slavery convenient for him. "I don't know why them traders don't just go up north and get them niggers up there what thinks they free. Yankees ain't doing nothing with their niggers, so we might as well take 'em." He smiled at the crowd, which was growing restless. "One fifty. Do I hear two hundred?"

"Two hundred," a well-to-do man called out.

"Do I hear two fifty?"

The auctioneer tried to keep the crowd focused on the woman's breasts and pelvis, but they were continually drawn to her eyes, which smoldered with the fire of a woman who wanted to be free. They saw the fear and they loved it. But they knew the inferno in her eyes would soon burn away that fear and they'd have to pay the patrollers to go fetch her when she ran away. So they remained silent.

"Going once. Going twice. Going three times. Sold to the gentlemen in white for two hundred dollars."

"Aaaaahhhhh!" Someone on the far side of the marketplace screamed at the top of her lungs. Chloe jumped, but no one else noticed. Then a woman in a skirt of every possible color emerged from between two buildings and approached Chloe. The woman's eyes were very large—much too large for her face. As she drew near, Chloe knew her. Those skirts lifted and swirled in a wind that blew nowhere else. It had been to this woman that Chloe had sung in the eye of the storm.

"Oya, Queen of the winds of fortune." Chloe thought she should prostrate herself before one so powerful, in whose hands lay her fate, but she decided to just bow her head.

"That's me, kiddo. You've no idea the great things I'll show you. I'm capable of blowing your mind. Great things, great things you will do. Yes you will, kiddo." The Orixa said without preamble.

Great things? What great things? And where were the others, Chloe wondered. "I thought I was supposed to meet Exu and Ayodele also."

"Oh, Exu. He's at the crossroads, you know. You'll meet him when you're ready.

As for Ayodele, this woman you see on the auction block is none other, kiddo."

"A slave?"

"Yes, kiddo, and your ancestor."

"Ancestor?"

"I hear an echo. She lived many years ago in the nineteenth century. Of course, that's as you measure time."

Chloe was really perplexed now. "How can a slave bring changes to my life? How can she help me do great things?"

"Oh, she won't. You'll change your own life, after you've learned what you need to learn, of course. She'll be your teacher. In her mind dwells all the knowledge you need."

"In her mind? How . . ." But before Chloe could ask the question, the winds that swirled around Oya caught Chloe up and she found herself floating toward Ayodele. Chloe didn't feel any part of her body moving. She didn't feel herself moving at all. She just knew she was moving. For an instant, all was darkness around her. She became pure consciousness, without any physical sensation or even a brain to think thoughts. Then the nothingness in which she existed turned into somethingness. Where there had been no corporeal body, she suddenly found physical substance and sensation. She found herself looking down, and to her astonishment, saw that she was on the auction block. But she wasn't standing beside Ayodele. Chloe was *in* Ayodele—in her mind, looking out through her eyes. Amazing.

Chloe thought she understood what Oya had meant. She thought inhabiting Ayodele's body with the knowledge of the twenty-first century would enable her to help Ayodele run away—escape using the information that was unavailable to slaves. That must be what Oya had in mind—escape and do great things. She, Chloe Marshall, could reshape history and life would be different for all her ancestors.

She tried to raise Ayodele's hands in triumph, but they didn't respond to her command. She tried again—nothing. She watched in horror as Ayodele's body moved, but not at Chloe's command. Rather than possessing Ayodele's body, Chloe was only an internal observer. Hearing what Ayodele heard and seeing what she saw, while having no control over what Ayodele did. Chloe wondered if she could talk to Ayodele and share her knowledge. Oya hadn't told her she could. But she hadn't told her not to try.

"Ayodele, it's me, Chloe. I'm your descendant."

There was no response. Chloe could hear Ayodele's thoughts like echoes from the past, but she couldn't influence them, for they had already happened.

Chloe felt like a parasite. She was actually inside someone else's body like a bacteria or a mental tapeworm. It was dehumanizing—unnatural. But this is where Oya had placed her. In this new world of the spirit, who was she to say what was natural and what wasn't? For all she knew, she might have played host to someone from her own future, looking through her eyes at her world and taking notes. That's what she should be doing. Oya had put her here to learn. She should be taking notes. But she had no paper. She could only pay attention and learn from what she saw, heard and felt.

"This one'll need breaking in," the auctioneer said when Ayodele's new slave master came to claim her.

The two men smirked when Ayodele pulled away from their grasping hands.

"Hold still, nigger." The slave master slapped her down. Chloe felt the blow but couldn't release her anger through her own physical body. She felt Ayodele respond, felt the pain when her bare knees hit the hard boards of the slave block and heard her anguished thoughts, but that only increased Chloe's helpless rage.

Ayodele cursed the dogs who abused her. She thought only of escaping at her first opportunity. She was no more a slave than Chloe was, but the captive daughter of the great babalawo, Kayode.

"Babalawo?" Chloe thought. Like Olumide at the *terreiro*. This was no coincidence. This was a connection between Africa past and African-American present. How Chloe wished she had some paper.

"I know how to break 'em. I'll break her in half if I have to."

The two beasts grinned. The slave master dropped a rope around Ayodele's neck that could've been a dog collar or a noose. He started to drag her away by the rope, but she rose quickly to her feet and stumbled down the steps. She could barely keep up with his long-legged stride, but she was determined not to be dragged, so she took three steps for his every one.

Presently, they came to a wagon where two black men waited. Ayodele's heart leapt at the sight of these men. Surely, they'd help her. Surely, they'd overpower the white beast and punish him.

"Help me! Help me!" she cried in her native tongue.

The Crossroads of Time

Chloe couldn't understand the words as they left Ayodele's lips, but she understood the thought those words represented.

Here it was two to one and the white beast had no fire stick. Yet the black men didn't move. Ayodele didn't understand why they didn't help her. Even if they were from some far away village and didn't understand her words, they could see what the white beast was doing to her, and yet, they didn't move.

Ayodele's heart sank as the two black men stared at her with incomprehension and revulsion. She remembered the black men on the ship who were helpless to aid her because of their chains and the fire sticks the white beasts carried. There were many who didn't speak her language, but none were repulsed by her nakedness. She couldn't think of anything else but her nakedness that could account for the bad manners of these black men.

They didn't leer at her as the Dahomey had. In their eyes, she saw a brief moment of shame, and then something akin to holy shock, as if they were gazing on an abomination against Olodumare himself. Beneath the revulsion, she saw something else. The men on the ship had been helpless in their bonds, but what she saw in the eyes of these black men went beyond helplessness. She saw defeat. The chains were not on their bodies but on their minds.

The slave master threw Ayodele into the bed of the wagon and barked at the slave men. "Get moving."

"Yes, sir."

Ayodele couldn't understand the speech of the white beast. On the ship, she had picked up a few words, but she wasn't fluent enough to hold a conversation. That these black men understood the white beast meant they'd totally capitulated to his will. They were slaves. She wasn't. She was a captive and soon she'd be free. She'd return to her village. Even if she died trying, as long as her head wasn't cut off, her spirit would return to her people.

In a way, Chloe was glad she couldn't tell Ayodele the truth. The woman was Chloe's ancestor, which meant she'd be in the United States the rest of her life. Ayodele had no idea how much water separated her from Africa—water and the will of her enslavers. There would be no going back. Truth would set you free, so they say. But how do you destroy someone's only hope in the name of truth—especially when you have nothing else to offer?

Chapter 16

The wagon pulled up to a large, white mansion. This had to be the "Big House." It probably had a name like Mount Vernon or something. Chloe realized all the cultivated land they had passed through probably belonged to this one man's plantation. She wondered if it was the same season here as it was in her real world. If so, then the slaves she had seen in the fields were harvesting for Thanksgiving.

Several black men and women pounced on the wagon, removing its cargo and carrying it through the back door of the mansion. The slave master threw an indifferent thumb towards Ayodele. "She's gonna be a wench. Pawny, take her in the kitchen."

Although Ayodele couldn't understand what the slave master had said, Chloe seethed at the thought of her ancestor being used this way. She knew she was sharing consciousness with a woman of impeccable elegance, but he thought nothing of assigning her as a kitchen wench. Chloe only wished she had a body with which to express her inexpressible rage.

"Yes, sir, Massa Keaton." A woman as round as a ball and brown as a paper bag reached for Ayodele. "Lawdy chile, we gone get some clothes on you. And look, you black as pitch. I'm sure some of that will wash off, 'cause I ain't never seen nobody that black les they was dirty."

Again, Chloe smoldered with indignation. Then she remembered she was in the South of the nineteenth century. She couldn't hold these people to twenty-first century standards. Still, the spirits of rebellion and dignity had to have been present even then or how could they have survived?

Pawny reached up to help Ayodele out of the wagon, but Ayodele scorned her help and climbed down the other side.

"Oh, she trying to act hinkty. One of them Africans, I reckon. She gone try to run fore long. She gone learn ain't no runnin' from Massa Keaton. She gone get whipped fore she learn she got to do what people say."

"Ain't nobody got to do what you say, Pawny." A man as black as the ace of spaces grinned toothlessly and hauled another sack out of the wagon. "But she sure gone get whipped if she don't do what the massa say."

"If she gone work in my kitchen, she got to do what I say."

Chloe wanted to shake her head, but couldn't. *Her* kitchen. Put a slave in a box and she convinces herself that it's her box. But what was the alternative? Despair. Like those kids standing around on Wesley Avenue, they chose the delusion of ownership over despair. Were those our only choices—delusion or despair? Chloe wondered what she'd have chosen if those were the only parameters of her life.

They walked to a little brick building that served as the kitchen. It wasn't far from the back door of the mansion so food could be carried in. Pawny gestured for Ayodele to sit on a three-legged stool. Then she went away and came back with a dress. "Put this on if you ain't too good for Miss Keaton's clothes."

Ayodele was eager to cover her nakedness, but she didn't want to act like she'd never had any clothes before. So she took the dress nonchalantly and examined it. It was different from anything she had ever seen, but it wasn't hard to figure out where her arms were supposed to go. She slipped it on and sat back down.

"What your name, chile?"

Ayodele rolled her eyes. She was actually counting in her mind to see how long it would take this woman to realize she didn't speak their language. She didn't want the woman to think she was the dumb one, so instead of giving her a blank look, she stared at her disdainfully.

Pawny pointed to herself. "My name Pawny. Paw-ny. What your name?"

Ayodele turned her regal gaze out the window.

"Is you deaf?" Pawny banged two pots together so loud it made Ayodele jump despite all her efforts to appear impervious. "No, you ain't deaf. If you heard that, then hear me. My name is Pawny. What your name, Miss Thang?"

If Chloe had been in her own body, she would've fallen out of her seat laughing at the sight of this butterball clanging pots and looking fit to burst. But Ayodele only composed herself and resumed an air of hauteur.

Chloe knew and understood Ayodele's thoughts. She also knew Ayodele would be in this country a long time and she'd only make life harder for herself if she couldn't get along with other blacks. But Chloe couldn't tell her that. She could only witness what had already transpired. Her ancestor in the raw. Chloe would see the unedited version with all the contradictions and foibles of the human character. Would Ayodele make her proud?

"She doesn't speak English," Keaton said, entering the kitchen. "You'll have to teach her."

"Why you bring this chile in my kitchen for and she don't even know how to talk?"

"*Your kitchen?* Yes, Pawny. This nigger'll be help enough for you in *your* kitchen once she learns how to talk like decent folks. Now, don't you let her run over your kitchen."

"When the last time I let a nigger run over me?"

"That's my girl. When you finish with her, send for Jimboy to take her over to the Sugar Shack. She's to go straight to the Sugar Shack and stay there until I see fit to visit her. Do you understand?" He leered at Ayodele with a hunger the three women understood perfectly well.

"Yes, Massa Keaton."

He grabbed a biscuit off the stove and left.

Pawny's eyes followed her master wistfully until he was gone. Then she turned to Ayodele. "So I got to teach you how to talk. Well, I ain't no teacher, but you better learn. That's all I got to say." She glanced around the kitchen and picked up a cooking spoon. "Spoon. They call this a spoon. Spoon." Then she picked up a fork, a rag, a pot, a jar, telling Ayodele the name of everything in the kitchen.

Ayodele realized the woman was trying to teach her the ghastly language of the beast, but she didn't open her mouth. She was learning the words. She'd been picking up words from the day they had captured her. But she wasn't going to let her enemies know what she knew.

"Look, I got to teach you and you got to learn," Pawny screeched. "Why don't you learn? How you gone stay here if you can't talk? You could just lie down to do what Massa want you to do in the Sugar Shack, but how you gone help me? You gone stay in that Sugar Shack and never be good for nothing else. Oh, why 'm I wasting words with you? You can't understand nothing."

Chloe understood. She knew the truth of Pawny's words. And she trembled at the realization that she herself would experience everything the slave master did to Ayodele.

Damn Oya. Why couldn't Chloe learn about slave life from a book? There were plenty of books. Slavery was horrid enough just to read about. Why did she have to experience it? She wanted to cry, but had no access to physical eyes. She wanted to scream, but had no access to a physical voice.

***

Ayodele shuddered when the beast who'd taken her from the market and brought her to this farm entered the kitchen. She saw the way he leered at her. She saw the way he fingered the biscuit suggestively while his eyes fixed on her breasts. She remembered the beast at Elmina Castle and cringed inside at the thought of this new beast doing that to her.

Why was she cringing? She didn't want to cringe. She wanted to feel rage—pure rage that would give her fighting power—but she thought of him touching her that way and all she felt was sick. She could only hope that she'd have an opportunity to escape before he touched her. "Olodumare, have you abandoned me?"

"No, he hasn't."

Ayodele looked around the kitchen, wondering who in this hellish land could speak in her native tongue. She saw only Pawny's exasperated gestures and knew that it'd been a spirit who'd spoken. "Who are you?"

"There are three who inhabit the Earth—the living, the dead and the yet to be born. I am Iyabo, the unborn of Ekundayo. I will comfort you if you keep your promise to remember my mother's name. I will bless you if you remember my name."

Hope bloomed in Ayodele's heart. "I remember Ekundayo. Can you help me escape? Will you punish these white beasts?"

"The only escape I know is that which my mother took. If that is what you want, I can help you, but I am not here to punish."

This wasn't what Ayodele wanted to hear. Her bloom faded. "I don't want to die. My Egun, Baba Abioye, promised me great things."

"And he promised that you'd have a price to pay."

"I don't know what is going on. I only know that I am far from where I should be for some great thing to happen as he promised. It's not happening."

"Would he make a promise with a price unless he knew you had the coin to pay it? Be comforted. I am gone."

Ayodele called, but there was no more answer. Every voice around her now was in the hateful tongue of the beast.

The toothless black man entered the kitchen. He grabbed a biscuit off the stove.

"Unhand my biscuits, nigga. Them is for Miss Keaton. 'Tween you and the massa, ain't gone be none left. Now, take this chile down to the Sugar Shack. And tell them she got to stay there 'til Massa Keaton say otherwise."

"I thought she s'pose to help you."

"How? She don't know how to talk. Massa want me to teach her, but she too full of herself to learn. I'm through with her today, so you take her on out of here."

Jimboy looked at Ayodele and there was sadness in his eyes. Chloe knew that unmasked sadness was a gift to Ayodele that he kept hidden from his master. Still, Keaton was his master, and his master's will he'd do. No matter what he felt in his heart, he'd take her inexorably to the Sugar Shack where nothing sweet awaited her.

***

Ayodele picked up her feet as she walked. She had no desire to return to this land once she escaped and wanted no dust to be on her feet. The dust from her home had washed off long ago, but she clung to the hope that its spiritual essence had seeped into her pores where neither brine nor wind could dislodge it.

Keeping her eyes open, she watched diligently for escape routes. The paths they'd taken so far were too crowded with people for stealth. Her captors had foolishly allowed her to remain conscious of the way to the great water. She might have to look for a less traveled road, but she knew the general direction, and once there, she'd be able to lose herself among the throng of people, board one of the great boats and return to her homeland. It was only a hope, but hope was all she had. She wouldn't discard it.

The toothless man brought her to a hut made of wood. He knocked on the door and a small, black woman answered.

She looked Ayodele up and down. "Got a new one for us, eh Jimboy?"

He didn't push Ayodele into the hut, as she expected, but gestured gently for her to enter.

Taking note of this, the little black woman said, "Jimboy's got a soft heart. Soft hearts break easy around here." She grabbed Ayodele by the arm and shoved her at the most bucolic-looking white beast imaginable or unimaginable. "If Jimboy's been soft with her, she'll prolly need breaking."

As gentle as he had been, Jimboy didn't betray so much as a wince in the presence of the white man. "Massa say she s'pose to stay here until he say otherwise. If you don't mind, Miss Rita, I'll be on my way." Then he bolted out the door before Rita could look up. Not that she did.

Ayodele remembered the sour odor of stale whiskey that had clung to her captors like wet cotton clothes. She thought she'd never get used to the stench. Now she knew she'd never get away from it either.

Chloe felt odd in this unique form of clairvoyance, eavesdropping on someone else's memories—someone else's experiences. And she knew she was eavesdropping, for she still had a sense of self, sharing the body and observing the mind of a distinct otherness.

She wondered what was going on with her own body while she wasn't in it. Was it in stasis? How were the people around her responding to her vacant body? She could only wonder and hope Oya knew what she was doing and wasn't indifferent about the things that were important to Chloe. That was the way of gods. "His ways are above our ways and his thoughts above our thoughts," her mother liked to say when inexplicably bad things happened.

Ayodele didn't know which was worse, the rheumy eyes or the pudgy fingers that raked her body. She tried to pull away, but the beast wrapped his arms around her— leaving her no room for pulling or pushing.

"I'm going to enjoy breaking you in. Ooh Lawd, yes. You can't be pulling away from the boys when they come. You got to give them what they want. I got to show you how to act."

"I don't think she can understand you, Harley. I heard Massa got this one straight off the boat from Africa. Can't speak a lick of English," Rita scoffed.

"She'll understand soon enough. The way I teach, unless she's dead or simple in the head, she got to understand. What's her name?"

"I forgot to ask."

"Don't matter. In here, we'll call her Polly. Niggers don't need a name except to be called by." He grabbed Ayodele by the chin. "First, I'll teach you not to pull away from me." He forced her face close to his. His breath reeked of whatever he'd been drinking for the last ten days, but she couldn't have pulled away without breaking her neck.

"Then I'll teach you to come when I call you—Polly."

And he took her in a back room and taught her. He grabbed her breast. She tried to pull away, but he slapped her. Chloe felt the slap and feared that Ayodele would continue to defy him until he slapped her to death. Ayodele had never heard of slapping someone's head off. That thought would've given her pause. He yanked her up off the floor by her hair. As soon as she was on her feet, she kicked him. This time he used his fist.

"Nigger bitch. I don't want to have to damage you. Lose a lot of money that way. You'd be worth a lot if you act right. Ain't worth nothing if you don't act right."

Finally, he just pinned her to the floor. She thrashed beneath his weight, but her little fists and feet could find no purchase on any part of his body. He laughed, taking pleasure in both her motion and her frustration.

His torso was long and Ayodele's was short, so his chest pressed against her face, nearly suffocating her. She turned her head to free her nose, but no air could reach her except that which had first passed under his arms, and it made her wheeze.

She could tell that her thrashing about pleased him, so she determined to do what she had done before and just lie still. She hated the thought of surrender. And how could she think of surrendering to such an atrocity as this? She wanted him to know how much she hated him. She wanted him to know how much she loathed what he was doing to her. But that wouldn't make him stop. Indeed, it egged him on. Lying still had made the beast at Elmina Castle grow tired of her and leave her alone. Maybe it would work with this beast as well.

"Nigger, you got to move. When them boys come in here, they want a good time. I ain't no bear, so playing dead won't work with me." He reached down and grabbed her hips and rocked them back and forth in a mockery of sexual passion. He slapped her again. "You got to move. Move, bitch. Move." Then he thrust himself inside her and pulled her hips against his, forcing her to move with him.

Chloe felt sick. Ayodele felt sick. But she didn't move. She was being forced to move, but she didn't move herself. As soon as he let her hips go in order to slap her, she slumped under his weight like a dead thing.

"Now nigger, I know you know how to move. You wasn't no virgin, easy as I got into you. Prolly been with one of them African monkeys. If you moved for a monkey, you better move for me, 'cause I'm a man—a white man, at that. Ain't a man better than a monkey, bitch?"

At that moment, Chloe wished that she had eyes to weep for the injustice of this accusation. She could read in Ayodele's memories the horrors of Elmina and the way she'd been used on the ship. Not even the monkeys, the hateful Dahomey, had abused her this way. If only Chloe could make Ayodele throw up for both of them.

She couldn't understand why he kept talking to Ayodele when he knew she couldn't understand him. When Ayodele looked into his eyes, Chloe understood what she had seen there. She read his thoughts like the pages of a history book. The fact that Ayodele couldn't understand him was part of his pleasure. He spoke words she couldn't understand to prove to himself that he was superior. Because she was too dumb to understand, he had to show her by force all the ugliness contained in his words. How did this mere nigger dare challenge him? He had a job to do. His job was to break her; and by damn, he'd do it. His pride was at stake, now and Chloe knew he wouldn't relent but would abuse Ayodele until she either broke or died.

Because he was doing all the moving, he was also doing all the perspiring. His unwashed body, reeking of whiskey and tobacco, produced every foul smell known to living flesh. When the odor of his semen was added to this miasma, Ayodele and Chloe thought it could get no worse.

Oblivious to her distress, he stopped only when his own body conked out. When Ayodele heard him snoring, she sighed with relief, knowing the ordeal was over—at least for that day. But she was now trapped under him. If she pushed too hard, he might waken and start all over again. Pushing gently did no good. So she heaved with all her might. He muttered in his sleep but didn't wake up. The greater part of his bulk was off her, but she was still imprisoned under one arm and leg. She eased out from under his grotesque limbs and crept to the door.

She heard no one. Could this be her chance to escape? She could hardly believe that after such an ordeal, escape would come so easily. Yet, she had been looking for the slightest opportunity, and if this wasn't her ideal chance, she'd make it so.

Carefully, she crept to the front room. She doused the lamp on the table so no one would see the light when she opened the door. Rusty hinges and old wood vied to see which could creek the loudest. She held her breath, waiting for his beefy paw to slam the door shut. But he snored on.

She peered through the darkness and listened. The only sounds she heard came from far away. Maybe everyone thought that beast would watch her and didn't bother to check on her. Whatever the reason, everyone gave her a wide berth. It might not last long, so she had to make the most of it. She closed the door behind her and stole toward the forest that lay between her and the sea.

She saw a path through the trees, but shunned it as a place where she'd most likely run into someone. The undergrowth was sparse and posed no great barrier. It was certainly easier walking than the trek from her village to Elmina Castle. Still, the trees grew where they pleased and kept her from walking in a straight line. She could get lost. *No*. This was a strange forest, but it was a forest made up of trees and she could use the skills she'd learned making her way through the trees at home.

But the foliage of these trees blocked out the stars that had guided her in Africa. Maybe if she kept to the same general direction sight, smell and hearing might tell her where she was. Opening her senses, she noted each tree and bush, but in the darkness, the trees looked alike. Her father had taught her to mark the trees to make sure she wasn't walking in circles. She couldn't do that here. The best she could do was make sure that for every left turn, she made a right turn and for every right turn, she made a left turn.

She walked cautiously. Her mother had taught her to be light-footed. Her father had shown her all the signs hunters looked for when following an animal, so she was careful not to leave any.

Chloe ached to tell Ayodele that she didn't need to leave signs. The dogs could follow her blindfolded. After all Ayodele had gone through, Chloe knew this displaced African was still blissfully ignorant of what was bound to happen next. In a way, Chloe was glad she couldn't shatter that brief moment of bliss by telling her about the dogs.

Chloe couldn't tell Ayodele about the slave catchers and how they'd beat her to the very doorstep of death. Or that they maybe even cut something off to teach her not to run again. She remembered *Roots* and knew that kind of thing happened. Out here in the forest, the slave catchers were free to do whatever entered their minds. Then again, Keaton might decide Ayodele was more trouble than she was worth and sell her to someone else—someone who might be kinder or crueler.

Both Chloe and Ayodele had their hopes for the future. They both felt destined to do something meritorious in life, but at the moment, neither of them had any say in the matter of what would befall them.

Unlike her host, Chloe had to live this coming terror twice—once when visualizing what she knew would happen and again when it actually happened. This was Oya's doing. *No.* Oya hadn't caused slavery, but she was causing Chloe's experience of the horrors of slavery.

Chloe wanted to seethe. She wanted Oya to release her and return her to her own body before this terrible thing happened. Then she remembered that this terrible thing had already happened hundreds of years ago. Even if she was spared, Ayodele hadn't been spared. Shame and dread warred for dominance in Chloe's consciousness. She could be neither an indifferent observer nor a disinterested judge of what she was experiencing. What could she possibly learn from this and how would it help her accomplish some great goal as Osa Meji had promised? She couldn't know. She could only wait and see.

From the direction of the plantation came the baying of dogs. Chloe cringed, but Ayodele didn't know what the sound pertained to. With all the twists and turns of the forest, she had walked a long way but still had not gone very far. Through the trees, she could see that she was approaching an open space. She paused behind the last tree to spy what lay ahead. She could see lights ahead, so she knew she was at the edge of the forest and not at a mere clearing. The baying of the dogs grew louder and she could hear individual barks. Ayodele couldn't help but notice this. Surely, even if they'd discovered her missing, she had been careful to leave no tracks, so how could they know where to look? She must not have been as careful as she'd thought. The barking grew louder. It didn't fluctuate or retreat. They were coming inerrantly toward her as if they knew exactly where she was.

She wondered what to do. Now wasn't the time to panic. She'd come too far, suffered too much to be undone by her own emotions. She thought of running away from the barking, but vetoed the idea. She'd be out in the open where she'd have no cover and no idea what lay ahead. She thought of climbing a tree. Her pursuers would pass right under her. With all the noise they were making, she'd hear them coming and going.

No, thought Chloe, it won't work. But Ayodele didn't hear her. She climbed a likely looking tree, pulling herself from limb to limb, careful not to disturb the bark, until she reached a high bough with lots of leaves between her and the ground. She straddled the bough and pressed her feet against it so they wouldn't dangle and betray her.

The hunters came right toward her. Ayodele wondered at the sound of the barking. What could that be? It wasn't human speech. Some kind of animal. The beasts of the beasts? To her dismay, they came straight to the tree where she sat supposedly hidden by the darkness. She could hear them below her feet, barking and clawing at the tree. Around them, the ghoulish faces of the hunters flickered in the light of the lanterns they carried. There was no escape. They barred her only way down.

The fangs of the animals gleamed in the lantern light. They looked like wolves but were smaller. Despite their size, she knew if she climbed down among them, they'd rip her to shards before she even touched the ground. If there was ever a time to panic, she knew this was the time, but she didn't. She couldn't afford to.

"You might as well come on down, nigger. Lest you plan to stay up there. We got all night."

She recognized the voice of the beast who had raped her. So he had awakened and found her gone. She shuddered. He wouldn't be kind.

"She can't understand you, Harley."

"Don't matter. Maybe she'll understand lead." The two-legged beasts grumbled—some nodding their heads in approval, some shifting their feet apprehensively.

"Naw, we got to bring her back live."

"But we ain't gotta bring her back whole." They all laughed.

"Or untouched." They found this funny, too.

"Got to get her down first, then y'all can have all the fun you want. Somebody got to go up there after her."

"What, and get kicked? Naw, you go."

"I think I will, coward. Call your dogs. I'm going up and get me some nigger flesh."

"I hope she kicks your fool head in."

"When we see Keaton, you gone forget you said that, but I ain't."

There was a low whistle and the dogs drew back. Chloe was glad Ayodele didn't mistake this as her chance to escape. The African woman knew something was going on, and she'd find out what it was before she moved an inch.

Then one of the white beasts started climbing the tree. Ayodele scrambled onto another higher bough, hoping to get as far from him as possible. This would only buy her a little time but not prevent the inevitable. As she climbed higher, the foliage closed out the lantern light. She noticed something strange about this other branch. It was getting thicker as it moved away from the tree instead of thinner, as she'd have expected. Following its thickness, she found that it led to another tree. She paused to thank Olodumare and Eshu, all the Orisha and Egun she'd ever heard of for this stroke of luck.

The light from the beasts' lanterns didn't reach to this tree. Now she could climb down on the far side of this other tree, and in the darkness, slip away while her enemies concentrated on the first tree.

She climbed down the other tree so silently there was no way they could hear her over the barking of their animals. The one who'd climbed up after her might discover she was gone and follow her on that branch, but it was dark and she was dark and swift. She'd be gone again and they wouldn't know in which direction she'd gone. Chloe wanted to shake her head, but she had no head to shake.

When Ayodele hit the ground, the dogs immediately plunged at her. One bit her on the thigh. They pinned her to the ground until the two-legged beasts called them back.

"Oh, looky here. Ain't smart enough to talk, but thought she was slick climbing down another tree."

Ayodele couldn't understand why it had not worked. She had been so silent. It should have worked. Maybe if she could understand their speech, she might find out what she'd done wrong. She'd learn the language, not to capitulate with her captivity, but so she could understand what was going on around her. Chloe jumped for joy that Ayodele was finally thinking clearly. But regret thwarted Ayodele's resolve. She thought that surely, they'd kill her now. She had learned her lesson too late. She looked at their leering smirks and knew what they'd do to her before they killed her.

One of the beasts pulled Ayodele to her feet and pushed her against a tree.

"Ah, nigger. Don't look so scared. We just some good ole boys. We don't mean no harm. Just want to have little fun. Not our fault if it ain't fun for you."

Then they all took turns, one after the other. Then two of them took her at once. Such pain she had never felt before. Such humiliation she had never imagined before. Then the fiend in front of her got down on his knees and licked her. He licked her and he licked the penis of the fiend behind her.

"Oh Jack, I like that. Never had fun like this with a white woman."

"They too precious. But with niggers you can do whatever you want."

"We shoulda brought something to smoke. Nothing to do while y'all over there having all the fun. Hurry up. I want my turn."

"Come on then."

And they abused her until the sun rose. Chloe felt sick. Body or no body, some part of her was retching—throwing up all the food she'd ever eaten in her life. But Ayodele didn't throw up. She didn't respond at all. She had gone inside herself to a place where the beasts couldn't touch her. Nine ghastly fiends in all. They'd beat her if she pulled away, run her down if she tried to flee and take pleasure if she thrashed in fury. So she

Rhonda Denise Johnson

entered her own mind and her body went
limp.

"You wanted to escape. Remember
my mother's name. She knows the way of
escape. Ekundayo knows the only way of
escape. I am gone."

Ayodele stayed within herself. She
was unaware of anything around her. She
couldn't have said how she got back to the
plantation, how she wound up in Pawny's
kitchen or what was done to her in the
interim. She only knew that she felt
unimaginable pain in unimaginable places.
She lay on a blanket in the corner of the
kitchen near the stove. How could she feel
such aches and weariness without
remembering exactly why? She remembered
climbing the tree and the fiends abusing her.
Then there were two of them and she
remembered no more.

Chloe only wished she'd been able to
block such horrors out of her own awareness,
but she'd experienced it all and remembered
it well.

"Ain't no need of raising your head
'cause you gone get a whipping soon as
Massa come in and find you woke. You just
got here. What possessed you to run away?
Just lay still."

Ayodele looked up at Pawny. This woman knew the language and had tried to teach her. Would she try again? Ayodele rose to her feet and walked over to the sideboard. It hurt, but lying down hurt, too, so she figured she might as well get up and try something.

"What you lost over there?" Pawny asked.

With trembling hands, Ayodele picked up a pot. She chose a small one so the woman wouldn't think she planned to hit her with it. Pointing to the pot, she turned what she hoped was a quizzical look at Pawny and asked "Bí?"

"What you say? Bee? No, that's a pot. So you want to learn to talk now. You didn't take long to get tired of not knowing what folks saying to you." She took the pot and pointed to it. "Pot. This a pot."

"Pot," Ayodele repeated.

"Yes, pot." Then she picked up a cooking spoon. "Spoon. This a spoon."

"This a spoon." Then Ayodele picked up a knife. "This a . . ."

"Knife. Put that thang down. You ain't dumb as we thought. Learn quick when you ain't trying to be uppity."

They went on until they had named everything in the kitchen. Then Pawny went back over everything to see what Ayodele remembered. *Yes.* She was a quick study. Pawny got friendly, but Ayodele never forgot that her purpose for learning to talk the beast's language wasn't to make friends with those who had submitted to his will, but so she'd be better prepared to escape and survive.

Pawny pointed to herself. "Pawny. My name is Pawny. Paw-ny."

"Pawny."

"Well now, I never thought I was much for teaching, but you never know, huh." She pointed to Ayodele. "Harley say your name is Polly. Pol-ly."

Ayodele recognized the word the beast had used. So, that was a name and he had given it to her as if she hadn't her own name. "Ayodele. My name is Ayodele. A-yo-de-le."

"Naw, ain't nobody gone twist they tongue trying to say all that just to call a nigger. Your name Polly, so get used to it."

This woman was definitely not a friend, Ayodele decided. Totally capitulated and trying to teach her to be, too. Ayodele wouldn't. She'd never. She lifted her chin defiantly. "Ayodele."

Pawny rolled her eyes and looked at Ayodele as if she knew something the

African didn't know. "You due for a whipping anyway for running. Keep up your ways and you gone be due for a whole lot of whippings."

Ayodele took note of Pawny's look and the condescending tone of her voice. What but meanness could make this woman act so smug? Mean or not, Pawny was willing to teach and Ayodele had to learn. She decided to be softer, but she'd never say Polly.

"Pawny, is that nigger woke yet?"

"Yes, Massa."

Keaton entered the kitchen and grabbed a biscuit off the stove. For the briefest second, Pawny's eyes decried her vanishing biscuits, but she had been trained not to let her master see anything he might interpret as the smallest protest.

"So you decided to wake up, did you? Well, too bad for you. I'll teach you to run from me. I didn't pay two hundred dollars for you to act a fool." He slapped Ayodele to the floor and placed a rope around her neck.

As she hit the floor, Ayodele caught a glimpse of Pawny's placid face. Common decency would've caused anyone else to wince, but Pawny was trained. She was well trained.

Chloe was beside herself with worry. That rope sure felt like a noose. Since Ayodele was her ancestor, she knew the woman wouldn't be killed, but that didn't mean she wouldn't be hanged. Chloe shuddered. What would she have to go through next? She didn't know if she could stand much more of this virtual reality.

Keaton grasped the loose end of the rope and walked out the door, still eating Pawny's biscuit. Ayodele stumbled after him, trying to gain her feet before he could drag her.

He tied his end of the rope to the branch of a tree that was just high enough that Ayodele had to rise onto her toes. She wore no shoes, so only her big toes touched the ground. Then he tied her hands to the branch. This relieved pressure from her neck and toes, but obstructed her breathing.

"I almost hate to damage your virgin back. But I'm not going to have no niggers thinking they can do what they please around me. So you never tasted a whip before, huh? Well, maybe that's what's wrong with you. You gone taste one today."

And she did. It was a bitter taste, seasoned with tears and marinated in blood. She wanted to cry out with each blow, but she hated this beast so much that she withheld the cries, knowing they would give him pleasure. The whip licked her back ten times and she thought she could bear no more, but he kept on until she had received twenty lashes.

Then it stopped and there was silence. She heard the thud of his boots walking away. Did he plan to leave her there until she died, Ayodele wondered. But soon Jimboy came and cut the ropes. He held her as he cut them so she wouldn't fall to the ground. She moaned at his touch. He held her gently, but there was nowhere that he could hold her that didn't hurt. She could moan for this man as she hadn't moaned for the beast. He was a man—weak in some ways but still a man. She had no cause to defy him, and without defiance to give her strength, she could do nothing but let herself go.

He took her back to the blanket on the kitchen floor. Pawny washed the blood from her back and shoulders, but Ayodele barely noticed. She didn't bother to rise again.

She didn't stir from the blanket that day, nor could she stir. For all anyone knew or cared, she was at the door of death. But the next day, feet began to kick at her and she heard hostile voices demanding that she do something. She had to get up, or be kicked more senseless than she already was.

Rhonda Denise Johnson

Pawny continued her language lessons and Ayodele augmented them by picking up conversations on the sly. After a few months, she was speaking passably and could understand most of what she was told to do. This didn't satisfy her. Her goal wasn't just to learn enough to be ordered about. She wouldn't be satisfied with her skills until she could understand everything that people said.

The price for this knowledge was that she sometimes caught herself thinking in this dreadful language. But that was how one learned a language, she reasoned. Still, it was the language of the beast and she hated such an encroachment on her mind.

Her nights in the Sugar Shack continued with every kind, shape and size of beast coming and going. She could block out the worst moments but kept her ears open to hear any information that might aid her next escape.

Once a week, a beast they called the parson came to the plantation. Keaton made everybody, young and old, big and small, slave and free, sit in a stone hut to listen to this parson speak.

When the parson arrived, Jimboy helped him down from his carriage and started to walk him into the stone hut they called the Meeting Hall. But the parson

232

wrenched himself out of Jimboy's grasp and turned his gaze toward the Sugar Shack. Clearly, he knew what went on there. Ayodele noted his look of displeasure when he addressed the beast who called himself her master.

"Den of sin. Abode of evil. How do you call yourself a Christian, Mr. Keaton, and allow such an abomination on your land?"

"Oh, that's just the boys having a little fun."

"But you allow it and you profit from it. Do you think you will enter Heaven with such sin on your conscience?

"Now see here, Parson. I'm saved by grace. Ain't nothing I can do on God's green Earth will keep me out of his white Heaven. I do what I please here. God will forgive me. Anyways, you ain't here to tell me about my sins." He patted his pocket meaningfully.

The parson clearly took Keaton's meaning and without another word, entered the Meeting Hall.

Everybody sat on wooden benches while the parson faced them from behind a tall, wooden box. Clearing his throat and removing his spectacles, he looked out over the people with muddy-grey eyes. He didn't particularly like what he saw or what he was doing. Sweat glistened on his forehead before he even started. He was there to do a job he had done many times without relish.

"When there's no one you can call on, that's the time to call on God."

So much of what he said, Ayodele couldn't comprehend, but she got the impression that when the beast said "God," he was referring to their version of Olodumare.

"If you put away the devils you worshipped before God's great mercy allowed you to serve good white folks in this land of plenty; if you call on Jesus, he'll ease your burdens and take you to your glorious rest after you lay your burden down."

"Yes, Lawd," some old black woman shouted. She was fanning herself with a piece of paper and looked like she was about to faint.

"And the burden of slavery is light, for Jesus said his burden would be light. Take his burden upon you as he commanded. Do all that your master tells you to do like a good servant of the Lord, and at the end of the day, give it all to Jesus."

This sounded so familiar to Chloe. She'd never heard it in the context of chattel slavery, but this is where it had come from. This was how the Bible had been used to enslave her ancestors' minds. Nothing had changed. Yes, the iron chains were gone, but the minds were still in shackles.

Ayodele regretted that she didn't have a better command of the language. But she knew the beast was talking about his corrupt version of Olodumare, so even if she could understand his words better, they still would make no sense. These white beasts and their black slaves could only insult and offend Olodumare by calling on him.

"We need to stop right now and pray." Then he bowed his head and muttered with his eyes closed as if invoking the Orishas.

Was this parson their babalawo? He clearly had no power. They worshipped without power or reverence. Ayodele only hoped she wasn't tainted just by being in this unholy place with these profane people. She thought Olodumare must be appalled to see her here when she hadn't spoken to him since she'd left her homeland. Was Eshu angry with her? Was that why her attempts to escape failed?

She remembered her father had told her she'd find her answer in the wind. She determined to build a shrine to Oya, the Orisha of the wind. She tuned out the rest of what the parson said and focused on the daunting decisions of when, how and where to build her shrine.

Oya? Chloe could hardly believe this. Ayodele spoke of building a shrine to *Oya?* Well, of course. The Orisha of the wind would be as old as the wind itself. Both Chloe and her host had been told they'd find their answer in the wind. To what question was Ayodele seeking an answer? She'd asked that question before she was taken captive. The plot was thickening. Chloe was so excited that she almost forgot to breathe. Then she remembered, she wasn't in her body and didn't need to breathe.

Her body? She had been out of it for months. What could be happening to it? She'd wondered about this before, and now that so much time had passed, craved an answer more urgently, yet one remained no less elusive.

Chapter 17

The forest was out, Ayodele thought. The beasts watched her like a lion watched zebra whenever she so much as glanced that way. She certainly wouldn't build her holy shrine in that torment pit they called the Sugar Shack.

She thought of that little corner of the kitchen where she slept—when they let her sleep. Would it be safe from discovery? She could place the items of her shrine under the blanket. Pawny never touched the blanket to wash it.

It would take time to find nine copper coins and a piece of burgundy cloth for Oya and three red or black canes for Eshu. She must not forget Eshu. There were enough calamities in her life.

One of the beasts who came to the Sugar Shack liked to wear a burgundy shirt and take it off so she could see what he mistakenly thought was an attractive torso.

She spirited a small sharp knife from the kitchen, and while he slept, cut off a small piece from the hem of his shirt. She looked at him as he snored contentedly and she thought of cutting other things, too, but didn't want to complicate her plans. Then she found three small, black sticks that could serve as the canes for Eshu.

Finding nine copper coins was going to be more challenging. Those coins the beasts called pennies were of copper. Pawny kept a jar of them on a cupboard in the kitchen. One penny could buy a sack of flour.

Ayodele knew she couldn't ask Pawny for nine pennies without telling her why she wanted them. She'd have to steal them. In her village, stealing was very wrong. As the daughter of the babalawo, she had been raised with the utmost moral standards. How could she lower those standards now? She thought about all the things these beasts stole from her—her freedom, her body, her dreams, her dignity and her life. How dare she be squeamish about taking from them? How could she let the thief determine what was rightfully his? She wouldn't be stealing. She'd be taking a small recompense of what she deserved.

But Pawny wasn't a beast. She owed Ayodele nothing. Then again, Pawny wouldn't be giving her anything. Those weren't Pawny's pennies any more than that was Pawny's kitchen, even though she thought of it as such. Nine sacks of flour couldn't begin to repay Ayodele for what was done to her. There was no payment for that.

Chloe couldn't fault her. It would be easy to read about this in a book and stand back in judgment about what she'd have done. But Chloe wasn't just reading a book. She was actually there—feeling, hearing and smelling the realities of Ayodele's world. It was no different from Chloe's own world. Trees were still trees. Water was still water. Dirt was still dirt. And the powers that be still thought they could determine what constituted moral standards for those from whom they had stolen. There could be no justification for stealing, but no rational being could call what Ayodele planned to do stealing. Certainly, no one would call it stealing if they themselves were in this situation. Chloe only dreaded what would happen if Ayodele was caught.

High on her plans, Ayodele forgot what she was in the kitchen to do. She forgot that other people thought her time belonged to them. She didn't want to think about what other people thought. Totally absorbed, she sat on the three-legged stool and surveyed the kitchen, taking note of every object and the distance between objects.

For a fleeting moment, she pictured how she must look—a slave just sitting there. Not a slave. A captive, she reminded herself. But in the eyes of the beasts, and even in Pawny's eyes, she was a slave, and she'd seen the beasts beat slaves who just sat. Getting a beating right then would mess up her plans.

She hadn't been on the stool long enough to warm it before she drew Pawny's ire.

"Trifling chile, Massa ain't send you in here to sit. There's a floor to scrub, if you can't find nothing to do."

Ayodele got up and fetched rags and a pail from the pantry. She wrapped a rag around her knees to protect them from the hard floor and the lye soap. To avoid Pawny's questions, she kept her head down and her eyes up.

Now she knew what she was going to do and where. All she needed was the when. The only "free" time she had was the nights of the days the parson came. They called those days Sunday. *Sun-day?* They worshipped their Olodumare on the day of the sun? Did they believe the sun was Olodumare? Such blasphemy. No wonder

Olodumare burned them with the very sun they worshipped.

On the nights of Sunday, the great beast didn't make her go to the Sugar Shack but let her sleep on her blanket in the kitchen. No one entered the kitchen on those nights. She was as dark as the darkness. Even if someone did look into the kitchen, as long as she didn't let them hear her, they wouldn't see her.

The following days she did everything she was told to do. She never so much as looked at the cupboard. She was silent but not rigid in the Sugar Shack. That was the hardest part. She couldn't betray her dignity—not even for her plans. Eshu wouldn't ask it of her. *Would he?*

But she had no say in what they made her do, so she could only define dignity as silence—though she knew they defined it as something else. Let them think she was being docile. Let them think she had learned her lesson and their brutality had finally broken her.

Building the shrine wouldn't set her free—and she was still determined to ultimately be free—but in some small way, the shrine would reclaim a part of herself— the part that belonged to Olodumare and not to them.

She went dutifully to the Meeting Hall on Sunday. The very same fiends who raped her nightly were there bowing to her, doffing their hats and calling her ma'am. She didn't know what ma'am meant. Under the circumstances, it was no different from Polly.

Thinking about her plans for the night made her even more impatient with the parson's inane speech. When the others rose to leave, she wanted to run out, but knew that would raise questions, so she disciplined herself to stay with the crowd and do what she was expected to do.

Everybody did what they were expected to do. It was Sunday and they were all on their best behavior. Ayodele knew they'd make up for that the next day. But then, she'd have her shrine, and with it, Eshu and Oya. And with them—a way to escape. After all, Eshu was the owner of the crossroads—the place of life-changing decisions. And Oya was the Orisha of the wind that executed change. No change would come without a decision. What decision would that be, she wondered.

That night, she lay down on her blanket, thinking and waiting. Pawny was gone, but Ayodele could still hear people meandering around near the kitchen. When she heard no more sounds and the glow of lantern lights disappeared from the windows, she still waited.

This was the boldest thing she had ever done in her life. She was acting on her own plans and her own strength, at the command of no one but herself. No one in her life had ever encouraged her to do this— not even in her village. She'd been the daughter everyone expected. She'd been the sister everyone expected. She'd been the villager everyone expected. The aspirant Egun of her people.

No one expected her to do this. No matter. What she expected of herself was all that mattered right now. She expected herself to act with fearless potency. Would she? She was sure she would—but she didn't move.

She lay there on the blanket, staring into the darkness as if the blanket were a precipice and the darkness were an abyss of unknown terrors.

Finally, her brain managed to send a signal to her backbone to rise from the blanket. Everything outside remained still and dark. The plantation was asleep. No one would brave the moonless night to get one of Pawny's biscuits. She could see nothing and was glad she had taken a careful survey of where everything was located—especially the jar of copper pennies. In the darkness, everything would still be in the same place where it was in the light. She told herself this.

Getting up, she placed her heels on the edge of the blanket and took ten paces until her thighs hit the table. Then she turned right and followed the table to its end. Now three paces and she'd be right in front of the cupboard. This was it. This was the door of no return. She must do it or forever chide herself as a coward.

She reached up and her hand hit the splintered edge of the cupboard. Stifling a cry of pain, she slid her fingers along the surface of the board until she felt the jar. Carefully, she held it in both hands and lowered it to her chest. It was heavy even in both hands. No way could she release one hand to unscrew the lid. If she dropped it, the heavy glass would break on the stone floor and she'd be undone.

This task was turning out to be more than a notion. She pivoted and returned to the table. Placing the jar on the table, she unscrewed the top and removed nine pennies. Then she replaced the top and put the jar back on the cupboard in, she hoped, exactly the spot where it had been. She'd leave nothing amiss—nothing that would raise the slightest suspicion.

With careful high hopes, she followed the edge of the table back to the place across from her blanket. Taking ten paces, she dropped to her knees and placed the coins in the corner. First, she had to acknowledge Eshu. She retrieved the three sticks from under the blanket and spread them out before her. These sticks were the canes Eshu often carried.

She wished she had some kind of food to give him. He loved food, and would eat anything. But he'd have to understand that she didn't want to push her luck by making the shrine more complicated than it needed to be. So three canes would have to suffice. She bowed her head in supplication.

"Eshu of the crossroads,
Divine messenger of the river,
Ayodele acknowledges you,
Ayodele bows to the majesty
            of your importance.
Bear a word from me to
            Olodumare.
Help me to escape this
            miserable place.
Return me to my home,
My mother, my father and
            Bamidele if he has
            come back."

She placed the canes under the blanket and spread out the coins on the burgundy cloth. Again, she bowed her head and prayed to the Orisha of the wind.

> "When it is time, you will tell
> me the answer to my
> heart's question.
> Blow away the beast in your
> mighty wind.
> Suck them down into the
> whirlpool of your
> wrath.
> Tear them in the storm of your
> anger.
> But lift me up and show me
> the way to safety."

Ayodele remembered the dance her villagers always did to honor the Orisha. They had danced to drums, but she had no drums to dance to and she dared not make noise that might be overheard by her captors.

Africa was in her, she reminded herself. And so were the drums of Africa. A drum beat in her mind, whipping up images of her brother Bamidele. She could smell the foods, hear the voices and see the colored strips of her last Egungun.

246

Rising to her feet, she danced. Chloe danced with her. She recognized the rhythms from her lonesome dances in her office and from the *toque* in Yara's house. Chloe felt exalted in the knowledge that she shared these rhythms, not only with the Africans in Brazil, but also with those who had come straight from Africa. These were her rhythms—her heritage from the Motherland. They danced together and Chloe vowed to remember every step.

Finally exhausted, sweaty, and tired, Ayodele put everything under her blanket and lay down to sleep.

Chloe didn't sleep. She was a soul, not a mind. The soul kept an unblinking eye on the mind. Chloe watched Ayodele's mind slip from the real world to a dream world in one seamless tapestry of consciousness.

"You didn't remember my mother's name in your prayers. Ekundayo knows the way of escape, and she knows the way of revenge."

Chapter 18

"Nine copper pennies!" Pawny screamed. "She done brought the Devil into my kitchen. Massa, she got the Devil and done brought him into this house."

"What you talking about, Pawny?" Jimboy asked. He was walking past the kitchen door and nearly jumped out of his britches. "Anybody don't know better'd think somebody in there killing you." He came through the door and stood looking at Pawny like she had lost a good part of her mind.

"Go get the massa. It's the Devil."

"What Massa gone do with the Devil? You got the Devil in your head if you think I'm gone run for you. What you talking about?"

Pawny was too frantic to acknowledge his jibe. She could barely get out an explanation. "See, Polly got nine copper pennies."

"So she stole some money. What the Devil got to do with that? What she gone do with them pennies anyway? She can't spend 'em. Soon as she try, everybody gone know they ain't hers."

"She ain't stole them to spend them, fool. She stole them to worship the Devil with them."

"Now I know you gone crazy."

"No, for real. I remember when I was little, my mammy showed me how she used nine copper pennies to conjure up some devil from Africa. I'm glad Massa turn me against her devilish ways. Parson say that's Satan. And Polly done brought Satan in my kitchen. *My kitchen.* Wait 'til Massa hear about this."

Jimboy grabbed Pawny by the shoulder. "No, you can't tell him. He'll kill her for sure. He'll do something to her we ain't never seen him do to nobody before."

"She shoulda thought about that before she bring the Devil in my kitchen."

"Pawny, listen . . ."

"What's all this commotion, Pawny?" Keaton entered the kitchen, saw the ashen horror on Jimboy's face and squared his shoulders like he'd come to mete out justice.

"Massa, oh Massa. That African you brought in here done brought some African devil into my kitchen."

"Calm down, Pawny, and tell me what ails you." Keaton was the image of composure before his flighty servants.

"Massa, I went to put them coins you give me in my little jar and I notice the clean spot on the cupboard. I never move that jar. I just drop the coins in the little slit on the top, so the dust don't never move. But somebody moved it last night and I could see where they wiped the dust with their fingers trying to find it in the dark. Now I say to myself, ain't but one person been in my kitchen, so I go over to that chile's blanket to see what she got under there. Bless me, Massa. She had nine copper pennies. Nine."

"What is that supposed to mean to me? She thought she was stealing from you. So make her put them back and be done with it."

Jimboy lost himself to the point where he actually sighed with relief. He silently reprimanded himself for letting his mask slip, but Keaton took no notice.

"You don't understand, Massa. Nine copper coins is what they use to worship the Devil in Africa. My mammy showed me when I was little. They pray to the Devil, Massa. They don't pray to Jesus."

Keaton was paying attention now. His face turned scarlet and his lips quivered as he said, "I don't allow that in my house. 'As for me and my house, we worship the Lord.' That's what the Good Book says."

Pawny nodded her head. "You got to put a stop to this, Massa. If she harkening to the Devil, ain't no telling what he tell her to do. He might tell her to put something in your food. She so full of hate; she might . . ."

"Stop right there, Pawny." His scarlet face turned to chalk as he envisioned the mayhem one freethinking African could commit. "I've heard enough. I'm going to nip this in the bud right now. Where is Polly?"

"Think she went to the outhouse. She s'pose to be here this time of day. Reckon she be back soon. Ain't nowhere else for her to go."

Pawny watched the little African saunter into the kitchen like everything was everything and wondered how that chile thought she was gone wiggle out of this. Did she think she could just lay down with the Devil and Massa wouldn't have nothing to say about it?

"Polly, we worship Jesus in this house," Keaton said.

Ayodele looked around as if to see who Polly might be.

"I know you know your name, nigger. I said we worship Jesus in this house. 'Thou shalt worship the Lord thy God, and Him alone shalt thou serve.' Didn't you hear the parson tell you that?"

"Yes. I heard him."

"Yes, you heard him what?" Pawny resented that Polly never called their master Massa. The insolent little African not only refused the nice little name the white folks had given her so they could call her, but she had the nerve to spurn her master's rightful name.

"Yes, I heard him say that."

Pawny knew Polly knew what she meant. She started to insist the Devil-worshipping wench show some respect for her master, but Keaton didn't notice their interchange.

"I don't care about you stealing from niggers. That's not the point. The point I'm making is you brought a false god into my house. You worshipped something that ain't Jesus and I won't have it."

Pawny almost winced. *Almost*. If her master didn't care about stealing from niggers, who was she to care about it? Still . . . no, she couldn't afford to think about still. If she wanted to live and work in her kitchen, wasn't no still about it.

One thing for sure, Polly's silent defiance was of the Devil and wouldn't get her nothing but a whipping. Pawny wanted to ask her just how she thought she wasn't gone get caught—wanted her to ask how they'd caught her. But their master was in charge now and Pawny knew the best thing for her was to keep quiet.

Keaton grabbed Ayodele and pulled her outside. "Jimboy, get my whip and bring it to the Meeting Hall."

"Yes, Massa." Jimboy could barely keep the question out of his voice. Pawny heard it and she knew how much effort it took. But Keaton was too occupied with Polly to notice. She was glad for Jimboy's sake. Wasn't nothing but trouble for a nigger to even look like he didn't like what his massa say. When it came to wearing the mask, Jimboy was good. Pawny was better. Polly had a long way to go—if she lived long enough to learn.

Ayodele did her best to keep up with Keaton's brisk pace as he marched her to the Meeting Hall. She wouldn't allow herself to be dragged. That was just one small act of control over her own body. It meant almost running. She couldn't maintain the elegant stride her mother had taught her, but at least, she wouldn't be dragged.

Inside the Meeting Hall, he pulled her to the front and made her face a picture of a

Rhonda Denise Johnson

beast with very pink skin and long, white hair on his head and chin. The hair on his head was long and flowing like the hair on one of the beast women she'd seen.

"This is God, nigger. You will worship him in my house."

Ayodele was appalled. These beasts actually thought Olodumare looked like them? Now she knew she must struggle against them with every ounce of her strength. How could Olodumare tolerate such an abomination?

Keaton slapped her to the floor. Yanking her head up by her hair, he snarled into her face, "You're a sinner. You were born in sin and conceived in iniquity. But this here Jesus will cleanse your soul of all your African depravity. Just say Jesus. Say it!"

She didn't open her mouth.

"Say Jesus! Everyone who calls on the name of the Lord will be saved—even niggers. Jesus loves niggers because he died for sinners. His blood will wash your black soul as white as snow, but you got to call his name. Say Jesus!"

Her brain flowed with magma. Her blood boiled in her veins. If she didn't get away from this beast and his white Olodumare, her brain would gush from her skull like lava from the Blu Plateau. She was

254

so determined not to open her mouth that she forgot to breathe. Her lips burst open in a gasp, but still, she didn't speak. She clamped her lips shut again.

Ayodele wasn't alone in her rage. Chloe bristled and grieved within her. This was the foundation of all that her own mother believed. This was how it all began. At some point in her family's legacy, some ancestor broke under the brutality of Christian evangelism and bowed to the white deity. The beatings were forgotten, the insults overlooked. The pink-faced Colonel Sanders picture her ancestors had been forced to pray to became sweet, olive-skinned Jesus with an aquiline nose and full lips. At that point, the African captive became an American slave.

Chloe marveled that Ayodele never said the word "God." To her African mind, it was just a corruption of the name of Olodumare and she refused to let it pass her lips. Chloe moaned, knowing that she'd soon experience another beating—a very violent beating fueled by righteous wrath and religious indignation. Ayodele and Keaton were at an impasse and neither of them would give ground.

Chapter 19

Chloe braced herself for the beating of her life, but the unleashing of Keaton's fury never came. Instead, she was wrenched from Ayodele's body and thrust back into her own. She found herself in the marketplace again. The auction block was empty and the crowd had dispersed. Chloe could jump around in time and space—experiencing only what Oya thought she needed to experience. She wondered what had happened while she was gone. Not that she could change anything for Ayodele. All that Chloe might have witnessed and experienced had already happened. Still, some macabre part of her mind wanted to know what had happened.

"Aaaaghhhah!" Oya announced herself in a whirlwind of screaming and bedeviled air.

"Oya," Chloe called. "What happened? Why did you bring me out of Ayodele just before her worst moment?"

"Kiddo, there was nothing you could have learned from that experience. And that wasn't her worst moment. Only a prelude to it."

"Learned?"

"Why yes, of course. Did you suppose I sent you there for a vacation? You have learned what you need to know for right now."

"No, I haven't. I was supposed to find the answer to my question in the wind. I didn't find it. I still don't know what I'm supposed to do in life, and I still don't know what message the spirits were trying to give me."

Oya pursed her lips and blew out a small tornado. She smoothed the ruffles in her skirt and blinked her large eyes. "Patience, kiddo. No one said you'd get it all in a truckload. You wanted to know what message the spirits have for you. Well, we're the spirits, and then there is your own spirit."

"So, what do I do now?"

"Do what you've always done. Live your life."

"*What?* I thought things were supposed to be different. I thought you're supposed to bring a big change in my life. What about the lesson I was supposed to learn? What about the great things I'm supposed to do? What's that all about? What was it all for if I'm just going back to the same old same old? And I still haven't met Exu."

"Kiddo, your head is full of Hollywood. You expect to sit back passively while something spectacular unfolds before your eyes. It doesn't work that way. Go back and live your life. You will see what you will see."

"I'll see what I will see?" Before the question left Chloe's mouth, she found herself caught in the embrace of a maelstrom. Its winds were not made of air but of spirit. Her second time in this vortex of quintessence was no less formidable than the first time. Here, the fifth element justified its status as an element—buffeting her like air, pummeling her like earth, drowning her like water, and searing her soul like fire. This ethereal cocoon swirled all around her, moving her body where it willed. And it was Oya. Chloe passed into the peace at the center of Oya and rested, knowing there was nothing she could accomplish by panicking.

Presently, Chloe felt herself descending. Her feet touched some surface and gravity reasserted its power on her body. She dared to open her eyes and found she was back in the courtyard of her apartment building. The key to her mailbox was still in her hand and the sun had not moved. But she had been gone for months. How could no time have passed? Did the Orixa have power over time as well as the elements? Chloe thought about it. Oya controlled the winds of change and change marked the passage of time. How could she control one unless she controlled the other?

Chloe could ask Yara. The Brazilian priestess could answer the question. *Couldn't she?* Ayodele knew nothing of Candomblé. Her Orishas came straight from Africa without a shade of Portuguese influence. That meant Oya's being wasn't etched in stone. Through Yara's Brazilian experience, she saw aspects of Oya not seen in Africa. It may be that in her time-traveling experiences, Chloe was seeing aspects of Oya not seen in Brazil or Africa, yet they were nonetheless valid. She'd ask Yara.

****

"*No!*" Olumide screamed. "Absolutely not. She has not been a student of Candomblé longer than a heartbeat and already she wants to westernize it. Time-travel? Out-of-body experiences? These have no place in the worship of the Orixa."

Rhonda Denise Johnson

The babalawo's rage made Yara's living room shrink. They'd have to take the couch out or something to make room for this man's paroxysms. Chloe took note, and didn't like the way he spoke about her, using the word "she" as if she weren't there. As babalawo, he was due some measure of respect, but she disdained giving anyone more respect than they were willing to return. She turned to Yara.

"He doesn't like the idea."

Comprehension shone in Yara's eyes. "No, he doesn't."

Olumide glared at Yara. "This is your fault. I told you this would happen. I told you when you first brought this Westerner to the *toque*."

Yara lowered her eyes, uncomfortable in such proximity to defiance, but the man had sparked some fire in her and she couldn't back down. "Yes, you did, and you saw how Xangô and then Omolu accepted her."

He gave the idea a backhanded slap. "That changes nothing. She is still a Westerner."

"How can you say that changes nothing? The approval of the Orixa changes everything."

"You dare to question your babalawo?"

260

"If you give yourself the right to question the Orixa, then you give me the right to question you."

Olumide straightened himself. "I see." His quiet tone thickened the air more ominously than all his torrents of wrath.

Yara shuddered and Chloe looked out the window. Still a Westerner? Still a proselyte—an adoptee—who could do what she wanted but never change the fact of who she was—an outsider. A part of her wanted to explain. Maybe if she could just make him see how sincere her heart was, he'd accept her. She immediately vetoed the idea of fawning for this man's acceptance. He wasn't concerned about being accepted by her, so why should she be concerned about him?

She remembered the hurt and humiliation she'd suffered inside Ayodele's body and vowed she'd never demean her ancestors by lowering her dignity. She was part of a community of black women past, present and future. Ayodele had no control over what men did to her. How dare Chloe relinquish the control that women like Ayodele had won for her?

Yara trembled. In her eyes, fear and rage warred for mastery. She soon composed herself and looked her babalawo directly in the eye. "You don't see. I mean no disrespect for you are the babalawo of this district. But Chloe has . . ."

"Enough! You have said quite enough. I will make my report to the temple in Brazil."

"

No." Yara gasped.

He sneered at Yara's distress and bore into her with predatory eyes. "I will stay my hand no longer. I warned you. Yet, you continue to compromise the integrity of orthodox Candomblé. Now the time of warning has passed. I will go to the Council."

Chloe thought of Keaton beating Christianity into Ayodele and realized Olumide was doing the same to Yara. All he lacked was a whip. Yara fixed her eyes on the fourth button on his shirt as if all her thoughts were concentrated in that one spot. She didn't move except to tremble. Would she be excommunicated? Chloe realized that this was all about her. Yara was losing the favor of her babalawo because of her and might soon lose the favor of her whole religion, all because of Chloe.

"Maybe I should just leave. I don't have to be here."

Yara started. She didn't want whatever Olumide was threatening, but neither did she want to succumb to his tyranny. Taking a deep breath, she swallowed hard and reconnected to her resolve. Turning to Chloe, she placed a reassuring hand on Chloe's arm. "No, that won't help. There are other things."

Chloe heard people ascending the outer stairs to the *terreiro*. Olumide looked somehow vindicated as if everything was going according to his plan and the people's presence only gave him another opportunity to impose his will. But Yara rose to her feet and walked past him as if he weren't there.

"The people are here for tonight's *toque*. This discussion must give way to my preparations."

Chloe followed Yara outside. In the distance, a crowd of humanoid shadows approaching. She couldn't distinguish shadow from substance in the moonless night. She shuddered. Strange things happen on moonless nights. Then she laughed. Wasn't it supposed to be the full moon that made people act crazy? Maybe it wasn't the moon. Maybe it was the night. Maybe it was just people. She turned the corner of the house and ascended the stairs to the *terreiro*.

"There she is, Charlotte. I told you she was up to no good."

To Chloe's horror, she heard her uncle Charlie's voice booming down the street. As she reached the top of the stairs, she turned to see an angry swarm emerge from the darkness into the light of a nearby streetlamp.

"Chloe, I didn't raise you to worship the Devil," her mother pleaded. "You come down from among those heathens and stand with Jesus."

Her mother and uncle stood at the head of a crowd of a dozen people carrying picket signs and chanting, "Jesus, Jesus, Jesus."

"The Westerner has brought this abomination to this holy *terreiro*," Olumide roared. His voice bristled with rage, but Chloe saw in his eyes a glint of satisfaction and even glee. With a triumphant glare, his eyes scraped past Chloe and he entered the *terreiro*.

Yara looked as mortified as Chloe felt.

"Thou shalt worship the Lord thy God, and Him alone shalt thou serve," someone in the crowd yelled.

Chloe remembered that this was the same scripture Keaton used on Ayodele when he prepared to beat her into submitting to his pink-skinned version of God. Did she finally submit? She may have. Either Ayodele or someone after her must have capitulated.

How could Chloe's mother act the way she did, otherwise?

Then someone took up a melody and the crowd began to sing.

> "Oh, how I love Jesus
> Because he first loved me."

Chloe could see Yara's neighbors peeking from their windows to see what the tumult was about. Yara could see them, too. She glanced anxiously at the door of the *terreiro* as if hoping Enriquo was calming the people who had come for the *toque*. All she could do was hope.

"That's my daughter. I'm going to bring my daughter home." To Chloe's utter alarm, her mother commenced to climb the stairs toward her. Yara pulled Chloe inside and slammed the door in her mother's face.

"I'm taking you back, Chloe. I'm bringing you back to Jesus."

Then Chloe heard sirens. *Oh, man.* That's all she needed. This wasn't her night. She remembered Oya and knew she wasn't alone. Chloe would see what she would see, the Orixa had told her. How could she have thought that meant things would be the same? The Orixa had foreseen what was happening and prepared her for it. Was she prepared?

She still didn't know what to do, but at least she knew she wasn't alone.

"Break it up! Break it up! This is private property."

The people in the *terreiro* listened to the policeman's voice. A preternatural serenity calmed them to silence.

"Officer, those heathens have my daughter in there. It's the Church of Satan and I've come to take her home."

"Is she a minor?" Chloe could almost see the police officer taking out his notepad to make a report. In her mind, she visualized every cop she'd ever seen on TV, from Kojak to Tenspeed and Brownshoe.

"Oh no," Her mother said. "She's grown, but she's still my daughter and I'm not leaving her to the Devil."

"If she is an adult, then you can't force her to come with you. That is considered abduction, and is punishable by law."

"But they put a hex on her. The Devil has my daughter under his spell."

"I understand that, ma'am, but this is private property and you are disturbing the peace." Kojak sounded tired and bored. Chloe knew there was nothing more dangerous than a bored cop. Her mother was sure to give him all the excitement he craved. "If you'll come with me, ma'am."

"Peace! Peace! I didn't come to bring peace. That's what Jesus said. He came to bring a sword. To divide mother and daughter—brother and sister. I'm not leaving my daughter in the jaws of the Devil. I'm taking her home."

"Amen."

"That's right, Sister Marshall."

Chloe couldn't believe her mother was actually defying the police. There was a time for defiance, but facing an armed officer wasn't one of them. Then again, if her mother really believed she was on the battlefield for the Lord—snatching her daughter out of the pit of Hell—yes, she'd defy the Devil himself. And Chloe knew that was exactly what her mother thought she was doing.

Chloe didn't move. Some part of her thought she should go out there. After all, it was her mother. Go out there and do what? If she were out there, her mother would try to grab her and then the police would move to stop her. Chloe didn't even know how many cops were out there. She'd only heard one, but she knew they came in teams—especially to a neighborhood like this. They might think they had to use force. Somebody might get hurt.

Chloe didn't move. She listened to the sounds of scuffling feet, police radios and barking dogs. She listened to the sound of an unstoppable object colliding with an immoveable object. There was the sound of many people moving away from the door without alacrity, climbing down the stairs and disappearing into the night. Then there was silence. Chloe listened to the silence as well. And it was louder than the mayhem of discordant zealots.

"What will you do now?" Yara asked.

That was the one question Chloe didn't want to deal with at the moment. She wanted someone else to deal with it— someone older, wiser, and stronger than she. But there was no one else to deal with it. Certainly, the other people in the mob had family members who'd bail them out of jail, but that was her mother and uncle and no one else's responsibility but hers.

"There's only one thing I can do. I must get my mother and uncle out of jail."

Yara came to her and took her hand. "First, you must honor Xangô. He will help you when you face opposition."

"Is he helping you, Yara?" Olumide growled. He never spoke. He roared or growled. Even his whispers hinted at menace.

Why was this man so baleful? Chloe wondered. There was something between him and Yara, and Chloe knew she was only his latest excuse for ire.

Yara wasn't in the mood to back down. She met his derision with equal disdain. "Yes, Xangô helps me. It is you who gives me reason to seek his help."

"I'll take note of that when I speak to the council."

But Yara didn't flinch away from this threat. Her concern for Chloe calcified her own backbone and she stood her ground. "So be it. I'll do what I will do. If I cannot make the right decisions, then I will make my decisions right."

"Will you now be your own babalawo?" He raised his eyebrows, daring her to challenge his unquestionable authority.

She didn't think his authority was as unquestionable as he imagined. "Babalawo? Did you ever consider the meaning of that word? Baba means father and *awo* is spirit. From the time you came here, your contempt for me never faltered. You're no father and your spirit is negating. I will find a real babalawo. You may leave if you wish."

269

Whoa. Chloe only wished she had brought some popcorn. She had a ringside seat to the bout of the century, and there were no corner men, no bell and no referee.

Trying to roll with the punches, Olumide delivered his own uppercut. "Must I remind you that you are in what is supposed to be a *terreiro* and your devotees are watching? Will you fight me here?"

Yara could roll, too. She parried the blow and whispered—hissed really, "No, I have nothing more to say to you. Try to act halfway civilized, if not pleasant, for the rest of the *toque*."

She went to Xangô's shrine and lit the candles. Enriquo commenced to play the drums and Yara danced over to Chloe. Taking Chloe by the hand, she pulled her into the middle of the floor where they both danced to the honor of Xangô. The rhythms were familiar to Chloe, but the brilliance that had filled her body the first time was now a burning fire. She knew it was the fire of Xangô, imbuing her body with the aspect of his father Aganyu. As they danced, Yara opened her mouth and began to speak, but it wasn't her voice. Chloe knew that the Orixa whose fire burned away their fears and sorrows now possessed her friend. She listened.

"Chloe, listen fluently. What I say I will say but once. Do not forget what I say, lest Exu forget to show mercy to you at the crossroads."

"I'm listening."

"Chloe, you are to build my temple. That is the great work of your life—the only true meaning of your life."

Chloe was perplexed now. Of course, it made sense that her great work would be something beyond her immediate abilities. Yet still, she was perplexed. "Build a temple? How? When? Where?"

The Orixa sighed. "Mortal minds are so inquisitive. You can only experience reality one moment at a time, yet you want to know everything at once. I will show you what you need to know, only set your *Axé* to obey."

Fearing the flames and the unpredictable temper of Xangô, the people had moved back. Olumide shook with rage. He was the babalawo, but the Orixa in Chloe didn't acknowledge him. When she looked at him through the flames, she saw only a man whose mind was consumed by impotent fury. He was the spiritual father, yet the spirits had no use for him.

Chloe wouldn't let her mother spend the night in jail. When Xangô departed, she left, too. She'd need bail money. Disturbing the peace shouldn't even be a misdemeanor. Fifty dollars, maybe? She'd do what she could for her mother. But she wouldn't pay to get her out of trouble she put herself in. Chloe pointed her car towards her mother's house. As she pulled into the driveway, she could see that her sister Lisa had turned on every light in the house. Sixteen and she still didn't like to be alone in the dark. Chloe shook her head and marched into the house.

Blaring music and raucous laughter told Chloe that her little sister wasn't alone and her reason for all the lights was different altogether.

"You know Mom's going to have a fit."

"You scared me," Lisa said running into the foyer to meet Chloe before she entered the living room where Lisa's friends were doing Olodumare-knows-what. "I thought you were Mom. Where is she?"

"In jail." No need to hide it. Lisa was sixteen and their mother wasn't likely to conceal her martyrdom.

"What?"

"I don't have time to explain," Chloe said, pushing past Lisa. She barely looked at Lisa's friends as she headed towards her mother's room.

Lisa followed her, overcome by consternation. "What's Mom doing in jail?"

"Where does she keep the grocery money?"

"Grocery money?" Lisa frowned.

"For bail. Where is it?"

"You're going to use our grocery money to bail Mom out of jail? That's not right. Use your own money. She's our mother. They probably have her down there sharing a cell with murderers and rapists."

"She's in jail because she and Uncle Charlie made public spectacles of themselves trying to break up something I was doing."

"Uncle Charlie's in there, too? Man, I thought we was having a party here. Mom and Uncle Charlie must have been partying hard to wind up in jail. What was y'all doing anyway?"

"What *were* you doing?" Chloe corrected. "Never mind." She didn't want to get into it about Candomblé right then. They had to get down to the jail. "They weren't partying. They were arguing with a cop and he took them in for disturbing the peace. Where's the money?"

"Why don't you use your own money?"

"I don't have money for foolishness."

"It's just money. It's no big deal."

273

Rhonda Denise Johnson

"It *is* a big deal if you have to work for it, kid."

"And it's a big deal if you have to eat with it, Miss Grown."

Any other time, they'd have laughed at this usually friendly banter. Under the circumstances, it wasn't completely friendly. Lisa opened a drawer in the long dresser and pulled out a sock. "How much you need?"

"Oh, I don't know. I guess fifty a piece should cover it."

Lisa peeled off a hundred-dollar bill and handed it to her big sister.

"Brace yourself, Lisa. All hell is about to break loose."

Chapter 20

The crowd of arrestees milling around the police station or handcuffed to arresting officers spoiled the grand entrance Charlotte Marshall would've liked to make. She settled for marching straight to the sergeant's desk.

"Officer, I don't know why I'm here. This is a crying shame. I'm an upright pillar of the Church. I haven't broken any laws. God gave us his law. He didn't break the laws."

The sergeant didn't look up from his paperwork. "No one here broke the law, ma'am. You're as innocent as the rest of them. If you haven't noticed, there's a line. Please wait your turn."

"I'm not waiting in no Godforsaken line." She couldn't remember ever being treated with such disrespect, and she wouldn't stand for it—not if her God was still in Heaven, and she knew that he was. "You're going to lose your blessing, treating the Lord's servant like a common criminal. I demand that I and all those with me be released."

The sergeant looked up, alarmed by her belligerence. "Where're the officers . . ." He spied the arresting officers helping themselves at the coffee machine. "Bates! Reynolds! Escort your detainees to seats."

Bares and Reynolds tossed their cups into a waste can and came over to escort Charlotte and her troop of seven to seats near the back of the station. To her credit, she had enough sense not to struggle with them, but when one of them touched her arm; she spurned his touch and marched off in the direction he indicated. She and Charlie sat next to each other.

"Lord, Charlie, I never thought I'd see the day when one of mine would give herself over to the Devil. You know I've done my best."

The police had let six of Charlotte's mob go because they had been on the street and had dispersed without incident. But six others had tried to forestall the police when they took Charlotte from that heathen woman's door, so they were all taken in. They sat around in a tight little conclave, regurgitating their righteousness among themselves.

Charlie nodded his head. "I know you did, Charlotte. I ain't faulting you. I fault that damn school. You know the Good Book say not many wise enter God's kingdom."

"That's right," said Big Mabel.

"Sure do," agreed Josephine.

"That's what it say," Nathan chimed in.

Charlie raised a finger in the air like he was raring up for a sermon. "Like a camel passing through the eye of a needle is them that's rich in intelligence—what the world calls intelligence, anyway."

Two hours passed, and finally, the sergeant called Charlotte's name. They went to the desk ready to state their case, but without looking up, the sergeant read their charges.

"Resisting arrest. Disturbing the peace. Trespassing on private property. You'll go to cell five to await trial or bail."

"Trial? For what?"

"Don't we get one phone call?"

Charlotte's bosom heaved, and she crossed her arms as if to keep it from bursting from this outrageous indignity. "I'm not calling anybody. I shouldn't be here. Officer, look . . ."

"Arthur Banks, come to the desk. Your case is next."

A guard escorted Charlotte and company to a cell while the sergeant went on with his day's work. There was one bench in the cell, but none of them wanted to sit on it. Sitting down would make it seem like they belonged there, and Charlotte refused to make herself comfortable in this dungeon of Pharaoh.

From their cell, they could see the front door and Charlotte glanced towards it every other heartbeat. They'd been there long enough and she was beginning to worry. She'd done the right thing by the Lord, but she knew her daughter thought she knew better than God knew and might decide to let her rot right there in the jailhouse. Not that she planned to stay. How could they keep a servant of God? Didn't God deliver Daniel from the mouth of the lion? "Reckon she'll come to fetch us?"

Nathan shrugged his massive shoulders. "If the Devil's guiding her, ain't no telling what she'll do. Shame will keep her away. She got to feel shame for all the trouble she's caused."

"Amen. They say we resisted arrest, but she's resisting the Lord. Shame on her," Margaret declared.

Dale raised his hands to Heaven. "Yes, Lord."

278

"God bless the child," continued Margaret, for she wasn't finished. "They don't need to have their own. Look at what they do with it."

Treese shook her head. "Naw, don't blame it on her being a child, 'cause we sure wasn't like this when we was young. Had the Devil whipped outta me."

"There she is," Charlie called out.

Charlotte looked up and saw Chloe walk in the door. Chloe stopped to speak to a guard and he pointed her towards cell five. As she approached them, Charlotte cocked an eyebrow and regarded her daughter with righteous indignation. What could that child possibly say for herself after this? Gave her soul to the Devil, running after heathens, and to top it off, let her own mother languish in jail for four hours before she stirred her behind to come see about her. Charlotte wanted to weep just thinking that she had raised a child like this.

Chloe peered at them through the bars. "Hi Mom, Uncle Charlie, Miss Mabel, Miss Margaret, Miss Josephine, Mr. Dale, Miss Treese, Mr. Nathan." She nodded to each in turn, addressing them as she had been raised to do. "I'll go talk to the sergeant to see about your bail." Then she turned and walked away.

"Just like that. Gone see about our bail like ain't nothing to it," huffed Margaret.

"Shameless," Josephine spat out. "She got no shame."

"I didn't raise her like this. Lord knows I didn't."

"Oh, she knows how to act like she was raised right," said Treese. "*Miss* Mabel and *Miss* Margaret. Like she think we don't know all about her ways."

Charlotte's friends and brother continued to remark on her daughter's selfish behavior, but Charlotte turned her attention inward as shame and wrath battled in her breast.

When Chloe returned, she didn't look happy. "The sergeant said he can't let you out until he contacts the people whose property you trespassed on to see if they will press charges. They're not answering the phone, so you have to stay here. I'm sorry. I really am."

"*What?!*" Charlotte screamed. This was too much. She couldn't take it. "That makes no sense."

Chloe looked away from her mother. "I know. I tried to talk to him, but he kept talking about the rules and his case-load and he won't budge."

Charlotte trembled. Her bosom swelled with rage. "You little heathen. It's your fault we're in here, so why should we expect you to make any effort to get us out."

"*Mom?*"

"YOU GOT THE DEVIL! YOU GOT SATAN! LEAVE YOUR MOTHER IN JAIL!" She was really screaming now. Her breath came in gasps. She couldn't breathe. The air refused to enter her nostrils. Pain seized her head as the grey cement floor rose to meet her. She heard Chloe and Charlie shout her name as darkness engulfed her.

***

Charlotte's next conscious thought was that the floor was no longer hard and cold. It yielded to the contours of her body and an orange light shone through her translucent eyelids. She listened. Instead of Chloe and Charlie, she heard clicking and whirring. The sounds were familiar, but she couldn't place them. She tried to open her eyes but couldn't.

Rising above the clicking and whirring, another sound came to her. It was a voice. Human but not quite human. An ethereal sound, soft and high-pitched, it came from inside her mind and drowned out the clicking and whirring, which came from outside.

"Poor Charlotte. What made you think you could raise a decent nigger child? There's no such thing as decent niggers. You know that. Niggers are niggers. If you'd whipped her like you were whipped, maybe the fear of God would be in her. Spare the rod, spoil the nigger. That's what you did, Charlotte."

In a flash, Charlotte remembered the voice as if she'd heard it only that morning. But it had been some forty years. It was the big white girl from her church. She'd been the perfect child—flaxen pigtails and sharp, blue eyes. She'd deigned to be Charlotte's friend and keep her black feet from straying off the way to righteousness. "Abigail? Where are you?"

"Right here, in your mind where I've always been."

Charlotte loved that voice—so melodious and sensible. How could she be hearing it now? She wouldn't question what God chose to do. She was tired. She was weary. Her daughter had worn her out. But this blessed voice could only be from the Lord. "It's been forty years since I've seen you."

"But it hasn't been forty years since I've seen you. Why did you let those heathens trouble you so? You should have put on the armor of God and fought the good fight."

Shame caught Charlotte's words in her mouth. What could she say? She could never be as good as Abigail was. She was too black to even think she could be as close to God as Abigail was, but the Lord knew she'd done her best. "She's my daughter. I didn't want those heathens to have her. I knew she could be saved if she just stayed away from the wrong influences."

Abigail laughed in that same way she'd always laughed whenever Charlotte said something foolish, which had been often. "What made you think a nigger like you could raise anything but a nigger? Your mama was a nigger. You're a nigger and your Chloe is a nigger. Now why did you act all surprised when she behaved like the nigger she is?"

"I didn't raise her to act that way. Lord knows I didn't."

"The Lord knows? Oh but the Lord made you my slave because Ham laughed at Noah and you people been swinging from trees and worshipping the Devil ever since. You may think you're free now because you wear no chains, but you're still my slave."

That must be true, Charlotte thought. Everything Abigail or any good white person said was true. Charlotte remembered how they used to play-act. "I remember we used to play slave and master. But we were just playing—just little kids having fun."

"Fun? Yes, you enjoyed being my slave, didn't you? And what a delightful little slave you were, too—always eager to please your master. What was it you used to say? 'Oh Master, thank you. I'm no longer a heathen. Bless the Lord for letting me serve you as the righteous servant of all that's good. I'm no longer a servant of sin. I serve the Lord.' Even as a child, you knew that serving white folks meant serving God."

Charlotte knew that somehow she had failed in that service. She was born to fail. They'd brought her out of that sinful African jungle, but like the pastor always said, the sin in her would stay in her until she reached that blessed place where the blood of Jesus would wash her as white as snow. "That's what the Good Book says."

"Does it, now?"

"Yes. It says, 'Servants obey your masters as is fitting in the Lord, not with eye service as men pleasers, but as unto the Lord.' It must have been talking about black servants serving white masters, 'cause I've never heard tell of white servants serving black masters."

Charlotte knew her Bible—knew what it said, and still, she had failed.

"And you believed that?"

"With all my heart, Abigail. Whatever God says is right, is right. I've never strayed from the place where the Lord put me. I've never raised my eyes to usurp the blessed dominion of whites. Pastor said that's what the Devil did, trying to be like God because he thought he was pretty. I'm not even pretty, and I sure don't want to do like the Devil."

Then Charlotte fell silent. She wanted to shift her position on the soft surface, but couldn't. She wanted to cough, but couldn't. Something was wrong, but she didn't know what.

"Charlotte?" Abigail called from somewhere in Charlotte's mind.

"Yes, I was saying, good white Christian folks took me out of the jungle. But I know as sure as my skin is black and my hair is nappy that the jungle is still in me. One day I'll wash all that black filth out of me in the blood of Jesus and be white as snow. Until then, I know my place. But my daughter, she doesn't know."

"Well, that's only to be expected. We've tried to help you, but like you just said, the jungle is in you and that nigger blood is going to show up somewhere."

"That's what the church people always told me when I was little. That's what you always told me. I could never forget that nigger blood in me."

"It's as true now as it was forty years ago."

"Yes, Lord. Sin as black as pitch. I don't understand why you set us free. You knew we weren't ready. Look at my Chloe. She's gone astray—turned away from the path of the Lord, talking about Africa and black history. What good is black history?"

"No good, if you ask me. But Charlotte, what makes you think you're free? You must remember what the Bible says in Isaiah. That was one of my favorite scriptures. 'Thus says the Lord: The labor of Egypt and merchandise of Cush and of the Sabeans, men of stature, shall come over to you, and they shall be yours; They shall walk behind you, They shall come over in chains; and they shall bow down to you. They will make supplication to you, saying, Surely, God is in you, and there is no other. There is no other God.' Charlotte, that's all still true."

"No other God but the Lord."

"Of course, Egypt today has nothing to do with you, but in the Bible, Egypt is that evil place—that black place. The Lord gave you to us and what the Lord joined, no president can put asunder. As long as you keep the words of the Lord in your heart, you'll never have to worry. There'll always be some good white folks to guide you in the right way of the Lord."

Charlotte sighed. "For me, yes, praise the Lord. But my daughter . . ."

"She's lost."

"*No!*"

"The God in Heaven brought you out of Africa and set you to good service. Anybody who turns back to Africa is lost. Once you come to Jesus, there's no turning back."

"No, not my child."

"No turning back."

Charlotte began to hear the clicking and whirring sounds again. She called for her master but instead heard a frightful voice.

"Mom? Are you awake?"

She didn't try to open her eyes. She didn't want to see that face—that lost, black African face. Abigail had always been right about everything, but Chloe was her daughter. She couldn't give her up to Satan. All her dreams for her children couldn't just be thrown away. She wanted them to get good jobs. She wanted them to know the Lord and follow his ways. "Charlotte Marshall," she commended herself. "Fight the good fight. You are more than a conqueror. Hallelujah! Hallelujah!" She'd win if it was the last thing she did.

Chapter 21

Daniel Freeman Hospital didn't feel the same. As Chloe sat in the waiting room with a horde of anxious people waiting to take a glimpse at her mother, she took no comfort in the room's elegant decor. How could she think about paintings and carpets when her mother had had a stroke? It had become a beige world now. She gave it no attention and it asked for none.

Beige was the perfect backdrop for the dreadful images that played in her mind. They weren't just thoughts. They were images. Her mother trapped in an emaciated body that failed to move at her command, somber men in long, white coats, and finally, iron fences, rolling hills and stone markers. Chloe felt relieved when a nurse came to escort her and Uncle Charlie to her mother's room. The twelve others who'd come with them would have to remain in the waiting room.

"Mom? Are you awake?"

Her mother's breathing was steady, but there was a troubled expression on her face. Chloe sighed with relief that there was any kind of expression on her mother's face. Things could have been worse. Even a troubled expression banished the dreadful images of twisted muscles from Chloe's mind. She wondered what could be troubling her mother and remembered the words of Omolu. Here was a woman who would never know peace as long as she hated herself and held onto beliefs that contradicted reality and one another.

"See what your handiwork has wrought?" Uncle Charlie snarled. "Is she awake? Why do you care all of a sudden? Why didn't you care when you were up there with those heathens?"

"I . . ." she started to answer, and then realized that an answer wasn't what he wanted. He wanted submission. She sighed and turned away from him. She knew he'd take her silence as admission to guilt, but she really didn't care what he thought. She was tired and couldn't house the shame he wanted to see in her heart.

She looked at her mother as if looking into her mind and it opened up for her. She saw a white woman sitting deviously in a well-worn groove. Her bobbed blonde hair flapped in Oya's wind and her blue eyes gleamed with a wickedness Chloe had never seen in human eyes. She winced in revulsion as the woman fed on her mother's self-hatred. Then Chloe understood that self-hatred was food and nourishment that kept the oppressor fat and healthy.

She felt Uncle Charlie nudging her.

"Why you staring at my sister? I know you got a devil, but you stop that right now in the name of Jesus. Woman's sick enough without you trying to put some hex on her."

"Uncle Charlie, I . . ." She stopped. She looked at him and just stopped. He didn't even know what was going on. He thought he had all the answers when he didn't even know the question. He thought she had a devil, and nothing she could say would convince him otherwise.

The nurse entered. "Visiting hours are over. You may speak to the doctor on your way out."

Chloe nodded and walked out without waiting to see what Uncle Charlie would do. She was done paying fiat deference to people who took every opportunity to show their absurdity. The twelve stooges in the waiting room looked up expectantly as she passed by, but she didn't stop for them.

In all the to-do, she'd almost forgotten there'd be a meeting of the Dance Ensemble the next night. They'd accepted her as a member—all except Yolanda, of course. Why did there have to be a miscreant in every group?

That morning, she packed her leotard and slippers into her back pack. She breezed through her classes and changed clothes before entering King Hall 213 carrying her books on her back and a set of conga drums in her arms. Enriquo had shown her how to select the best quality drum from an African shop in the Hawthorne Mall. When he pointed out the cherry wood Latin Percussion Exquisite to her on the shelf at Cream of Niger Boutique, she knew she'd buy it.

Even after all she'd been through, Chloe never got used to the way Ted beamed when she walked in that door, and he beamed with curiosity when he saw the drums. She had a surprise for him—for all of them. She put everything on a desk and joined them in their warm-up routines. As the *Carousel* ballet chinned, Bert pranced over to the congas and beat out a calypso rhythm.

Yolanda froze in mid-brisé. "Oh, stop. That really messes me up. Pay attention to what you're supposed to be doing, please. You're not even supposed to be over there."

"Oh, I forgot, Yolanda's the star tonight. I don't want to mess her up. Sorry Miss Yolanda." He sprang into the air in a spin that was anything but sorry.

"What do you mean, 'Miss Yolanda?' Don't get thorough with me."

But he wasn't listening. At the end of the piece, they all stretched their legs and flexed their ankles, awaiting Ted's next instructions.

"What do you have there?" Ted asked Chloe.

"African congas. I thought we'd try a little rhythm. I've been into African dances and it's really deep. Did you know that the rhythms we dance to today are the same ones our ancestors danced to in Africa long before we came here?"

"Really?" Debbie asked. "How do you know? Have you been to Africa?"

"Well, let's just say, I know. I brought the drums to introduce you guys to some of the rhythms I've heard. Since we do all kinds of dance, I thought maybe we could incorporate some African dance routines into our repertoire."

Yolanda started to protest, but the others drowned her out.

"Sounds like it's all that."

"I'm down."

"Let's do it."

So Chloe sat Ted in a chair and placed the congas between his legs. She beat out a rhythm for him and he caught it right away.

"Keep doing whatchu doing," she instructed.

Then she took the floor and everyone moved out of her way, taking seats as if the fires of Xangô were burning through the pores of her body—and maybe they were. She danced—sliding and stepping, jumping and pivoting. Her whole body had a part to play and so played it well.

"This is dreadful," Yolanda grumbled. "Surely, we aren't going to do this."

"Why not? I like it," said Bert, nodding his head to the beat.

"You would," Yolanda snapped. "It's all percussion. It has no melody—nothing to arch the time."

"But we all like it and we will do it," Mark assured her.

Yolanda leapt to her feet and glared at them all. "No, I'll not." All she needed to do was stamp her foot and the picture would have been complete. "If you insist on bringing this dreadful stomping atrocity into our ensemble, then I will leave."

Bert appeared saddened by the news. "Gee, Yolanda, we'll surely miss you, but we wish you well in all your endeavors. Honest we do."

"You foolish boy. Don't you understand that I'm the star dancer for our next show? If I leave, what will you tell the manager?"

Ted cocked an eyebrow at her self-important assumptions. "That's what understudies are for," he reminded her. "We'll tell him to be sure to buy tickets for his family."

Here Yolanda checked herself. She glared at Ann, her understudy in the show. The thought of someone else taking her place didn't sit well with her, so she sat down— though not without some dirty looks at Ann and Chloe.

Because of Yolanda's attitude, nobody felt like practicing the ballet anymore that night. They spent the rest of the evening practicing different African dances to rhythms Chloe taught Ted and Charlie.

Chloe could feel things coming together now. The world of her visions dovetailed with the world of her reality. Dancing in the wind was more than a notion—much more than a silly dream. It wouldn't help her get a good job, and so, would never win the endorsement of her family—especially not her mother's. The thought of her mother brought Chloe down a notch. Who or what was that white woman she'd seen in her mother's mind? How had the woman gotten there? What was she doing? And more importantly, how could she be excised? For she'd definitely have to be excised—or should she be exorcised? Her mother had dreams for Chloe, and now Chloe had dreams for her mother. Was this the temple symbolized by the task Xangô had set before her, or was he speaking of a real temple? She had to find out. He had warned her of dire consequences if she didn't comply, but she could do nothing until she knew what she was supposed to do. Maybe Oya would tell her or maybe Yara knew the answer. Yara? Yes, she'd know.

Chapter 22

"You've got to be kidding?" Chloe couldn't believe what Yara was telling her. Why was everything happening so fast?

"I wish I were. I read the letter thrice, and each time, it said the same thing. The babalawo in Brazil has forbidden me to practice Candomblé priesthood in my home."

"Olumide?"

"Yes, and my friendly neighbors. After the thing with your mother, they called the authorities. Olumide got wind of this without telling me. He procured statements from my neighbors and sent copies to Brazil. And now I get this." She threw an angry fist at the letter on her coffee table. "They're going to put legal power behind this by looking for some obscure zoning law. I've tried to do right. How could Olodumare allow things to go so wrong?"

Chloe shrugged. Every religious person asked the same question no matter who their god was. She figured that the same answer probably applied. "What's gone wrong, really?"

Yara glared at her as if she were obtuse. "What has gone wrong? Oh nothing. Everything's wonderful. Don't trouble yourself."

"I don't mean it like that. But think, Yara. You're being forced to make a change that you otherwise wouldn't make if everything were going along smoothly. This is Oya. I go through changes, too. I wish she'd ask me nicely whether or not I'd like to change. If it would be convenient for me at this time or if I had other plans. But like the wind, she doesn't."

Enriquo entered unobtrusively, bearing a tea set of dark brown, handcrafted stoneware. Yara poured herself and Chloe a cup and sat back on the couch as Enriquo departed without a sound. "I don't know what kind of change I could make. This isn't something I'd expected or asked for. I haven't even contacted the devotees yet. That's where the real trouble starts. They've nowhere to go if they can't come here. How could this possibly be the work of the Orixa?"

"Maybe it's the work of the Devil."

Yara almost gagged on her tea. "There is no devil in Candomblé. There are negating spirits, but I have protections against them. Only the spirits of Candomblé can work, but what could they possibly be doing?"

"Well, first Xangô charged me with building a temple and now you are forbidden to stay here." She gave Yara a look that said, "Do the math," and sipped her tea.

"That has nothing to do with . . ."

Chloe sighed. Clearly, arithmetic wasn't Yara's forte. Chloe persisted. "Do you really believe in coincidences?"

"Of course not. Everything happens for a reason."

Now they were getting somewhere. Chloe drove her point home. "If that's true, then why fret?"

A smile of comprehension crept over Yara's face. She set her cup down and looked at Chloe. "Because I'm not in control of the reason."

"What control do you have?"

Yara glanced at the letter. "Well, I can cry."

They both laughed. Chloe patted her friend's shoulder. "It's usually you who pats me on the shoulder, but I guess today was just too much."

"Today and yesterday—the whole week really has been a drain."

Then an idea occurred to Chloe. She mulled it over for a few seconds and decided it was worth bringing to the table. "I work in Senator Braxbury's office. Maybe I can find something out about the zoning issue."

Yara shook her head. "If this is the hand of Olodumare, shouldn't we wait to see what he will do?"

Chloe sighed again. She sighed a lot when she talked to religious people. Although Candomblé was worlds different from Christianity, and her mother would never admit to sharing anything in common with Yara, the same theme of trying to relinquish personal responsibility worked through them all.

She didn't know a lot about the esoteric teachings of any religion, but she knew about life. She knew that no matter who the god was, life just didn't work without human effort. "If Olodumare opens a door, we have to be there to go through it. And tell the truth, he seldom opens any doors but simply points them out to us so we can open them."

"Don't let Olumide hear you say that. He'll burn us for witchcraft."

"The truth is often more sacrilegious than a lie. But I'll look into this—and you, too."

Chloe didn't want to dismiss her friend's troubles, but she hadn't forgotten her own reason for coming. She couldn't forget, though she talked about everything else. "There's something I want to ask you. I wonder, considering the prohibition from Brazil, can you still perform divinations?"

"Yes, of course. The Orixa aren't subject to the prohibitions of men."

"I know, but will they still listen to you if you're under censure by your superiors?"

"They've been answering me in this house for as long as I've been here. It's not likely that they didn't know it was wrong and needed Brazil to tell them."

"Good, because I have a problem and it's of a spiritual nature."

"Most problems are at their root."

"Well, this one is of the spirit root, trunk and bough. It involves my mother."

Now it was Yara's turn to sigh. "Oh boy. I told you the herbs I gave you would only help her so much."

Chloe knew this and hoped Yara wouldn't just dismiss her mother as a hopeless case. Surely, the new developments would make a difference. She could only hope. "I doubt if she even drank the tea. But Yara, when I looked into her mind at the hospital, I saw a white woman."

"Looked into her mind? What do you mean?"

This Chloe didn't want to explain. She hardly understood it herself, much less how to tell someone else what happened. She evaded the question and hoped Yara wouldn't press it. "It's a long story. I don't fully understand it, but Oya sometimes takes me into people's minds and I see things. I have visions. That's why I came to you the first time to try to understand the nature of these visions. Anyway, I saw a white woman in my mother's mind, just sitting there looking evil and feeding off my mother's self-hatred. The woman was weaving the fabric of my mother's thoughts—directing them, so to speak."

"That's interesting." Yara poured herself more tea and stared into the cup, as if to find enlightenment there. "A white woman or maybe the memory of a white woman from your mother's past."

"A memory." Chloe was glad Yara wasn't being dismissive. She showed interest, but could she help?

The Crossroads of Time

Yara sipped her tea thoughtfully. "When words are repeated over and over, they form a groove in our brains and all our thoughts can fall into this groove if we don't take control. We tend to reject any information that doesn't fit this groove. The more compelling the information, the more violently we reject it."

"That's irrational. Compelling knowledge is, well . . . compelling."

"True, but compelling knowledge doesn't meet our emotional needs the way the groove does, so we feel threatened."

This was making sense. Chloe envisioned a groove along which all her mother's thoughts traveled. Her mother interpreted every idea in a way that fit into that groove. "And my mother has definitely accepted this self-hatred groove as her comfort zone."

"So many of us have, to one degree or another. Let's see what the Odu have to say."

"The *jogo de buzios*."

"You remember. When you first came here, you knew nothing—painfully ignorant of the spirit, you were. Now you know things I didn't teach you. Where does your knowledge come from?"

"Ask the spirits."

"I just might. After all, it's not fair that you can look into my mind if I can't look into yours."

"I don't do it with deliberate intent. It just happens when Oya wants to show me something. I couldn't look into your mind if I wanted to."

"But if Oya wanted you to, you could."

"And if she wants to show you where I got my knowledge, she will. So we're even."

"I guess so. We'll go up to the *terreiro* for the divination. It still requires a holy place. Unfortunately, with my neighbors watching and communicating with Olumide, we must enter the *terreiro* from the profane inner door."

Chloe still didn't understand how Yara could think of her home as profane. Maybe she did understand it as Yara had explained it to her before, but she still didn't fully accept the necessity of the idea. They walked to a door in the hallway.

"What's profane about this door?"

"It's not so much the door itself that's profane. It's the mundane thoughts we carry with us. We go straight from the mundane to the holy without an in-between place where we can prepare our minds."

"If it's not the door but our minds that are profane, then let's close our eyes right here and clear our minds of all mundane thoughts before we go through the door."

Yara looked at her skeptically, as if still unwilling to believe Chloe knew things Yara hadn't taught her. "Can *you* do that? Do you know how to clear your mind in meditation?"

"I guess. I don't know. I've never done it before. Sometimes when I dance, I meditate, not to clear my mind but to fill it. Clearing my mind seems self-defeating. I mean, I have to think about the thing I'm trying not to think about."

Then Yara's eyes widened as an idea popped into her mind. "We must still climb stairs before we enter the *terreiro* proper. While on the stairs, let's fill our minds with the reverences of the Odu." She smiled with newfound confidence in her ability to solve an old problem with a new idea.

"Will do."

Yara opened the door and they began to climb.

"Odu Odu, corpus of the
divine,
Speak to mortal flesh
Reveal the secrets of time

And life and Earth
Measure the days as they are
known to you."

Once again, Chloe found herself staring at sixteen cowry shells as Yara scattered them onto an ornate tray. They fell within a circle made of runes Chloe couldn't decipher.

Rune? Bewildered, Chloe wondered what Candomblé had to do with European sorcery? Yara would know, and she'd have the esoteric knowledge to read these symbols. But would she tell Chloe what the symbols meant? *No,* Chloe conceded. Why would a priestess give her esoteric knowledge? Such knowledge wasn't for the laity. Despite all Chloe had been through and seen, she knew she was still in the laity of Candomblé—not even a full-fledged devotee. How did the saying go? Those who know, don't tell and those who tell, don't know.

Suddenly, the room went dark. It was already dark because they didn't dare turn on the lights for Yara's neighbors to see, but suddenly, an opaque blackness engulfed the room. Chloe could see the street lamps outside, but their light no longer penetrated the frosted-glass window. Chloe and Yara were in a black hole that admitted no light.

Chloe became aware of a heat like fire crackling at her back.

"Oyeku Meji!" Yara exclaimed.

Chloe turned and saw a wall of fire rising from floor to ceiling and giving off heat that was minimal compared to its size. She'd have expired in the heat that much fire could generate. But even though its heat was diminished, the conflagration shone brilliantly in the darkness. In the center of it was a black hole—a disk of blackness even blacker than that which engulfed the room.

"This Odu symbolizes death and transformation," Yara said. "Somebody or perhaps something is going to die."

Chloe thought Yara's voice was inexplicably calm when she said this. The priestess was making a totally professional assessment of the situation without the slightest emotional involvement. "Something?"

"Yes." Yara nodded. "Death is the end of any cycle. It could mark the end of the life cycle or it could be the end of something intangible like fear or oppression."

Chloe shook her head. She doubted that all that fire marked the end of fear. If anything, it heralded the beginning of fear—of incessant terror. "It looks so ominous. How can it mean the end of anything bad?

Rhonda Denise Johnson

Yara, I'm scared. I came to ask about my mother and I see this. Does this mean my mother is going to die?"

"Of course, she's going to die . . ."

Chloe started. She couldn't believe Yara would say something so cold. It occurred to her that she really didn't know Yara—a classmate. Did she relish the death of a woman who'd caused her so much trouble?

But Yara went on. ". . . and so will you and I. Everything that lives must die."

Chloe sighed with relief. She'd just have to understand that that's how Yara said things. "Well I know that, but does this Odu mean she'll die soon?"

"That, I don't know. The good news is every ending is followed by a beginning. That's why we shouldn't fear Oyeku Meji, no matter how frightening the Odu seems."

"So what's going to end and what's going to begin?"

"Hopefully, the Odu will deign to tell us."

There was silence for more than a moment. Then Yara began to speak. Her voice was deeper than it had been when Osa Meji spoke through her. Strangely enough, the words and the rhythm of crackling fire

308

created a music that made Chloe want to dance, despite her fear.

"Chloe, the darkness rises and it will consume as surely as fire unless you turn the key."

"Key? What key?"

"You have the key."

Chloe sighed. This was just the kind of cryptic answer she'd come to expect. He might as well have been the Magic Negro in some Hollywood fantasy adventure. "Okay, then where's the lock the key that I already have is supposed to open?"

She didn't mean to sound so tart with an Odu. Why bother coming into a holy place if she acted insolently? But she couldn't help feeling disappointed in his answers. Why couldn't they just lay it out on the table like it is?

"The lock is in the door of the temple you will build, and that is in the wind. When you have reached the crossroads with Exu, you will have the key and you will see the lock."

Naturally. Chloe sat back and closed her eyes just to take a break from this frustrating situation. The glow of the fire didn't shine through her translucent eyelids, but she felt the heat. She wanted to block this maddening messenger of unknowable doom out of all five senses—out of her mind.

As she sat there with her eyes closed, the heat faded and she felt a sudden chill. She opened her eyes and saw that the Odu was gone along with the impenetrable darkness. Light from the street lamps shone through the window once again. Yara sat silhouetted against the window, just as ordinary as ever. The inexorable enigma of *jogo de buzios* was over.

Chloe studied the wall where the fire had been. "I still want to know about that white woman I saw in my mother's mind."

Yara looked sort of relieved. She had control of her own voice again, after all, and despite knowing better, probably felt relieved seeing that the fire had done no damage. That would only be a normal human reaction. She put the cowry shells away as she spoke. "The Orixa know that you want to know."

"Then why don't they tell me?"

"I don't know. I guess if we knew everything we thought we wanted to know, we'd never get out of bed in the morning."

"The truth will make you free."

"Quoting the Bible, are we, you little heathen? No, the truth makes us responsible for making the right choices with that truth. It doesn't necessarily tell us which choices are right. We still have to figure that out."

Chloe pouted like a little girl. "So the Odu don't trust me to make the right choice?"

"Maybe. Or maybe they know that you won't."

"They know the future?"

"They know you."

Chloe didn't like this. She felt like Yara was toying with her. Why stay and be toyed with? She could leave now. She could walk away and not look back. *No*. That option wasn't open. The powers controlling her life now were very powerful—more powerful than anything her mother had shown her. Xangô had warned her there would be consequences—unspecified, but dire consequences—if she didn't obey him.

So they weren't showing her what she wanted to know at the speed she wanted to know it, but they were showing her many things she'd never have thought of. She wondered if she'd ever see Ayodele again, or if she was done with that part of her education. "Well, I don't suppose I'll get any more answers tonight, and it's late. I've got a long drive."

They said good night, and Chloe walked to her car. When she turned the ignition, Smokey Robinson came on the radio singing "Just to See Her Again." Chloe was used to these "coincidences" now. She had seen greater wonders from the spirit world, but still appreciated these little reminders that the spirits knew what was going on and could respond to the real world.

When she got home, she ran a bath and got in while the water was still running. As the tub filled, inch by inch, she watched the spray rebounding from the surface like white water rapids or water churned by a hurricane. Why was she thinking about a hurricane? She closed her eyes and someone screamed.

"Aaaaahhhghhhhaah!"

Her eyes flew open and she looked around frantically, wondering how anyone could have possibly sneaked into her apartment. To her astonishment, she found herself sitting in a trough for watering horses and a big-eyed black woman in a highly mobile and colorful skirt was laughing down at her.

Chapter 23

"Oya."

"None other, kiddo. You'd better get out of there. You don't look water-tight."

Chloe looked down at the water glistening on her bare chest. "I can't. I'm not dressed for the occasion."

"Devil in the details. Oh well, wait. I'll get something."

"How long do you expect me to wait in here?"

But the Orixa blew a gust of wind from her mouth that rushed toward the nearby shops. It came back bearing a long granny dress with a high neck. Chloe knew the pattern on the dress was called calico from watching episodes of *Little House on the Prairie*.

Oya snatched the dress off the draft that stopped right in front of her. She held it up for Chloe to see. "There now. With this, you'll fit right in. I dare say; these people had some kind of color phobia. Their garments are so plain, but this was in a dress shop down the street, so this must be what they were wearing."

But Chloe didn't reach for the dress or move out of the trough. "So, am I supposed to stand up for the world to see me while I dress?"

Oya wove a translucent whirlwind around them. Chloe had been in the eye of Oya's storms before, but this one was up-close and personal. The swirling wind created a vacuum that drew the water off her body, but thankfully, didn't pull her off her feet. She took the dress and pulled it over her head.

"How did they wear these? I can't reach all those little buttons down the back."

"Now that will have to be done by hand. Of course, I could pull up a wind to do it, but it might tickle your backside. Are you ticklish?"

"No, thank you. I hate to ask you to do something so menial. You're an Orixa, after all."

"I'm also the mother of nine children. Turn around, kiddo."

Chloe turned around, expecting to feel some out-of-this-world thrill as the great Orixa of the wind buttoned her dress. Instead, she felt Oya's maternal touch. The warm, motherly fingers were something Chloe couldn't recall experiencing with her own mother. She was glad the feeling was cozy instead of exotic.

Oya drew in her breath and the whirlwind disappeared. Chloe looked around the marketplace. The auctioneer was on his block extolling the physical virtues of some hapless black captive. The crowd milled around the block or jumped out of the way of some passing wagon loaded with tobacco, pigs or more slaves. She didn't have time to look too long before she felt that familiar darkness as she left her body.

Chloe braced herself to see as Ayodele opened her eyes, but it was still just as dark. Stale whiskey and sex told her she was back in the Sugar Shack. Ayodele lay on her stomach, for her back oozed with the welts of a fresh beating. How much time had elapsed? Was this the same beating Ayodele was about to get when Chloe had left her, or was this a new one?

The pain between Ayodele's legs told Chloe her host had just been raped. At first, Chloe wondered that it would still be painful, but then she remembered what it was like. She knew that even without a hymen to break, an invading phallus would always bring pain when it wielded as a weapon. What did soldiers say? "This is my weapon. This is my gun. One is for killing. One is for fun."

So the gun wasn't the weapon of choice in war or slavery. This was the life of a slave. Her first experience of what was supposed to be a beautiful union was forever marred by the cold indifference of enslavers.

Chloe grimaced, thinking about how so many politicians and Hollywood producers in the twenty-first century tried to whitewash and romanticize slavery as a mutually beneficial relationship between puerile black slaves and their benign masters. How divergent from the truth this picture was.

A shaft of light split the darkness and widened as Chloe watched. A shadow loomed in the light. It wasn't a friendly shadow and it didn't promise relief. The shadow had broad shoulders and an angular head.

"Nigger, get your black carcass up. Can't be lazing about when there's tobacco to harvest."

Chloe recognized Keaton's voice. So Ayodele was out of the kitchen and was now a field hand. That meant harder work but more opportunity to run, if she still had a mind to do so. Why not? What could've happened in the space of a whirlwind that would dull the edge of Ayodele's determination? One beating too many? Chloe didn't believe that.

Ayodele rose to her feet and pulled on a dress that had been lying in a corner. It smelled horrendous, but in the darkness, she couldn't isolate the smell of one dress from the general stench of the room.

It was still dark when she went outside. Working from can't-see-in-the-morning to can't-see-at-night. That's what they did with never a hope of anything else to look forward to until they died—and if they were lucky, that would come soon. Dozens of other slaves joined Ayodele in a loose group, all headed for the field.

"Step lively," the overseer barked. "Why y'all niggers so lazy? Can't even appreciate a good day's work. Don't y'all know hard labor is good for the soul?"

Chloe wondered if that was why these slaver's souls were so feeble. They left all the hard, soul-nourishing labor to the slaves and received none of its benefits.

And the work was hard. Picking tobacco could break all but the strongest backs. Chloe noticed that the slaves moved in a rhythm. Every reach of the hand, every step, every bending of the back was in time with some silent tempo. Then they began to sing.

> "Keep your hand on the
>   plough
> Keep your hand on the plough
> Gotta keep your hand right on
>   the plough
> Hold on
> Hold on
> Hold on."

Chloe was astonished. She'd heard that song before in a vision about the Abyssinian Baptist Church. Clearly, it was about more than that. Much more.

Ayodele was appalled. How could these people honor slavery with song? Did they enjoy being slaves? She didn't believe that. She had seen others get beaten and even killed at the whim of some beast. No one in their right mind would enjoy that. Were these people in their right minds?

Then she listened—not to the words but to the soul behind the words. Then she realized that the words were just a code for something else—something that the beasts, having no souls, could never hear.

"Lord if I could
If I could
If I could, y'all I would
Know I would
I'd stand up there on the rock
Stand on the rock
I'd stand right where Moses
                stood
Moses stood."

Ayodele remembered that in the Meeting Hall, the parson had told them how Moses had led his people out of slavery. Keaton nearly had the parson himself whipped for teaching them that. But it was too late. The remnant of true African spirituality would never allow them to fully embrace the pink-skinned, silver-haired picture on the Meeting Hall wall as Olodumare.

Although the parson extolled the blessed rest of Heaven where they could lay their burdens down at last, they knew that they'd never find rest in a Heaven full of the same white Christians who beat, raped, sold and humiliated them in unspeakable ways. The story of Moses provided a code language for secret rebellion. Still, the slaves were taking a chance that the white beasts wouldn't understand what they were saying, and she wondered that they sang so boldly right in the overseer's face.

She didn't have to wonder long. He soon cracked his whip. "What're you darkies singing about?"

The whip really did let out a cracking sound, and Chloe remembered that this was one of the legends of why whites were called crackers. Far from being a racial slur, it was a reminder that those who once were masters and bosses still thought of themselves as such.

"Nothing boss. We just singing 'bout the good Lawd. You know us."

> "Oh Mary, don't you weep.
> Mary, don't weep.
> Tell Martha not to moan.
> Tell Martha don't you moan."

When the overseer's attention was satisfied and turned elsewhere, the singers resumed their code without missing a beat.

> "Some of these mornings
> bright and fair,
> Morning bright and fair,
> Take my wings and cleave the
> air.
> Cleave the air.

> Pharaoh's army got drowned
> Drowned in the Red Sea.
> Well, Jesus said, 'Mary.'"

Chloe marveled at the brilliance of her ancestors. Outwardly, they were shiftless, dull-witted and just barely human beasts of burden whom the white man had taught to talk. It made him comfortable to believe that, and like the song goes, what a fool believes, he sees. She knew that if she had a radio, that song would be playing right then.

Ayodele faltered under the weight of the heavy sand lugs. A recent rain had splashed these early leaves with pounds of sand and clay. She bent and stood, bent and stood like a jackknife, pulling the plants off their stalks to be lugged to the curing house. It was hard, heavy, dirty work that turned her dress into an itchy torture chamber. Ayodele wasn't used to it, and sometime between noon and sunset, her body just gave out. She fell to the ground and didn't move.

"Get up, you lazy nigger," the overseer barked. "We don't have time to fool with you."

He beat Ayodele with his whip. She groaned with each lash but didn't move. He grew even angrier and whipped her even more until her blood began to spurt onto the tobacco plants. Jimboy covered her with his body so that the whip fell on him.

"So you want to play the hero, huh, nigger? Then you take what she's got coming."

And he whipped Jimboy until his own strength gave out. Powered by rage, he had a lot of strength, and when he finished, the two captives lay in a pool of blood, their muscles glistening through broken flesh.

Eight black men moved to carry Jimboy and Ayodele away from the field.

"I didn't tell you niggers to stop working. You get back where you belong and leave them two to rot."

But they paid no attention to his slashing whip and curses. The whip fell on their strong black bodies like lightning bolts, but they shrugged it off like spider webbing. Seeing that his whip didn't scare them and that he was outnumbered, the overseer got scared, wheeled his horse around and sped away. Everyone knew he was going for reinforcements, but the eight didn't break their stride.

Ayodele was out cold, but Chloe was acutely conscious when they entered the kitchen. The man carrying Ayodele laid her on the blanket by the stove. Pawny hadn't moved that blanket, though Chloe suspected

Ayodele hadn't slept there since she'd tried to make her shrine. They laid Jimboy on the floor.

"Why y'all niggers trailing all that blood into my kitchen?" Pawny objected.

The eight men gave each other an exasperated look. This was Pawny, but couldn't she see that now wasn't the time?

One of them decided to try reasoning with Pawny. "These two need caring for."

"Them two always making trouble for themselves and everybody else. Well, I ain't no nurse. What you 'spect me to do?"

Chloe listened as Ayodele's rescuer tried to explain the situation. It was like trying to explain the basics of human interaction to someone who had just arrived from another planet. "A little hot water to wash the blood off their bodies, maybe? Just act halfway decent is all we 'spect, Miss Pawny. Just a little loving kindness."

Pawny headed for the stove. "Hot water? Where you think I'm gone get hot water? This water is for Massa's stew tonight. If I waste it on these niggers, I'll have to haul more water and boil it all over again—just for two no-count niggers."

But she got rags to clean their wounds, and one of the eight took the steaming pot off the stove and placed it on the floor near them. Pawny took some herbs from a jar on the cupboard and placed them in the hot water to steep. As horrible as they smelled, Chloe figured they must be medicinal. Pawny certainly wasn't making tea.

Chloe watched in terror as fifteen white men barged into the kitchen and grabbed the eight black men. It took fifteen armed white men to confront eight unarmed black men. She thought of the KKK, which didn't exist yet. Things wouldn't change from the nineteenth to the twenty-first centuries.

"I hear you niggers were trying to run in broad daylight. What's the matter with you?"

Keaton bogarted his way through the horde of slave catchers and faced the eight black men.

The black men looked at each other as if they had known it would come to this. They knew which one of them would speak to Keaton while the rest gave their tacit support. Chloe was glad he wasn't wearing a hat. She'd hate to see him take it off while he spoke to the man who thought he was his master.

"No, sir. We wasn't running. See, we just brought Jimboy and Polly to the kitchen.

They was bleeding all over your tobaccky and we know blood ain't good for tobaccky and you'd be mad if you lost money 'cause of them, so we brought them here."

"Bleeding? Why were they bleeding?"

"Well Massa, they was so tired and couldn't work no more. The boss man beat 'em and beat 'em, but they couldn't get up. So he kept on beating 'em 'til I reckon there was more blood on the ground than in they bodies."

Chloe noticed he left out the part about Jimboy taking the whip for Ayodele. She guessed they knew a black hero wouldn't last long around here. There was no betrayal, mistrust or meritorious manumission among the slaves on this plantation—Pawny notwithstanding. But she wasn't much liked anyway. Though, naturally, Keaton loved her like a boy loves a faithful spaniel but hates his brother the fox.

"So you defied Jason to bring them here?" Keaton smirked, knowing this was a dangerous question.

The eight knew it was a dangerous question, too. They sashayed the danger expertly—if a bit obsequiously. "No, Massa. We wasn't trying to defy nobody. We was just protecting your investment. Begging your pardon, Massa, but the boss man don't care how much money you lose when a nigger dies, long as he gets his pay."

"And you were protecting my investment?" Keaton put a baleful tone in this question, as if he knew otherwise.

"Yes, Massa."

"And what do you niggers know about investments?"

Oops. Time to backtrack. "Nothing, Massa. Not a blessed thing. We just heard tell . . . well, we thought we heard somebody use the word. It don't mean nothing to us."

This chosen prophet looked slightly crestfallen. Just slightly, but even that was gross on a face that he had trained to not show any emotion. Chloe guessed that to Keaton, it probably came across as the look of proper humility, but she knew the black man must have been wondering why he couldn't just be a man and die rather than go through all these convolutions. But if they had done that—if all the black slaves had chosen to die on their feet rather than live on their knees, she'd have never been born. Dead people have no posterity.

Keaton shook his head. "It don't mean nothing to you, but you know what it means and you know that niggers are my investment."

The eight remained silent. Caught in a damned-if-you-do-damned-if-you-don't situation, all they could do was study the patterns on the kitchen tiles.

"Well, niggers are my investment, and I can't have my investment beat to death. So this is what I'll do: Jason will walk tonight. Tomorrow, you eight boys will be my new overseers."

"Massa?"

Chloe caught this stroke of genius. Unlike Jason, the eight didn't have to be paid. By making them overseers, Keaton had turned them from folk heroes to objects of resentment among the other slaves, and at the same time, kept his investment.

"Keaton, are you sure you know what you're doing?" Harley asked.

"Course I'm sure. Never been surer."

"Jason's gonna be plenty mad losing his job to a bunch of niggers. He's got a wife and three kids to feed."

"He'll find another job. They're looking for a patroller over on the Drew plantation right now."

"Yes, I reckon you won't have to worry about runaway niggers with Jason on the patrol. Of course, there's no guarantee your slaves will be brought back to you alive

if Jason catches them. You better protect
your investment, Keaton."

Chloe saw the eight pass each other
surreptitious glances. Their eyes didn't move.
They had more sense than to let whites see
them respond to what would happen to
runaways. As far as the whites were
concerned, they weren't thinking about
running away and had no need to worry. The
whites had no need to worry. They were all
one big, happy family. As a soul, Chloe could
hear their whispering eyes. There was no fear
in them. Their eyes said nothing has changed.
We'll deal with Jason, if we must.

The slavers kept babbling, and Pawny
kept swabbing Ayodele and Jimboy with the
medicine/tea. Despite her own pain, Chloe
felt Pawny's hands tremble. Clearly, she
didn't want to be there. She looked like a
mouse ready to bolt into the nearest hole, but
with the white men's attention on the eight
black men, she didn't want to draw it to
herself by doing anything other than what she
had been doing when they entered.

Chloe had always marveled at this
woman. With the kitchen as her domain, she
was able to keep herself fat so the white men
wouldn't desire her. Although she loved her
massa and might have entertained fantasies
of him deigning to touch her, she didn't want

the lower class white men to ravish her. So she nibbled and tasted everything edible within her reach until she was sure they wouldn't dream of touching her.

Chloe realized that this wouldn't change in her own time. Large women still commanded more respect in the black communities of the twentieth and twenty-first centuries. To disrespect a large black woman was like disrespecting your mother. It just wasn't done. Did these modern women know the root of this phenomenon? Did they know that their corpulent foremothers had been at the vanguard of black resistance, repudiating everything the white world deemed beautiful? Perhaps Pawny's mind was too occupied with mere survival to formulate such lofty political theories. Still, she knew what she was doing.

"Well now," said Keaton, "I reckon I've got everything under control here. So you boys can go on back to your work. You're still being paid to work, you know."

Harley looked uneasy and not a little suspicious. "Are you sure you'll be all right alone with all these niggers, Keaton?"

"I'm sure as all get out. I've always been safe with these bucks. Can't say how safe you'll be if I set them on you. They're my niggers—my mastiffs, under my control. Get my meaning?"

"Now see here," Harley protested. But the other white men shuffled out the door, mumbling to themselves about highfalutin nigger overseers and reckless plantation royalty.

"I know what I'm doing," Keaton said to Harley. "And so do you."

Comprehension dawned in Harley's eyes and hatred brewed in Chloe's heart. She, too, knew what Keaton was doing. This wasn't just genius—this was diabolic. By surrounding the eight black men with resentment and mistrust from both blacks and whites, he was isolating them so their bravery couldn't influence the other slaves. At the same time, he was eroding solidarity among his slaves.

Chloe looked at the eight. They knew what Keaton was doing also, and they were not happy. *Good*. Keaton's whole plan rested on the idea that blacks were dull-witted and predictable. Granted, some were. Some blacks fell for whatever scheme whites concocted for them. But would the blacks on this plantation—the plantation of Chloe's direct ancestor? She thought of her mother and shuddered before falling into a dark vortex of wind.

Chapter 24

"We'll be home before the streetlights come on, Uncle Charlie," Lisa said, with Tonyeesha nodding in agreement.

With her mother in the hospital, Lisa had to endure Uncle Charlie as her live-in chaperone. She had to be very careful broaching this subject. "Yes" would be the only acceptable answer. She couldn't lie to her uncle—not even to a man as opposed to the truth as he was. She stuck to the truth. The truth was, she was going to watch a modern-dance performance, and that is what she'd told him. The truth was, if he knew Chloe was in that dance, he'd put his foot down and hit the roof at the same time. She had to go to her sister's dance, and this man had the power to stop her for no other reason than his own hatred. That was her truth. She'd be lying to herself if she thought otherwise. So she left Chloe's name out of it.

Rhonda Denise Johnson

Uncle Charlie flicked his newspaper and harrumphed. "I ain't thinking about that. There's just as much mischief for young'uns to get in before the streetlights come on as after. Where is this place? Who's gonna pay to let you in? I know it ain't free. Salvation is the only thing free in this world. Everything else has to be paid for."

Lisa hadn't planned for this question. But she was a senior at Washington High and was used to pop quizzes. Without missing more than a quarter of a beat, she said, "No, Uncle Charlie. It's not free. But we've been knowing about it for a long time and saved up enough money to get in."

"You've been knowing about it for a long time? You ain't told me about it. That don't sound right. Why you wait 'til the last minute to tell me about something if you been knowing about it for so long? Tell me that."

Lisa and Tonyeesha sighed together. What could Lisa say? You didn't need to know or it wasn't your business? That would be the truth, but it wouldn't be all that tactful. She settled on this tried-and-true teenage standard. "We forgot. You know, with school and homework and all, we just weren't thinking about it."

"You were thinking about it enough to save your money."

Lisa knew they'd never win this way. Uncle Charlie was an expert in giving two for one, though he didn't like it when anybody gave it to him. She had to get the conversation back on track. "Can we go?"

"I guess it will get you out of my hair for a spell. Just don't come back pregnant, and don't have none of them hoodlums coming 'round asking about you."

"Oh thanks, Uncle Charlie. You know we never do anything bad like that." They tried to hug him, but he pushed them away, muttering something about rotten juvenile delinquents.

***

The Nubian Lounge and Grill was huge. It was the main attraction of the Westside Shopping Plaza. You could buy the latest Nikes at JC Penney, and then chill at the Grill with your bags under your stool at the fifteen-foot black and grey marble bar.

Lisa thought that Chloe hadn't been exaggerating when she told them to dress to the nines. Lisa wasn't coming out to catch boys, so no high heels and miniskirts would do. Chloe had shown her how to apply make-up for subtle elegance and dress in a way that only suggested what men wished they could see but couldn't. Tonight, she and Tonyeesha looked like stately queens. Lisa could have been on her way to the White House in midnight blue silk. The doorman smiled at Tonyeesha, clearly appreciating the way she made even leopard skin look unassuming and graceful.

Lisa showed the doorman the passes Chloe had given her and an usher escorted them backstage. They passed by dancers stretching their bodies and legs or doing excruciating-looking things with their feet. Chloe was having her eyes, mouth and cheeks painted with African symbols. Her costume consisted of a skirt of multicolored strips and a skin-colored Danskin. Her ballet slippers were also skin-colored. On the dressing table lay an exotic mask of some African spirit.

"Who's that supposed to be?" Lisa asked, pointing to the mask.

"That's Oya, the Orixa of the wind," Chloe answered.

Tonyeesha tried to look at the mask without looking like she was looking at the mask. "What's an Orisha?"

"They're like angels, except they have names and personalities and they can actually do things and show you things."

"Really?" Lisa asked. "What can they show us?"

"Whatever you need to see."

"Like the stuff you were doing when Uncle Charlie threw you out the house?"

"Unc . . . yeah. Stuff like that. I'm surprised he let you come."

"Do you think I told him we were coming to see you? He knows where we are, but he doesn't know you're here."

"That's a shame. We're supposed to be family. He should be proud that I'm doing something."

Lisa laughed. "Yeah, you're doing something—dancing with demons."

Tonyeesha looked bewildered, so Lisa explained. "She brought the Devil's broom into our house and tried to sweep the good Lord right out from under our mother's bed."

"I didn't know the Devil had a broom," Tonyeesha laughed. "I thought he had a pitchfork."

"Curtain call in five minutes," a woman yelled as she passed through the dressing room.

"You guys need to go out front and take your seats."

Rhonda Denise Johnson

"Chloe."

Lisa's eyes bugged out of their sockets as a tall, muscular man entered the dressing room and kissed her sister on the cheek. Ooh Wee! Lisa squealed to herself. Chloe had a boyfriend. Wait until she told Unc . . . no she couldn't tell him. She wasn't supposed to be with Chloe. Oh well, she was sharing the dawn of history with Tonyeesha, her best friend, and that was all that mattered.

"Ted, this is my sister Lisa and her friend Tonyeesha."

His name is Ted, Lisa thought. How romantic.

"Okay, you guys go on out front." Chloe said this to the girls, but her eyes were on Ted, so Lisa knew it was time to go.

The two teens walked out front trying to see how many broom jokes they could make. Once seated, they gazed transfixed at the humongous stage. When the lights went out, the audience fell silent and the girls followed suit.

A low drum beat swelled until it reached the farthest corners of the theater. Then a male voiceover joined the drum.

> "Deep in the heart of Africa,
> African hearts beat to the
> rhythm

336

Of black hands on wooden
drums.
The people pluck the kalimba
And watch the spirits dance.
Behind the mask lives a spirit
Within the body lives an
ancestor.
Each colored strip of the
Egungun dress
Is a memory of the eternal
African soul."

A single spotlight shone center stage with Chloe at its nucleus. She rose up on her toes and began to undulate with the drum. As she danced, the strips of her skirt spun in a spiritual vortex. The mask of Oya covered her face. Bracelets of beads and shells adorned her arms and ankles. Other dancers swirled onto the stage.

At once, Lisa knew the Electric Slide must have begun in Africa. She recognized the rhythms and the movements. It was hiphop, but it wasn't hiphop. It was jazz and soul, rap and house. It was audible blackness and the dancers were Africa in motion.

In a crescendo of heartbeats, Chloe's dancing became wild. The other dancers scurried away from Oya's fury. In that moment, Chloe became Oya. Lisa could feel the wind raging as this great Orixa moved. Oya's arms, her skirt and her feet became a living whirlwind. How she kept from leaping off the stage, Lisa didn't know. She knew only that she was proud of her big sister.

Ted danced onto the stage. Lisa had never seen such a tall man move so gracefully. His smooth muscles only added power to his elegance. He approached Oya forming his own vortex, while lightning and thunder special effects filled the stage.

"Xangô!" the dancers cried.

Xangô took Oya's hand and they danced together. Then he removed her mask, revealing the symbols on Chloe's face. He fell to one knee and kissed her hand. The dancers all began to sing.

"Goddess of the wind,
Mother of the nine,
I implore you with the
      lightning bolt
This day you will be mine.
Your eyes are darkest onyx.
Your hair is spun like wool.
Your skin is woven smooth as
      silk.
Do not make me a fool
For loving you.
Loving you.

Queen of the wind,
Loving you."

The audience rose in a standing ovation as the curtains fell. But Lisa felt kind of sad when she realized that this kind of thing never happened in her neighborhood. The kids she knew loved to dance, but they had nowhere to go, so they danced on the street or at house parties. They didn't put on shows. They did nothing on which they could look and say, "We did this—we achieved this." Their energy was unfocused and often expressed itself in violent, self-destructive acts. She'd talk to Chloe about this. Maybe her big sister would come up with a solution if she were pushed in the right direction.

Lisa and Tonyeesha headed for the lobby to get snacks during the intermission. She was learning new words like "intermission" and "kalimba." A lot of her friends didn't like to learn new words. New words, big words, anything they hadn't learned by age five, were "acting white." From the time she was little, Chloe had taught her not to hate people who taught her new things. "If you're going to hate anybody, hate the ones who think you're too dumb to learn."

But if her friends could learn by dancing and the new words meant something in the real world, Lisa thought, maybe they'd embrace education. Lisa could kind of understand kids thinking that being good in school was for white kids. She couldn't think of one thing from her schoolwork that was worth anything. She thought of Carla Jackson, an honor student who had a scholarship to Cal State, gunned down by a high school dropout. Lisa's mother didn't understand why she didn't get better marks in school. Lisa didn't think she could explain it in a way her mother would understand. She'd never known her mother to understand any idea different from her own. So with the way her mother harped on good marks, Lisa didn't even try to explain that she didn't care about getting honors in a school that wasn't teaching her anything valuable. Certainly not anything worth dying for.

They stayed for the second half of the show, but Lisa wasn't watching. Her mind was too full of her own thoughts. She wondered what Chloe would do. What could she do? Lisa could think of fifty-eleven things that needed to be done, and she knew one person with no money couldn't do it all. Still, Chloe worked for the senator. There was something she could do—something that would be the start. Even if someone else had to finish it, at least Chloe could get it started.

The rest of the evening went by in a blur. After the show, all the dancers gathered around the bar for drinks. Someone offered Lisa a cognac, which she absent-mindedly accepted.

"Since when?" Chloe exclaimed.

"Oh, sorry. I wasn't thinking. I'll have a juice, thank you."

The juice went down her throat untasted. Nothing registered in her mind until she and Tonyeesha got into Chloe's car and she was able to bring up the crucial subject. "Chloe, this show was all that. I was thinking if we had something like this in our neighborhood, maybe we could keep kids off the street. You know—give them somewhere to go."

Chloe looked thoughtful, as if she had been thinking the same thing. "You're right. That would get them off the street. But we don't have anything like this."

Tonyeesha sat up and grasped the back of the front seat. Lisa had been too self-absorbed to share her thoughts with her friend, but Tonyeesha caught on quickly. "No, not now, but maybe if you try you could change that."

Rhonda Denise Johnson

"How? I'm just one person. I can't erase the problems that plague our community. They were here before I got here. They'll be here when I'm gone."

Somehow, Lisa wasn't convinced that Chloe believed what she was saying. It didn't sound like her and she was protesting too much.

As if reading Lisa's thoughts, Tonyeesha said, "I heard somebody say, 'I'm just one person, but I'm one. I can't do everything, but I can do something.'"

"Right," Lisa agreed. "You are one, Chloe, and you can do something. You work in the senator's office. For what?"

Chloe clenched the steering wheel so hard that it shook, and she had to pull over and stop the car. "You know better than to push that button."

"I'm sorry. I didn't mean to. It's just that there's so much to do and we're just sitting back waiting for somebody else to come into our neighborhood with a lot of money and good intentions."

"And maybe a magic wand," put in Tonyeesha.

"May need that, too," Lisa agreed. "If we just sit back and don't even try to do nothing."

342

"What makes you think no one is trying to do anything?" Chloe snapped.

"Gee, I'm sorry. It was just a thought. Forget it." Lisa sat back and said nothing else until Chloe pulled into her driveway. When Chloe unlocked her door, Lisa muttered "Good night" to no one in particular and went into the house.

Chapter 25

"Build it and watch them
come.
Cook it and watch them eat.
The hunger of the people
Turns stone soup to a feast."

Chloe felt ashamed. She hadn't meant to snap at Lisa and her friend. There was just so much to think about—so much she was trying to do, and she had told her family not to take her on a guilt trip because of her job. She could only do so much with her position. Still, she reminded herself, being under pressure was no excuse for being rude.

Then, too, when she told herself the truth, she wasn't doing anything with her position. She saw the dystopia black people called home, though she didn't try to pull any strings to change even a small part of it. Faced with the expectations of her family, she had been so intent on defending her inability to do it all that she never even thought about what she could do.

What was staying her hand? She'd told herself it was the limits of her position, but truth be told, she was just afraid. The job was too important to risk trying to be a civil rights champion. She had no money. The problems facing the black community were multifarious. Solving the problems involved complex legal processes. It was reasonable to consider such things when forming a plan of action, but when she let them immobilize her, they were just rationalizations for her fear.

Most shameful of all, on some level, Chloe knew Lisa was aware of all this. If Chloe didn't overcome her fear, it would come back to haunt her in a very ugly and painful way. Still, what could she do?

After dropping Tonyeesha off, Chloe found herself on Wesley heading north. The forty-fifth block looked like a vista of ancient ruins. Its abandoned buildings and empty lots were home to pigeons and hoboes. Why were they there? To whom did they belong? This was fallow real estate right in the neighborhood that could be turned into somebody's dream.

At work the next day, Chloe went through the escrow records for that property

Rhonda Denise Johnson

and discovered that it belonged to the city who had used it for public housing. When the housing inspector declared it unfit for habitation, they tore it down. Why was it unfit for habitation, Chloe wondered. She researched farther and discovered that the city council had cut funds for maintenance and pest control. Residents had petitioned for deadbolts on their doors, but no money was allocated for that. Thus, crime had escalated beyond the police department's control. A bid to sell the property to a shopping mall developer fell through, so it just stood there.

Chloe narrowed her eyes at this totally unacceptable situation. *Unacceptable to whom.* Unacceptable to *her,* maybe. But what about her boss? Did Senator Braxbury even realize what was going on, or rather, what wasn't going on? Didn't he ever drive by that area? Didn't he know the story behind that eyesore in his own district? Did he care? *No.* He didn't know. He stayed in his office and knew nothing unless she told him. She'd have to tell him. She'd have to assume that once told, he'd care. Chloe reassured herself that it wouldn't hurt to ask. *Would it?* It might hurt her. It might really hurt if her assumption proved wrong, but she had to take that chance. She drew in a deep, deep breath and entered her boss' office.

346

He was at his computer examining something. She cleared her throat to get his attention. The throat clearing and tightness of her face betrayed her apprehension. At the sound, he turned his attention to her.

"Senator Braxbury, I noticed the condition of the forty-fifth block of Wesley Boulevard."

For a brief moment, displeasure clouded his eyes. Chloe gulped. Why had she called him that? *Senator Braxbury*. So formal—a dead giveaway to her frayed nerves.

He regained his accustomed smile and turned back to his computer. "Yes, yes, what about it?"

She wanted to say, "Nothing," and scurry out of his office while she still could, but she had come this far. There was nothing to do but proceed. "I understand that it belongs to the city and was just wondering what we're doing with it."

"Doing with it? Nothing at the moment, Chloe. But the city planners will think of something. I guess you could call it growing room. Why do you ask?"

If there was ever a decisive question, that was it. That question was her door of no return, and all she could do was plough on. So plough on, she did. "Well, I was just thinking that maybe it could be used to build something for the community—something that could get the kids off the street. That would solve a lot of problems."

Braxbury paused briefly, clearly displeased with what she was saying. "Yes, well, perhaps it would, but that's out of the question. It smacks of socialism. You don't want to be accused of socialism, do you?"

"Soci . . . I don't understand. What does socialism have to do with using public property to help the public? It already belongs to the people. Why not use it in a way that will help the people?"

"The people?" his voice rose. "That's what's wrong now. The people always want something for nothing. They want someone to help them for free. Nothing is free. That property has to be bid on in the free market. The highest bidder will decide what to do with it."

Chloe wanted to remind him that wealthy people were always getting stuff for free. Only poor people were under moral obligation to pay for everything they got. But this was her boss. She could be bold, but she still had to be careful. "But if it's public property, they'd already be paying for whatever the city does through their taxes. I don't understand . . ."

Braxbury turned baleful eyes on her. "Stop right there. You don't understand and I don't want to discuss this anymore. Perhaps you need me to find more work for you since you have so much free time on your hands to discuss inconsequential matters."

"No, sir, I don't."

"More work or a cut in your hours. Perhaps you've been promoted to your level of incompetence and the strain is getting to you."

Chloe looked into his eyes. They were the same eyes that Ayodele saw when she looked at Keaton—the very same. She felt Jimboy's shame as she said, "No, sir," and went back into her office.

How she got through the rest of the day without strangling Braxbury, she didn't know. All this time, she had thought he was different. She had thought he was a relatively sensible man just because he didn't fit her caricature of a racist. Was this about racism or classism? Maybe the man was just an equal opportunity asshole. She'd been sure he'd never dream of using the 'N' word and had probably helped a few blacks get appointments in the government. Yes, as long as she smiled and danced around the real issues, he was kewl. Dance? She had always known on some level that she must wear the mask around him. Why else had she been so apprehensive about confronting him in the first place? Yet, whereas before he had had the benefit of the doubt, now he had none.

And now, perhaps, neither did she. He'd be watching her. She couldn't do what she had to do on her computer at work. She needed more information about the property. She'd get as much information as she needed at home and in the library.

She had to think. The property had to be bid on. She couldn't bid without money. Where would she get money and how much would she need? She'd have to use OPM— other people's money—just like the rich did. How much and where from? She had to think.

At home, she looked up the company that had reneged on their bid for the property and found their offer had been 1.1 billion dollars. Oh, damn. It would have to be OPM. The price was actually low because of the unsavory neighborhood. Perhaps that would be a plus. Perhaps the first bid would be the only bid and the price would come down.

She googled for urban development grants and found several that looked promising. Of course, they wouldn't give the money to her, a private citizen, but if she could get the city council to work with these grantors, maybe things would get done.

Then she remembered Xangô. With mounting excitement, it dawned on her that this might be the temple he wanted her to build. It could be. She had thought that other things might symbolize temple building in some oblique way. She didn't want to be like those religious folks who forged God's signature onto their own agendas. Chloe wondered why no god gave specific instructions today—thou shalt build an ark of gopher wood and it shall look like this and thou shalt do that. Instead, all the contemporary gods left it up to humans to figure out their divine will by puzzling through a maze of possibilities. People could only discern the will of any god in hindsight.

Still, she had this task on her and couldn't deny it. Unlike the things she'd thought might symbolize Xangô's will, this was more than a symbol. This was something that might actually turn into a real edifice to the Orixa. It had to happen. It *would* happen. So help her, Olodumare, it would happen.

She needed to think strategically. Oya was the Orixa of change and Xangô was the Orixa to turn to when facing enemies. She needed them both. She wanted change and she'd have enemies—probably, powerful enemies. She thought of the book Yara had given her. It wouldn't provide any specific strategies for her situation, but it might put her in the frame of mind to think more clearly and make the right decisions. She retrieved the book from a drawer in the nightstand beside her bed and opened it to the section on facing challenges.

> "The winds of change blow
>   through the mountains;
> Which to the short-lived
>   mortal eye never
>   change.
> But Oya finds every nook and
>   cranny
> And shapes them to her will.
> From the eternal eye of her
>   whirlwind,
> You will see impervious rock
> Shift and wear down."

The eternal eye. Chloe envisioned herself in the eye of the whirlwind—a place of peace. From there, she'd see the movement of everything around her. To get her mind to work, she had to find the center of peace. It was late and she knew no greater peace than the peace of sleep.

The Crossroads of Time

Towards morning, she dreamed of people marching. She watched in awe as every black man, woman and child in Los Angeles marched around the forty-fifth block of Wesley singing:

> "Sing a song full of the faith
>   that the dark past has
>   taught us.
> Sing a song full of the hope
>   that the present has
>   brought us.
> Facing the rising sun
> Of our new day begun.
> Let us march on 'til victory is
>   won."

In the surreal kaleidoscope of her dreams, every black in Los Angeles marched toward the door of one dilapidated shell of a building, and when they crossed the threshold, they found themselves in a grand cathedral—the temple of Xangô. There were no electric lights. Instead, a perpetual lightning bolt streaked across the ceiling, casting the entire edifice in brilliance. Chloe slipped through the throng and ascended a dais where she could touch the lightning bolt. Its brilliance shone through her. Then the crowd began to shout, "Hosanna! Hosanna in the highest! Crucify her! Crucify her! Every savior of the people must die!"

Every savior? Chloe felt perplexed. She was no savior. She was just Chloe. She was just one woman. She was just wide-awake lying beneath the covers wondering what on Earth she'd have to endure.

And how was she to reach that peaceful center with dreams like these clouding her mind? True, she had slept peacefully through most of the night. Her mind had been percolating. Drop by drop, the substance of an answer pulled together into a plan. Obviously, her mind had concluded that she'd reach her goals and there would be a price to pay—the price of Oyeku Meji.

There's always a price to pay. Nothing was free, Braxbury had told her. *Every savior of the people must die.* What was the plan? It was still inchoate in her subconscious mind. In time, it would come to conscious awareness.

***

She drove to the property and parked across the street. A group of hoboes was camped on one of the cement foundations. Where would they go if she turned this property into a temple? Every change meant the displacement of those who didn't want to or couldn't change. But there would be a place for these men in her plan. She'd need workers. Yes, Chloe exalted as she visualized these men working at something they could be proud of.

She pursed her lips as another thought occurred to her. She could give them work, but where would they live? It would have to be more than a temple. It would have to be a dance school, a theater and a residence. The block was big enough for all that.

She could see Ted teaching the kids ballet and African dance. He'd love that and so would they. Surely, among the older kids, there would be writers, choreographers, musicians and stage directors. The theater would house their own repertoire of dance.

What a big dream! Chloe decided to let her dream grow as big as her mind could take it. Without dreams, people would still live in caves instead of houses. If you can't visualize a house, you can't build one. And others would be involved, taking the dream even further than her own mind could working alone.

She crossed the street and began taking pictures of the property. Up close, everything looked exactly as it had in her dream that morning. Even the crumbling buildings crumbled in precise places.

Across from where the hoboes sat was the very door the people in her dream had gone through. She knew the inside was a far cry from the temple lit by Xangô's lightning. Did the hoboes go in there when the weather turned really cold? Despite what foreigners might think, it did get cold in California. As ramshackle as the building was, going inside couldn't be much different from being outside. Huge chunks of the wall and ceiling were missing. Within the helpless stones, Oya reigned invincible and uncontested.

The hoboes watched Chloe from behind the fire they'd built for cooking and heat. One of them got up and approached her. His smell preceded him like a heralding shadow. "What you doing taking pictures of our home?"

"Leave her alone, Lloyd," one of the other hoboes called. "Can't you see she's a lady?"

Chloe suddenly realized where she was—a woman out here alone with all these strange men. Traffic sped up and down the street and pedestrians went about their business on the other side, but no one walked over here. She swallowed that thought. If they were going to be part of her plan, she couldn't be afraid of them. Besides, if they were wolves, they'd smell her fear more than she could smell this man. "We're going to be building around here."

Lloyd drew closer. His bright grey eyes shone with a menacing light. "You can't build around here. This is our home."

Chloe hadn't planned for this. Not until she'd seen the men had she considered the possibility that her dream might disrupt other people's lives. The Devil was always in the details, but this was no game changer. "You can be a part of it."

"A part of losing our home?" Lloyd cocked an eyebrow and looked at her like he might have to help her find her lost mind.

Chloe knew she couldn't afford to lose a beat here. "A part of making a better home."

The men around the fire began to grumble and Chloe heard one of them say, "Neighborhood improvement always means we get pushed out. We don't want it."

"What will you be building?" One of the other hoboes asked.

"A theater and a school. We'll need people to work on the grounds, so we'll also have residences where you can live if you work. You'll be like resident managers."

Lloyd turned his gaze heavenward as if talking this over with God. "Sounds too good to be true. Outsiders always making promises."

"I'm not an outsider," Chloe protested, glad at last to have some advantage. "This is my neighborhood and I just want to have a place where the kids can go and get off the street. You can be a part of the solution or a part of the problem."

"What do you want us to do?"

"Just be willing and be ready. This is going to take some time." Chloe wished she had something definite to tell them, but she didn't and that was a challenge to her credibility. All she could do was work with what she had. "I'm going to have to fight some powerful people, but if we all fight together, I think we can all work out a solution."

"Solution to what? You're the one with the problem. We's doing all right."

"Lloyd, chill," another hobo warned.

"I just don't want to lose my home."

Chloe's eyes brightened. If that were his only concern, maybe she could deal with it. "You won't lose it if you're willing to work. I won't have any freeloaders."

Lloyd turned to the other hoboes as if to say, *You see.* "Why should I work for something that's already mine?"

"Because it's not yours." Chloe thought of Pawny, puttering around in what she referred to as "my kitchen," even though she was as much a slave as the field hands. Chloe hesitated to destroy this man's illusion when she could replace it with nothing but her own insubstantial dreams. "This property belongs to the city. I'm trying to claim it for the people before the city sells it to some shopping mall. Then you really will lose your home."

"How do we know you don't work for some shopping mall?"

"Be serious." She didn't want to tell them she worked for the senator. If word got back to Braxbury she was out here talking to hoboes about building a theater, that would be the end of that. "Right now, you don't know. But I'll show you."

A squad car pulled up beside them and the cop driving it leaned out and eyed the hoboes suspiciously. "Are you okay, ma'am?"

Chloe tried not to eye the cop the same way. "Oh yes, officer. Everything is fine." She saw no need to offer an explanation if none was asked for.

Lloyd walked back over to the fire where the other hoboes sat studying the cop until he drove away snarling something about Negro women and useless eaters.

Chapter 26

"A dance school and a theater? That sounds wonderful,"
Ted exclaimed.

The whole Dance Ensemble was on fire with Chloe's idea. They were all there: Carol, Debbie, Bert, Charlie, Mark, Tommie and Ann—all except the one Chloe really didn't need to see today.

Ever since they'd decided to do the African dance routine, Yolanda had stopped coming. *Good.* That meant less antagonism to a plan for which she already had enough opposition. She knew Debbie still kept contact with Yolanda. How much of what they talked about here would reach Yolanda via Debbie? Though Chloe wasn't sure of what Yolanda could do with that information, something told her she had to be careful. There were some things she'd only tell Ted.

The plan couldn't stay secret, of course. She needed public support, and as soon as she reached for it, the tiger would be out of his cage. Braxbury, Yolanda, Chloe's mother, Uncle Charlie and everybody else would know what she was doing. Although her mother was out of the hospital and well on her way to recovery, that white woman still enthralled her mind. Chloe could only imagine what a hateful negating spirit might convince her mother and Uncle Charlie to do.

Chloe had to move this thing beyond her. She had to put it in the hands of people her mother and uncle couldn't attack. As for Braxbury . . . well, she'd just have to work around him. Could she do that? Could she keep it secret until the right time?

"Tell us more about your plan, Chloe," Debbie asked.

Chloe thought Debbie's question came a little too close on the heels of her thoughts. But then maybe it was unfair to suspect her just for asking. It was a simple question—one any of them might have asked. But none of them had. Only Debbie, and fair or not, Chloe knew what was at stake. "It's still very inchoate right now. There's still a lot I need to work out."

"That's why you need to tell us," Debbie smiled. "Two heads are better than one."

Yeah. But if I tell her, there'd be more than two heads. Chloe just smiled. "Thanks, Debbie. I'll keep that in mind."

As if reading Chloe's mind, Ted announced, "Well, we still have a lot of work to do to prepare for our next performance. Debbie, I want to see you master the jeté."

Debbie took the center of the floor and they carried on with rehearsal. Nothing more was said about Chloe's plan. At least she knew she'd have their support when she needed it.

At home, she emailed Ted and laid out the first part of her plan.

"We need a petition with five thousand signatures to let the city council know there's a public outcry against the latent property on Wesley."

"Why not just write your congressman?" Ted wrote back.

"Very funny. No, Braxbury isn't to know about this," Chloe started to write but changed her mind. An old woman had once told her to never put anything in writing that anybody can't read. Instead, she wrote, "For what we're doing at the moment, the city council would be more appropriate."

He must have been write there on his computer because she didn't have to wait long for his reply. "So what do you want me to do?"

"I'll write the first draft of the petition. You put in your two cents. We put our heads together and come up with a final draft."

"While we're at it, can we put our lips together?"

Chloe was glad they weren't using video. It was bad enough that she was blushing without him seeing it. "I'm only letting you get away with that one because I handed it to you on a silver platter."

He'd come a long way from the insufferable nerd she'd first met. She could tell herself that it wasn't just his dancing. And it wasn't. Ted didn't just dance. He was the embodiment of the very concept of dance. Fortunately, she was able to keep her head around him.

She started thinking about the petition. What should go in it? The pictures, of course. And a description of what the property is doing to bring down the neighborhood along with what developing the property could do to enhance the neighborhood. She needed a contractor—an African-American contractor who'd develop the property the way she wanted it developed once the council received the money. Once the council got the money, the contractor would come in with the best deal for development. The public outcry and continued pressure would guarantee the council wouldn't turn around and build a shopping mall. It was a good plan. She could only hope that it worked.

Chloe opened Microsoft Word and began to type. "We, the undersigned residents of Wesley County, hereby decry the deplorable state of property owned by the city to which we pay taxes . . ."

***

Later, Ted downloaded a municipal petition prototype, and he and Chloe customized it to their specific petition. Once they were satisfied, they took it to a notary public to have it certified, and then distributed copies.

Yolanda showed up at the next Dance Ensemble rehearsal.

Chloe looked from Yolanda to Debbie. Debbie's eyes were just a little too wide. "Why, Yolanda, what a surprise to see you here. Welcome back."

"So, Yolanda, did you lose something in here?" Bert asked.

"If she did, it's long gone by now," Mark added.

Yolanda turned up her nose. She actually turned up her nose and sniffed at the lot of them. "I didn't come to engage in your foolishness. I came to give Chloe this signed petition."

Stunned could hardly describe Chloe when Yolanda handed her a copy of the petition with a signature as close to Edwardian Script font as was humanly possible.

"I just wanted to give this to you personally. I wish you well in all your endeavors. Honest I do. And do keep me posted. I'm very interested in what you're doing."

"Sure," said Chloe. Sure, she is, thought Chloe, as all the others probably thought, too. Yolanda was interested, all right. Just what her interest was, none of them knew—except Debbie, perhaps.

Yolanda swept out of the room like some melodramatic diva. Chloe thought all she needed was a long, black gown hugging her hips and a hunchbacked sycophant trailing her heels. So now she knew. Oh well, there was nothing to be done but hope. What more had she ever had but hope?

They went on with their rehearsal as if everything was everything, but Chloe could tell they were all a little frayed at the nerves.

It took time, but finally, they had the five thousand signatures they needed to take the petition to the city council. To Chloe's utter relief, Braxbury was in Washington at the time the council met, so she wouldn't have to worry about him for a while. At least for a while.

Chloe knew that while this petition might be important to her, it wouldn't be important to the council—no more important than the hundreds of other petitions it received. So she called the council chair's office and spoke to his administrative assistant, asking for general information about when the council met and how to submit a petition.

As Braxbury's administrative assistant, she'd had countless conversations just like this from the other end, so she knew what to do to expedite her petition. She got the assistant's name and thanked him for his time.

When she submitted the petition, she included a cover letter. "Your administrative assistant, Don Hamilton, was extremely helpful, courteous and knowledgeable." This, she knew, would get her letter to the top of the pile.

She went on to let the council know which contractor and grantors were available to meet the people's concerns.

After three weeks, she was ready to follow up when she received a letter from the council chair's office. Her hands shook so badly that she could hardly open the envelope. It didn't help that the thing had been sealed with an epoxy. She read the preliminaries and stopped. *Five thousand dollars!*

"Tacoma Urban Development Foundation has agreed to make the grant if you submit the first five thousand dollars. Make all checks payable to Wesley County City Council."

Chloe should've suspected something when she first opened the envelope and saw the business-reply envelope, imprinted with "Post office will not deliver mail without postage." But she'd been so excited that small suspicions hadn't registered. Now what was she going to do? She'd come too far— talked to too many people—to quit now. But from where was she going to get five thousand dollars?

"OPM," Ted said. "We'll do a benefit concert. It'll give all the people who signed the petition a chance to see just what urban development will bring to the neighborhood."

Chloe wanted to kiss him. She knew that with this man, a kiss wasn't just a kiss, so she decided against it.

***

"We'll do it," declared Tommy.

"I'm studying commercial art," Mark put in. "I can make a stunning flyer and a website."

"Let people know to keep writing the city council. We can't let the council forget what this is all about; otherwise they'll take the money and run." Carol, usually quiet, voiced this concern that had already occurred to Chloe. This was neither an accident nor a coincidence, but a warning for her to take heed.

Though she doubted that her mother or Uncle Charlie would have anything good to say, Chloe saw no harm in telling Lisa and Tonyeesha. The girls were excited, too, and wanted to help. They weren't dancers, but they could get the word out.

"What do you mean, I'm not a dancer?" wailed Lisa. She had taken to slipping out of the house while Uncle Charlie was asleep. Luckily, he and her mother slept a lot because that was the only time Chloe could see her sister. The name Chloe would send them into pyrotechnics. Lisa stood in Chloe's living room cutting a step to Jay-Z to prove her dancing expertise. "I can dance."

"There's more to being a dancer than knowing all the latest steps. You have to be committed and you have to train. I don't mean to discourage you, little sister. There may be a great dancer inside of you, but you still have to commit yourself to learning the techniques of the art."

Lisa raised her head defiantly. "Who knows? Maybe one day I will."

"I honestly think that would be wonderful. Maybe one day, we'll dance together. But I'm good and if you want to dance with me, you've got to be more than a wannabe."

"Broadway, here we come."

"Hey, we'll just hop into Hollywood." Chloe gave her sister a high five and they fell into giggles.

"Oh, Yara." Chloe's hand went to her mouth.

"What?" Lisa asked.

"Yara. This is for her. Her temple. She needs to come to the benefit and bring all her devotees."

"Devotees? What are you talking about?"

"That's just people who come to worship. You make the word sound so horrible."

"It *is* horrible. I'd never be a devotee. Sounds like a zombie. Someone who's totally brainwashed. I hope you're not a devotee of nothing."

"No, indeed. I'll sit right here on the fence where I can see."

"And you can dance on the fence."

They fell into giggles again.

Chloe turned sober. "Seriously though, I'm not on the fence about this project we're building. There are some powerful people who don't want this to happen, so we can't afford to play."

"No," Lisa agreed. "And we can't afford to be devotees. We have to think."

"And plan."

"And work."

"Oh yes."

***

The place was packed. The line outside wrapped around the Los Angeles Metropolitan Theatre and people were still coming. To Chloe's amazement, every ethnic group was represented that night—European Americans, African Americans, Asian

Americans, Latino Americans—everybody
had come out to support an American dream
and see it come true.

Chloe had never felt so exalted. She
kissed Ted, and damn the consequences. Let
the consequences happen. They were on top
of the world. Why not add a little "and they
lived happily ever after" to the mix? He had
the same idea.

"So, Ted, is it free admission to the
sideshow?" Bert teased.

"No admission. It's a party for two."

The couple's eyes made love as their
bodies drifted into their respective dressing
rooms to prepare for the show.

Chloe hardly heard the continual buzz
of the audience as she donned her costume.
The dancers were dressed as construction
workers. When the curtain rose, they spread
across the stage wielding saws and hammers,
pushing wheelbarrows and carrying sheets of
glass as they performed the *Ballet of the
Dream Builders*.

Chloe twirled and leaped with
controlled abandon. Finally, she was a part of
something that was bigger than she was,
beyond her meager contribution. It would
grow and help others reach their dreams as
well. She remembered seeing Tonyeesha and

the other kids standing on the street with nothing to do and no one to care. But now . . .

As Chloe danced, she became a human jackhammer spinning in Ted's hands in a perfect pirouette. It dawned on her to wonder why all their choreographies involved Ted touching her in some way. Sure, other dancers had touched her from time to time, but with Ted, there was always a spotlight, as if they were in a Kodak moment whenever he touched her. That could just be an accident, a coincidence—or a choreographic conspiracy.

As she turned, her eyes panned the audience. They were wild with excitement. But they were the kind of audience you'd expect at a ballet, not a basketball game. So their wildness was subdued—a cultivated but powerful hush. Lisa and Tonyeesha were down front with Yara and some of the people from the *toque*.

Ted released her and she leapt away, but as she did, she caught a glimpse of a private box to the right of the balcony . . . and almost lost her step. In the box were Yolanda, Braxbury and the chair of the city council.

Chapter 27

But she didn't lose her balance. Trouble would begin tomorrow when she went to work. Chloe vowed to make whatever trouble tomorrow held for her worth it. She'd be ready for Braxbury with the entire city behind her. But she knew they wouldn't be behind her if she lost her footing tonight.

When the curtain fell, Chloe stood with the other dancers listening to thunderous applause. The curtain rose again for an encore and she saw the audience was on its feet—a standing ovation. Let tomorrow take care of itself. This was worth it. Was it the dancers or the cause they danced for that roused the audience? Chloe didn't know. Whichever it was, they loved it and demanded three encores.

***

Chloe was so tired when she fell into bed that night, but she didn't go to sleep—she fell asleep.

The temple of Xangô dissolved into a Sears and Roebuck department store. Above the entrance, a gigantic neon "For Sale" sign flashed among the stars. The stars bowed down to the neon sign. This made Olumide angry, so he swept the stars with Omolu's broom and they fell to the ground, where they became politicians who turned into pigs and flew away. A lady appeared. She had huge eyes, bigger than the neon sign, and a colorful skirt that filled the sky with a rainbow. Drawing into her lungs the four winds of the Earth, she blew on the sign and it fluttered away, taking the entire façade of the store with it and revealing the temple underneath. The pigs tried to prevent people from entering the temple, but the lady blew them away, too.

When Chloe awoke, she remembered none of this. She knew only that she had dreamed of something and now felt peace. With the dreadful meeting awaiting her in the morning, she couldn't imagine why she felt peace. She just did.

She entered her office and turned on her computer like everything was everything and this were just one of many workdays with many more to come. She knew better but decided to play along, if only to keep from going crazy with apprehension. Hadn't Braxbury heard her? But he didn't open his door, so Chloe figured he wanted her to sweat a little, but she'd be damned if she did. She'd just go about her work and cross him like a bridge—when she came to him.

The Energy Star logo faded away, replaced by the prompt for her password to open Windows. It didn't work. She checked the caps lock key and re-entered it. Again, she was denied access. So, he wanted to use a suspension bridge, did he? *Okay*. Be prepared for anything.

Then she heard laughter—familiar laughter. It wasn't the laughter of someone who was having a good time but of someone who saw the fruition of some dastardly plot.

"Oh, I can start today." It was Yolanda.

Chloe gasped. If Yolanda was in Braxbury's office, how had she been so quiet all this time? What was she doing here? Yolanda worked as a waitress. She never referred to herself as a waitress in the high-class establishment where she worked, but she was, nonetheless, a waitress. The restaurant would be open, and she should be there. What was she doing here? Was the bridge raising or lowering? It made no difference to Chloe. She just didn't want to get caught in the middle of it, where one side separated from the other and the fall was a long way down.

"Chloe, what are you doing here?" Braxbury asked when he opened the door. "Didn't you get my email?"

"Chloe," Yolanda beamed, extending her hand. "What a surprise and a pleasure to see you here."

"Well, I don't suppose introductions are necessary. Chloe, you know Yolanda. She's going to be my administrative assistant since you have to leave so suddenly."

"*I do?*" Chloe asked, ignoring Yolanda's hand.

"Well, of course. You've got that big project you're working on for the city. It would take up far too much of your time, and there'd be a conflict of interests, you know."

"Conflict of interest? Whose interest?"

"Mine, of course. Chloe, you're interfering with people who're much bigger than you are and have a lot more money. Take this as a warning—cease and desist."

"And if I don't?"

"Chloe, things don't have to get ugly. I'm just trying to give you an incentive to reconsider what you're doing. A theater won't help those people. The city council has decided to build a casino. That will bring in revenue. We'll use the money you raised to get the project started."

"The people won't be happy when learn you plan to take their money and build a casino instead of a theater."

"*When they learn . . .?* Listen Chloe, this isn't something you can fight against, so don't try."

"You've never been the voice of discouragement before."

Braxbury drew in a breath and sat on the edge of the desk. He examined Chloe's blank computer screen and looked at her. "I was a senator before you were born, and one thing I know about people, they have very short memories. They'll forget all about your ill-conceived theater once they see all the money a casino brings in. Everybody wins."

"Everybody except the people who lose their money gambling. No, Braxbury, I've considered what I'm doing and the whole city thinks I'm doing the right thing."

"Yes well, I hope someone in the city can give you a job. Funny, I always thought you were intelligent, Chloe. I guess even intelligent people need more than an incentive to see the consequences of their actions."

"What does that mean?"

"It means you're dismissed. I need someone who can give her full attention to serving me—someone like Yolanda here."

"Her full attention," Chloe repeated. She took note of his hand on the small of Yolanda's back and overstood his meaning.

"Yes, indeed. And she'll be dancing with her fingers—on the keyboard, of course."

"Of course," Chloe repeated.

Yolanda passed the hand that Chloe hadn't shaken over Chloe's desk. Chloe corrected herself—the desk she had been using while she worked here. It was no more hers than Pawny's kitchen.

"Is this real oak?" Yolanda cooed.

Braxbury preened on the balls of his feet. "Why, yes, Ms. Perry. And as soon as Chloe here vacates that chair, you'll notice that it's upholstered with genuine leather."

Malaise turned Chloe's stomach. So, she was Ms. Perry and Chloe was just Chloe. Why didn't he just call her Polly? Oh well, there was nothing to do but leave. So, depriving the two conspirators of any theatrics, she just left.

But leaving was more than a notion, because now she didn't have a job. What was she going to do? First thing to do was update her résumé.

"References available upon request." What kind of reference would Braxbury give her? She needed a job where references weren't an issue. That meant a job with someone who already knew her. She went to the student employment office at Cal State.

"There's an opening in the cafeteria," the employment specialist said after typing in a few words on her computer.

Chloe thought the woman must be daft. "No, I don't think so."

The specialist sighed with exasperation meant, Chloe supposed, to make her feel like a nuisance. "Well, I don't know what else to tell you. I've shown you nine positions, and you've turned them all down. Are you sure you want to work?"

"Yes, I'm very sure. What's in that other book?" Chloe pointed to a suspiciously exclusive e looking book tucked away on a shelf. "Specialty Positions?"

The specialist's eyes darted to that book as if she wondered why it was even in Chloe's line of vision. "Oh, those are just high-level jobs. I'm sure you wouldn't be interested in those. They're very demanding."

"Let's see them."

"If the low-level jobs are too much for you, Ms. Marshall, I'm sure the high-level jobs will prove overwhelming. Why don't you come back tomorrow? Maybe something suitable for you will open up."

"I'd really like to see the high-level jobs, Ms. Claris. It's not that the low-level jobs are too much for me. I'm just not interested in them."

Chloe didn't want to say any more. It was clear by the look on Ms. Claris' face that she thought Chloe was an arrogant Negro— as clear as if the woman had said the words out loud. But she hadn't said them out loud. She gave Chloe the book with the air of a woman who thought she was wasting her time.

Chloe perused the pages carefully and discovered that one of her professors was looking for a research assistant. She didn't want Ms. Claris to know which job she was interested in, so she just took a mental note of the information and kept flipping pages. She closed the book and pushed it aside.

"Didn't find anything suitable to your taste?" Ms. Claris said. She looked like she thought she'd been vindicated.

Good, Chloe mused. Let her keep thinking that. "I'll have to give it some consideration." Then she walked away.

***

Getting the job was a snap. Chloe had been a straight-A student in Dr. Dervin's class, and he was very personable.

"Ah, Ms. Marshall. One of my star students. What can I do for you?"

"Hello, Dr. Dervin. I understand you're looking for a research assistant."

"That's correct. I'll be writing a book, of sorts. A treatise, you might say. It'll have to do with the business opportunities of war."

Chloe appreciated Dervin's British accent. He spoke the King's English, which made him sound intelligent and made her want to put her best foot forward, as well. Was this a result of slavery—love the massa? Nonsense. Slave masters aspired not so much to make slaves love white people as to make them hate black people. She felt no self-hatred around Dervin. He didn't leave her feeling inadequate. If anything, he left her feeling up to any task. No vestige of slavery would do that.

"That sounds interesting," she said. "Are you thinking about the way World War II pulled us out of the Great Depression?"

"Precisely."

"Perhaps you could pinpoint what's missing in the current war that hasn't pulled us out of the current depression."

"I say, you could be on to something, Ms. Marshall. If you're trying to convince me that you're the right person for the job, you're on the right track. A research assistant must be able to think—to put two and two together and get forty-four. I have my ideas, of course, but any new ideas can only enhance them."

Yes. She was on the right track. Dervin introduced her to research databases she'd never heard of: CARL, ERIC and Melvyl. Taking the job would provide her with invaluable resources. Proxies between the Internet and the databases meant she could do most of her work at home. That was good, because the job also meant a hefty cut in her income.

From then on, she'd have to use public transportation. She drove home one more time. Taking the scenic route, she cruised up and down the hills of Eagle Rock as if for the last time.

At home, she parked her car in the apartment garage—something she'd never done before. It had always been more convenient to park on the street and run in real quick. But she didn't want to have to see the car everyday as she walked to the bus stop. It would be like running into an old friend to whom she wasn't speaking. So she stowed it in the garage where she wouldn't have to think about it.

To her surprise, Chloe felt herself cringe at the thought of having to catch the bus. What was wrong with that? Lisa caught the bus. Was Chloe now too good to catch the bus? She questioned her qualms. It would be a change, and why not let someone else do the driving for once?

Standing at the bus stop meant worrying about what Oya was doing to her hair. She wore it pressed and curled in a soft, pretty style. To her dismay, when she got to school and looked in the bathroom mirror, it had completely reverted to its natural state. Her hair was all over her head in no kind of style at all. No wonder people had been staring at her like she'd just arrived from another planet. The Orixa wasn't Chloe's preferred hairdresser. She picked it out into an afro and vowed to start wearing cornrows.

Let's see Oya blow them away. She'd have to blow Chloe's whole head away.

Chloe had to leave her apartment before dawn and return after sunset. As she walked across the courtyard, she somehow felt more comfortable in the morning than in the evening. True, the mornings were just as dark, but in the morning, she could comfort herself with thoughts of the coming sunrise. In the evenings, she had nothing to look forward to but deepening darkness.

What was she afraid of, she chided herself. She was a big girl, but she had read one vampire novel too many and as she crossed the courtyard or walked past an alley, every shadow brought those novels to life. One of the shadows coughed and Chloe felt relieved to hear such a human sound.

Being outside meant she finally had a reason to wear her fleece-lined bomber jacket, which had always been too hot and bulky for the car. It was perfect for walking the streets and made her feel big and dangerous. She stuck her hands in the pockets and put a look on her face that said, "If you mess with me, you won't mess with nobody else." Her legs wanted to tremble, but she commanded them to keep a steady yet relaxed pace. Meandering along like she wasn't paying attention to her surroundings would make someone decide she was an easy target. Yet, rushing would make her look like she was carrying a million dollars in her pocket. So she had to find the perfect medium.

After a few anxious days, Chloe got tired of putting herself through so many emotional changes over nothing. There was nothing there in the dark that wasn't there in the daytime. She used to tell her little sister Lisa the same thing when Chloe had to turn off the lights.

She was walking across an alley when a human-shaped shadow detached itself from someone's back fence. The human-shaped shadow never ceased to be a shadow as it approached her, but it was corporeal and it had hands and it was strong—too strong for Chloe to resist when it pulled her into the alley.

"Cooperate, bitch, and I won't hurt you. You might even have a little fun. I sure will, so why shouldn't you?"

Chloe remembered what she'd learned about self-defense, so she screamed, *"Fire!"*

He slapped her before she could scream again. "I told you to cooperate, bitch. Do I have to hurt you? I get no fun outta hurting people. I just wanna fuck. So make it easy on yourself. Gimme a little pussy and go on about your business. It's not that deep, honey."

His slap had left her reeling. His words left her wondering if she were crazy. Not that deep? How could this shadow make something so bizarre sound so reasonable? "*No! Fire! Fire!*" she screamed.

And he slapped her to the ground. Barely conscious, she felt his big, clumsy fingers struggle with the stiff metal button of her jeans. Some part of her mind that was still able to think hoped the ornery button would deter him—discourage him and make him go away before he . . . before he—"*No!*" she screamed again, but the words didn't leave her mouth. She couldn't speak. She could scream, but she couldn't speak.

Not that deep? It was the deepest part of her body, and he entered it like he had a right to be there. Her holy ground was his playground.

Why had she yelled fire? That's what the self-defense experts had told her would make people come to help her. No one came. Everyone could see that the fireman was already there. He'd turn the nozzle on his fire hose and release his foam inside her, but it wouldn't put out the fire. It might even start a fire. Please, Olodumare, no.

387

She wasn't a guest, witnessing the rape of Ayodele's body. She was in her own body, and she had control over it. No, she didn't. She felt this shadow thrashing away inside her and knew she didn't. Her whole body was Pawny's kitchen. She lived in it, worked in it, but it didn't belong to her.

***

"Mama, call the ambulance. There's a lady out here. Somebody hurt her. Call the ambulance."

The sun had risen and Chloe could hear the city making its way to work and school. She had trusted the morning more than the night—the coming light more than the coming dark, and now she didn't want to open her eyes to the mocking morning sun. She heard feet running and people yelling. She heard the ambulance and felt shadow hands lift her onto a gurney to take her somewhere. Where were they taking her? Why care about where they were taking a body that wasn't hers?

In a moment that Chloe knew wasn't a dream, she felt someone hold her hand. She looked up and it was Ted. Yara sat beside him. When they saw her lucid eyes, they smiled at her and Ted squeezed her hand.

"Chloe, can you understand me?" he asked.

Chloe nodded. She didn't speak. Every part of her hurt but especially her mind. She could barely remember, but something had been taken from her and these friends had come to help her recover it. She knew. She didn't know how she knew, or exactly what it was that she knew, but these friends would help her get back a sense of something that was hers.

A nurse entered. "Ms. Marshall's family is here to see her. I'm afraid five visitors may be too much for her. Could the two of you leave, at least while her family is here?"

Ted and Yara nodded. When they rose, Chloe heard Ted's bones crack as if they'd been sitting there a long time. When they stepped out of the room, Chloe heard Uncle Charlie's voice before he, Lisa and her mother entered.

"What are you doing here? I hope you ain't put a hex on my niece. You're the reason she's here, you heathen."

Lisa was practically dragging Uncle Charlie into the room. The violence in his eyes made Chloe suspect Lisa was pulling him away from a fight. The man was loud and totally oblivious to the fact that he was in a hospital.

"Please keep your voice down or I shall have to ask you to leave," the nurse said before she closed the door behind her.

Uncle Charlie fumed, "What does God have to do to you to make you see the light? If getting raped wasn't enough to make you leave those heathens alone, I don't know what to tell you."

Her mother shook her head at her. "You just got the Devil in you. You're my daughter, and I hate to say it, but it's the Lord's truth."

Chloe looked at them in disbelief. Of the three of them, Lisa was the only sane one. No, it's not possible to stay sane in an insane world. So Chloe had a devil in her, did she? Well at least her devil wasn't white. Her mother had no idea what was inside her own mind. She was no temple for Xangô or any wholesome being.

Then her mother screamed, "*No!*"

She grabbed Chloe's head and rocked it back and forth. "Devil, you take your filthy hands off my daughter. You can't have her. She belongs to Jesus and in Jesus' name, I rebuke you."

"Amen," said Uncle Charlie.

Chloe felt her mother's hands, the hands of a shadow, on her head. Even her head didn't belong to her. Belonged to Jesus? Belonged to the Devil? Belonged to her mother? But not to Chloe. Whatever Ted and Yara had tried to return to her was fading away again. She was fading. She was barely aware when Lisa opened the door to summon the nurse. It took five men to pull her mother off her.

"Unhand me, you who love darkness. Will you persecute the Lord's servants?"

The rest was lost on Chloe as she slipped into the eye of Oya.

Rhonda Denise Johnson

Chapter 28

Ayodele studied the old scars on the man
they called Jimboy. They were long welts,
the same as were on her arms and legs from
the times Keaton had whipped her. At night,
after they had all dragged themselves from
the tobacco field and seen to their children,
Ayodele heard whispers that these were the
scars of his love for her. The people
whispered low. The massa could never hear
of it, and she could hardly hear it herself. For
a long time, she didn't even know who the
"her" was they whispered about. She just
knew the man was in love with some young
thing. Gradually, it dawned on her that she
was "her."

His love for her? What room was
there for love in the life of a captive? She
was far from home—far from a community
of people with whom she shared blood and
heritage. Without that sharing, what purpose
could love serve? It would be like a solitary

leaf of tobacco, fluttering in the wind, cut off from its root and forgotten.

She watched him haul the sand lugs away. The sun played among the beads of sweat on his back. When he tapped sand off the leaves, she saw her brother Bamidele tapping the Egungun drums in their village. Jimboy looked sad as he worked. Ayodele understood his sadness. He wasn't sad because of the work, nor because of the burning sun. He was sad because when the sun went down, he'd have nothing to show for all his labor—nothing except those scars. Even the sweat dried and evaporated. Even the heat of his body cooled and was gone.

Chloe never would have thought— Ayodele and Jimboy. But if the man loved her, she could deny it all she wanted. This was a happy development to return to. Jimboy would be good to Ayodele. Chloe tried to be happy for her ancestor, but there was a shadow over Chloe's heart.

"You hold it like this and pinch the top off." Jimboy was showing Ayodele how to open the top of a tobacco plant so it would yield more.

She looked at him the same way Chloe looked at Ted. Because Chloe could sense Ayodele's thoughts and feelings, she recognized that look that could lift any shadow. But it was a brief look.

Ayodele turned her attention to the plant and took note of exactly what he told her to do. Suckering tobacco plants wasn't Chloe's idea of a romantic encounter, but how else could it happen for slaves on a tobacco plantation? He couldn't ask her the conventional questions like "So, what do you do for fun?" Chloe squealed inside, wondering how this worked out. It had to work out some kind of way, or she never would have been born.

Chloe gasped at this thought. Was Jimboy her ancestor, too? Oya hadn't said he was. She hadn't said any man was and there had to be a man in the mix somewhere. She began to look at Jimboy with new eyes.

Ayodele pinched and Jimboy came behind her, opening the plants one at a time. Whenever they stole a glance or a touch, the eight black overseers were looking another way.

Chloe didn't know anything about growing tobacco, but she recalled that they were harvesting it when she was here before. So this had to be a different year. Ayodele had been in the field for a while—long enough for Jimboy's wounds to heal and form a latticework across his back and shoulders. Ayodele had been unconscious when the overseer whipped him and she had never known that he took those lashes for her. It wasn't the kind of question that one slave asked another. "What you do this time to get all them welts?" But the other slaves knew. The path between the fields and the slave quarters was the only time they really had to gossip; and even though Jimboy's scars were old and healed, the story of how he got them remained new.

"I wish somebody loved me like that," Millie complained. She was young and dark. Almost as dark as Ayodele and just old enough to walk with the adults. But she walked like a discarded thing that no one could possibly love.

Jackie, always the devil's advocate, threw a glance Ayodele's way. "I hope they don't get sold off."

"Long as they stay useful, Massa won't sell 'em." Cotton always picked up his feet like he really believed being useful to Keaton would make him sell proof.

"What use is love?" Jackie sighed and shook her head.

They couldn't walk hand in hand. They couldn't really gaze into one another's eyes. Such liberties would only get the black overseers in trouble and make everybody suffer. So every moment was brief and stolen.

The little black children encouraged Ayodele. "Miss Polly, Miss Polly, there go Mr. Jimboy."

Only among themselves did they say Miss and Mr. As little as the children were, they knew not to use such titles around the massa or any white person. Still, although Ayodele hated the name Polly, she had decided to keep her true name secret rather than have people make fun of her precious anchor to life. The people in her village knew her true name. They'd remember it and sing of it and her spirit would return there. She didn't want to return here, so she kept her name to herself.

Ayodele remembered her village. She remembered how close everyone was and how they drew together in times of need. She didn't want to stay among the slaves, but did that mean she couldn't touch them? She had been there long enough to notice people. She knew their names and personalities. Before, she had only seen how different the slaves were from her own people, but she began to notice that each of them had a counterpart in her village. Ma Verl commanded the respect of all, and like Kiki, was everyone's healer and confidant. Bubba reminded her of

Omotunde, who was loved by all the women. Was it possible they got the name Bubba from the African name Baba and this lost son was really a father? While she was here, could she be part of the community?

But she couldn't see how there could be a real community without some kind of culture. The only culture was the rhythm with which they worked. Their feet were their hands, and the ground was the drum on which they played continuously. But Ayodele saw no time when they could pass on knowledge to the children. The children had common sense. They knew what to do and what not to do around the beast, but the elder slaves could give them no knowledge beyond that. The "free time" after meeting on Sundays was given to washing, mending and doing all the things they'd no time to do for themselves during the week.

As they walked from the Meeting Hall to their cabins, Ayodele decided that was the only time she'd have to pass something to the children as her village elders had passed knowledge on to her.

The children walked a few yards ahead of the adults, so Ayodele quickened her pace to catch up with them. She listened to what they were saying.

"You know, God look a lot like Massa," Jessie Mae was saying.

"No, Massa look like God. God don't look like nobody," Lil George countered.

"He must look like somebody for them to paint his picture. He looks like he could be Massa's grand pappy."

"That's silly. Don't nobody know what God looks like. Somebody just painted a picture to look like them and told folks it was God." That was Peewee, who, over the summer, had outgrown his name and kept to himself now that he was taller than the other children were.

Then the children noticed Ayodele walking with them and fell silent.

She chuckled that these children were much like the children in her own village. They spoke when spoken to around adults, but among themselves, they said things that they thought the adults knew nothing about. Their conversation gave her the perfect opening for what she wanted to say. "Did you know that in Africa the Creator doesn't look like that picture at all? His skin isn't pink. His hair isn't white."

"What do God look like in Africa?" Molly asked.

Ayodele didn't like using the beast's word for Olodumare. It was short and

irreverent. She couldn't imagine that
Olodumare liked being called God any more
than she liked when they shortened her name
to Polly.

She didn't like it, but this is what the
children understood. Until they understood
better, she'd use the words they knew. They
didn't know Olodumare, but if she used the
word "Creator," she could honor
Olodumare's creative power and they would
still understand her. "The Creator looks like
us."

"God looks like niggers?"

To whatever power kept Ayodele
from slapping this boy, she could only be
grateful. But she was more saddened than
angered. "Don't ever call yourself that. It's
an ugly word. If you wash the dust from your
face, you will find that you are beautiful. You
look like my brother Bamidele."

"I do? I look like somebody in
Africa?"

"Of course, you look like the people
you come from. You don't look like that pink
picture and neither does the Creator."

"You have pictures of God in
Africa?"

Ayodele winced at this question.
What a revolting idea—a picture of
Olodumare. "No, but the Creator paints his

own picture in the sky, on the land and in the water. Everything that we see is a vision of his power. The same moon that shines here, shines in Africa. Our Creator is that powerful."

"If your African god is so powerful, why you a slave?" Buckeye asked, jutting out his chin.

The other children gasped at this insolent boy. They moved away from him. They were always moving away from Buckeye who unleashed on them all the anger he felt towards Keaton but couldn't express.

Ayodele had kept this one question at bay ever since she'd been stolen from her village. *Why?* She had no answer for such a question. The question would consume her mind if she let it. So she had buried it. "I don't know. I only know that a pink Creator somebody painted on a picture isn't helping us either."

The insolence left Buckeye's face for a moment. Ayodele felt a small triumph because she knew he had never heard any adult admit to not knowing something. Any other adult would have boxed his ears for asking a question to which they had no answer.

The other children shot questioning looks at one another. They'd always been told that the big pink Massa would always help them. They'd just heard the parson say he would. The other slaves said he would. Yet, here was this adult saying he wouldn't, and on some level, they knew that she was right. The god who looked like the massa would always help the massa.

"Polly, what are you doing up there with them chillun?" It was Pawny.

"Aw you know, she be thinking about Jimboy and probably want some chillun of her own."

"She going get herself whipped fooling with them chillun." Pawny snapped. "They belong to Massa. And what she got to say to them anyway?"

What indeed? Ayodele mused. But why would she be whipped for talking to the children? *The* children? Whose children were they? Unlike the children in her village, they were slaves. Like the adults, they belonged to the beast. Ayodele wondered how any woman could go through the pain of childbearing and then just hand the child over to the beast.

She knew now why she had not felt any community among the slaves. There could be no community without children—

without shared and inherited knowledge. In Africa, the elders taught the young. Here in this place, their only purpose was to work for the master, so when they became too old to work, they lost their purpose. She'd watched from a safe distance as lion cubs played around their watchful mother lioness. Even dumb animals had some kind of community, while these slaves had nothing.

As she thought about these things, the parson came up to her. "Polly, I've noticed you and Jimboy are um . . . well, you seem to be . . . um . . . what I'm trying to say is, I hope there's no sin going on between you."

Sin? Ayodele frowned at the word. She knew what the parson was trying to say and filed it away with the other idiotic things he said. *Sin.* As if they had time. As if they had a private place. "No, sir."

"If you ask your master, I can marry you."

"Marry?"

"Well, it won't be as grand as white folks' weddings, but every union has to have the sanctity of the Lord."

Ayodele marveled at how different the parson was from Keaton. The parson all but apologized simply for existing. Still, he wasn't doing anything to set her free. In fact, his words were only designed to make her accept what Keaton did. "Union? Sanctity?"

"When a man and a woman come together . . . you know. God has to approve, and to get God's approval, you have to be married."

Not for the first time, Ayodele thought this beast must be out of his mind, but the other slaves were nodding their approval.

"Yes, Polly. Oh we knew it was bound to happen."

"Oh, if I could see one marriage before I die."

Jimboy was listening to all this, too. He cocked an eyebrow at all of them. "I've never heard of slaves getting married. That's for white folks."

"That's why y'all got to do it. For once do something proper," Jackie insisted.

Then, as if by one silent thought, they all began to herd Ayodele and Jimboy toward the big, white house where Keaton lived.

"But that's Keaton's house," Ayodele protested.

"What did you call your master, slave?" the parson demanded.

The other slaves choreographed a flurry of business between Ayodele and the parson. They'd given up long ago trying to get Polly to say "Massa." She just wouldn't do it. In his presence, she avoided calling him anything. They held their breaths, hoping the parson wouldn't insist that she answer. But Ayodele let herself get caught up in the flurry and the parson didn't assert his authority. So the procession marched on.

At the foot of the garden, they stopped and shooed Ayodele and Jimboy toward the back door.

"Go on. We'll wait here. It's just you two now," said Ma Verl.

Jimboy took Ayodele's hand and they walked around the garden, past the brick kitchen, to the back of the house. They found Keaton in his study reading. He looked up when they entered, saw it was just them, and returned to his book.

"Have you taken a wrong turn? Looks like you niggers would know where the dust mops are by now."

"We didn't come for dust mops," Jimboy said.

Jimboy's statement was plain enough, but plain speech coming from a slave sounded bold, and this was certainly out of the ordinary. Keaton's head jerked up as if he expected an insurrection. "What did you come for, Jimboy?" He put an emphasis on "boy."

"We want to get married."

"Do you, now?" He eyed them like the parent of naughty children who were too young to know they were being naughty and just looked cute. "Is there so little work for slaves on a tobacco plantation that you now have time for frivolities like marriage?"

"The parson said we got to get married to make it right with the Lord," Jimboy said calmly, but Ayodele could feel his hand tremble—or was that her own hand trembling? Perhaps they were both feeling that this wasn't going well.

"To make what right?" Keaton smiled as if a stroke of genius had entered his mind. "All you need is a dime to get in the Sugar Shack to make it all right with me, Jimboy. Now, to make it right with the Lord, you might need two dimes."

"Sir?"

"Since you're so idle, you'll both work in the Sugar Shack for two months. You'll get a dime a month. When you have two dimes, you can get married. It's time you slaves learned about money."

"Me, work in the Sugar Shack?" Jimboy gasped.

"Why not? Polly here worked in the Sugar Shack. Think you're too precious, huh? If it's good enough for Polly, it's good enough for you. Isn't that right, Polly?"

Ayodele's mouth was stunned shut.

"I said, isn't that right, Polly? I should not have to ask you twice. If I have to ask again, I'll knock your teeth out. Answer me."

"Yes."

"Yes, what?"

"Yes, that's right."

Keaton took two strides and knocked Ayodele across the floor. One of her teeth did come out.

"You're going to be as toothless as this nigger if you don't call me Massa."

"Massa, please," Jimboy begged.

"Massa, please what? Two months in the Sugar Shack and you can have your wife. I know some fellas who would take to a buck like you—fresh and young."

"But sir, they're men and I'm a . . ."

"You're a what? You're a coward. You don't love Polly. If you loved her, you'd do anything for her—*anything*."

"Not that, Massa. Please not that." Jimboy stared straight ahead in apoplectic despair.

Keaton picked Ayodele up off the floor with mock gentleness. "I love you, Polly. I'll do anything for you. I won't even make you call me Massa, right now. Why you want to marry this no-count nigger? There's limits to his love. There's things he won't do for you."

"No," Ayodele moaned, too dazed by his blow and disgusted to fully comprehend him. She'd known he was a beast, but she had not known anyone could be so vile. If Keaton had not been holding her up, she might have sunk to the floor.

"I'm being nice giving you a dime to do this. I'm your master and I can send you out there right now."

Jimboy's eyes bugged and he fell to his knees. "Please, Massa. Please, Massa. Please, Massa."

"Get up, you coward, and act like a man. Oh, but I forgot, you're a nigger and niggers can never be men. I'm the only man around here. If you want to prove your love for Polly and get married, report to the Sugar Shack at moonrise tonight."

Ayodele slumped to the floor when Keaton released her and returned to his book. Seeing that his audience with his master was over, Jimboy helped Ayodele to her feet and out the door. When they got outside, the slaves looked at them expectantly, but the two could meet none of their eyes. Ayodele followed Jimboy to the cabin where he slept.

They fell silently to the dirt floor and wept. The parson knocked on the door and entered.

"Well, what did he say?"

"He said no," Jimboy answered.

Ayodele knew neither she nor Jimboy could ever tell anyone the shameful things the beast had told them to do if they wanted to get married.

"Are you going to continue your . . . um . . . courtship?"

Jimboy took Ayodele's hand and dared to look the parson straight in the eyes. "Yes."

"You know the Lord won't bless a sinful union."

There were things Ayodele wanted to tell the parson about his Lord—things that would probably get her and Jimboy worse than whipped. So she said nothing and neither did Jimboy. She contemplated how he must have felt. Jimboy was always silent in the Meeting Hall. While the other slaves jumped and hollered, he just sat there. She had never heard the name Jesus pass from his lips. She suspected that he felt the same way she did about the Olodumare of the beasts and knew she wanted to be with him always.

They couldn't get married. There was just no way they'd meet Keaton's demands, but maybe they could still be together. They said good night to the parson and for the first time in her life, Ayodele slept in the arms of a man she loved.

"So, you think you can find happiness as a slave?" Iyabo whispered in Ayodele's ear.

"I am not a slave. I am a captive."

The baby laughed. "A captive thinks of escape from captivity. Looks like you're thinking of settling down. You are no longer a captive. You are a slave."

This troubled Ayodele. Had she indeed become a slave? True, she now thought more of surviving than escaping. Hers wasn't the survival Pawny had chosen. She couldn't think of anything on this plantation as her own and she harbored no fantasies that Keaton would ever love her if she was good enough. To claim anything here as her own would tie her to this place. Pawny would never think of escaping to some place where someone else claimed the kitchen. Still, Ayodele hadn't planned an escape in she didn't know how long.

Chloe had wanted to be happy about Ayodele's union with Jimboy. Together, the couple had banished the pain she'd felt when her own body was ravished and they had introduced her to the joy that sex could bring when people loved one another. True, Chloe didn't love Jimboy the way Ayodele did, but she'd shared vicariously in her ancestor's joy.

It wasn't to last. Joy in slavery? It couldn't last. Late one night, as Ayodele and Jimboy lay together, Keaton entered their cabin. "Get up, Jimboy."

Jimboy didn't hear his master. He was so into Ayodele, he had not even noticed the man's entrance. Keaton grabbed Jimboy by his neck and yanked him to his feet. "I said, get up, nigger. Can't you hear?"

Keaton leered at Jimboy's erect phallus and sneered. "I guess not. Stand aside and keep your eyes on me. I'll show you how a real man makes love to a nigger bitch."

Jimboy watched in horror as Keaton doffed his pants and plunged into Ayodele. Jimboy turned away, unable to watch any longer.

"No, don't turn away," Keaton laughed as he pounded against Ayodele. "I told you to watch me. You might learn something from a real man, boy."

If it had been Keaton's plan to humiliate Jimboy, the plan failed. Ayodele saw the rage in Jimboy's eyes. Part of her wanted him to be a man and kill this white monster, but part of her knew they'd both die if he did, and she didn't want to die. She'd never see the promise Baba Abioye had given her if she were dead. What could that promise possibly be that it was worth enduring this horrid beast? Sweat poured off his body into her eyes. He smelled like swine and his bloated body only added to the effect. She struggled inside herself, not knowing if she wanted to live or die.

Chapter 29

"Oh Polly, you got two babies in there!" Ma Verl squealed. "You gone have twins."

It felt to Ayodele like the whole world was trying to come out of her womb. What had the parson said about fitting a camel through the eye of a needle? Well, this needle was about to break. Sweat poured down the sides of her face into her ears—blood and sweat and plenty of tears. She hadn't cried like this since she was a little thing in Africa. But the tears came now, mixing with the sweat so she couldn't tell which was which. So much pain. Did everyone who came into the world put some poor woman through all this?

She looked around. There was the parson and the same bent-over doctor that came when the horses foaled. She had suffered too many humiliations in this place. Why fall apart now over a horse doctor? She knew who she was, even if they didn't. Still, it hurt inside—deeper inside than the pain of the birthing. She didn't want this beast to touch her or her baby, but as always, she had no choice. She heard the first baby crying in Pawny's arms, waiting for its brother or sister to come out.

Her eyes rolled around toward the other side of the room and there she saw Keaton. What was he doing here? He had attended the birthing of his prize horses. So was she a prize horse?

She gave one final heaving push and the second baby slipped out. The miraculous thing about childbearing was that with all the pain of getting the baby out, once it passed through, the pain vanished. She felt wonderful, tired, but elated. She looked around, hoping that at least Ma Verl would share her joy, but the faces around her were ashen. Keaton coughed softly. Ma Verl muttered a prayer. The parson crossed himself. The doctor closed his eyes. And Pawny turned away. Ayodele followed Keaton's gaze to the baby in Ma Verl's arms. It was white and the baby Pawny held was black.

They laid the babies on her breast and she stared at the white baby like it was something out of a nightmare. Nothing white had ever been kind to her. The thought that she had given birth to this thing appalled her. The thought that her black baby had shared her womb with a white baby and had probably been abused by it, horrified her. Keaton's eyes were fixated on the white baby—not with love, but with possession. It was his. That was why he was here. How had he known? He had suspected, Ayodele decided, and he had wanted to see.

Ayodele moaned. No, she wouldn't love this baby. She wouldn't feed the offspring of the beast with the milk of her breast. Though it had shared her womb, it wouldn't share her heart with the child of Jimboy. She vowed to make one last act of defiance, if it was the last thing she did and she knew it might be. As sure as Olodumare gave her breath to draw, she'd kill the baby of the beast.

Jimboy stood quietly in the corner. His skin was so like the wood in the shadow of the corner that she could barely see him. But Ayodele saw him and they shared a look of woe. Would he help her? Would he hate her? Would he die with her?

She closed her eyes and saw Iyabo.

"My mother gave me a name. You know my name is Iyabo. That is why I am here, because I have a name. Do not give the baby of the beast a name and it will not come to me."

At last, Ayodele thought. Ekundayo's baby had given her advice that she could use. What would happen to Baba Abioye's promise once she was dead? She didn't care. What could she care about now that she had given birth to a beast? What was worth having that would banish the shame that had passed through her body?

Chloe was alarmed at this. Now that Ayodele had a child, she could die and Chloe would still be born. She didn't want Ayodele to die. Would Oya make Chloe share that experience, too? What could she possibly learn from it? Or would Oya take Chloe out so she'd spend the rest of her life wondering what had happened? What could she learn from that? She wished she could close her eyes like Ayodele and just block out all this horror. But she was pure spirit, and right now that meant pure hell.

Everyone left Ayodele alone with Jimboy and her babies. She put Keaton's baby face down in a corner while she cuddled and nursed Jimboy's baby.

"You have two babies, Polly," Jimboy reminded her. "Ain't you gone feed the other one?"

"Why you worried about it?"

"I mean, I know it ain't mine, but it's yours, and it's just a baby."

"It's just a beast. It belongs to the beast. You know whose baby that is. So again, why do you care?"

"I know the baby is yours." He picked the baby up off the floor. It wasn't completely white. It had some color—just a faint glow, but enough for anybody to tell it wasn't white. Its hair was slightly curled and its little nose turned up like Ayodele's did. "This is your baby, Polly. Feed it."

She shoved the baby away when he thrust it at her. He tried again, and she shoved it away with her fingernails in its chest.

Jimboy pulled away. "Woman, I didn't know you was full of so much hate."

"For nine months, I didn't know I was full of the white beast's baby. If I had known . . ."

"If you had known, what would you have done? You act like you the only one hurt. This hurts me, too. You think I don't feel pain?"

She looked at him, hardly believing he'd try this. "Pain? No, you don't know nothing about it. All you've ever had to do is watch. I was the one raped. I was the one who bore this horrid creature in my body and

416

suffered while it crawled out of me. What do you know about pain?"

Jimboy stood up straight and stared at her as if she had gone too far. She defied the very thought, but then he doffed his shirt and showed her his bare back. She stared at the risen white keloids there and fell silent. She knew they were there because he had taken a whipping meant for her. With this one tacit act, he had humbled her, but he had not quelled her rage or made her love Keaton's baby.

She didn't understand why he felt no rage himself. She didn't understand why he wasn't screaming for blood. Had years of slavery quenched the fire of retribution that any man would feel when his woman had been violated?

***

She turned into a lioness. She'd be the backbone for both of them. She found six thunderstones near a tree that had been struck by lightning and lined them up in a corner with four candles she purloined from the kitchen.

"Woman, what are you doing?" Jimboy asked. "You gone burn the place down."

She struck a wooden match on the wall and lit the candles. "Xangô will help us deal with our enemies if we aren't strong enough."

She wouldn't blame Jimboy for his timidity nor even for wanting to protect the baby of the beast. He was a slave, yes, but he was her man and they'd move forward together, even if she had to drag him. They'd die fighting this madness.

As they worked in the field, they placed the babies on the grass under a tree. Keaton rode by and frowned at the babies.

"What are their names?" he asked Ayodele.

"We'll name them on the eighth day." She didn't expect Keaton's baby to last that long. It would die without a name. Jimboy would have one baby to present to Olodumare—one beautiful, black African baby to whom he'd first whisper the name that anchored its *Asé* among the living and the Egun.

"Why is my son in the grass like some nigger?"

"Your son?"

"Don't act like you didn't know, nigger. You just held the cargo. He's half a nigger, but he's half mine, which means he's all mine. He don't belong in the grass. Take him in the kitchen and leave him with Pawny."

"If that's what you want." She let go of the leaf she was about to sucker and went to pick up the baby. She held it away from her body and looked at it with utter distaste.

"Why does he look so sickly?" Keaton demanded.

"Weak, I reckon."

"He looks like he's dying. He looks like he ain't been fed."

"Some babies just not meant to live. I'll take it in the kitchen."

"*It?* He's a *he*. That black devil baby over there is an *it*. But, nigger, my son better live or I'm going to know why."

She didn't stay to take note of his quivering jowls or to tremble under his disgusted glare. Instead, she turned and headed for the kitchen.

"What you done to this chile?" asked Pawny.

"I ain't done nothing to it. Not a thing in the world. You're supposed to keep it while I'm in the field."

"Who said?"

Ayodele didn't take this bait. Of all the slaves on the plantation, Pawny was the only one who still tried to get her to say

"Massa." Instead, she said, "Just keep it. I wouldn't be here if I hadn't been sent."

"Sent by who?"

"Just keep it. Do whatever you want. I have to get back to the field." And she left before Pawny could say anything more.

A wicked wind blew through the tobacco leaves, rustling Ayodele's skirt and worrying Jimboy's hat. They worked on until suddenly a scream erupted from the kitchen and Pawny came running.

"Oh Massa! Massa! Polly, I'm so sorry. That baby done died."

"Say what!" Keaton bellowed.

Pawny fell to her knees before Keaton. "He just up and died, Massa. He was crying and wasn't no tears coming out his eyes. He look like he didn't have a drop of water in his little body."

Keaton glared at Ayodele, who suddenly found the tobacco leaves more interesting than what Pawny was saying. "I told you . . . nigger bitch! I told you!" Then he stormed over to Jimboy's baby, picked it up and bashed its head against the tree. The baby didn't even cry. The part of its brain that registered pain was smeared on the bark of the tree. An innocent tree that had provided shade in the summer and wood in the winter, now displayed the blood of a baby not one week old—a baby that had no name.

"*No!*" Ayodele screamed. "You beast!" She snatched her baby from Keaton with the strength of an enraged mother and ran to the cabin she shared with Jimboy. There, she fell to the dirt floor holding the baby in her arms. It was bleeding. She ripped strips from her dress and wrapped the baby's head. Then she held it tightly to her breast and rocked back and forth as if rocking it to sleep.

"This is my baby," she moaned to herself.

"He has no name," Iyabo reminded her. "How can anyone remember a baby that has no name? With what shall I call his spirit to be with me?"

Ayodele bared her breast and placed it in the baby's mouth to suckle once again. "Mother's milk is life. Mother's milk is Asé. Your name is mother's milk, and with it I call you. Why didn't he kill me?"

This is how Jimboy found his woman when he came in that night. For the second time he queried her, "Woman, what are you doing?"

"Can't you see, I'm feeding our baby?"

Jimboy closed his eyes. He knelt down on the floor and put an arm around Ayodele. "The baby is dead, Polly. We have to bury it. You need to sleep."

"*No!*" Ayodele jumped up and pushed Jimboy away from her. Still holding the baby to her breast, she rushed out of the cabin.

"I must die. I will die. My baby has no name and I must die."

"Go to the sea. That's where my mother lies."

"You were right. There's only one escape. If I do not want to be a slave, I must die."

From far in the distance, she heard Jimboy call her name—her slave name. "Polly! Polly!" But her mother hadn't given her that name. She had loved Jimboy but had never trusted him enough to tell him her true name. He was of this life—the slave's life—and she'd soon leave.

She ran on until she felt her feet leave the ground. A wind wrapped around her. The wind was made of spirits, and the spirits had arms strong enough to bear her up into the night sky. She was in the eye of Oya headed for the sea.

Iyabo squealed with delight. Ayodele braced herself for the unknown. She closed her eyes and prayed to Oya.

>"Orisha of the wind,
>Take me on the journey
>From which no flesh returns.
>On your gentle breeze,
>Set me down in Orun Rere."

That's where she thought she was going, but when she opened her eyes, she found herself at a crossroads. In the center sat a man and beside him sat a woman. She knew the man immediately. He wore a hat that was black on one side and red on the other. Around his neck, he wore a leather thong with three kola nuts. She fell to her knees at the feet of Eshu, owner of the crossroads.

"Eshu, which road leads to death?"

He pointed to the road running east and west. "That one."

She rose to her feet and headed for that road.

"Are you sure that's the road you want to take?"

Iyabo stepped forward, hands on her hips. "Of course. That's the only road to freedom. It's where my mother lies. It's where I am. And we are free. So take that road, Ayodele—unless you want to go back and be Polly all your miserable life."

"Silence, Ajogan!" Eshu barked. He rose to his feet, looming over them like the night itself. "I am the protector of this traveler. She will choose her path and you'll keep silent."

Iyabo trembled under the Orisha's baleful glare, but she needn't have worried, Ayodele was already headed for the road that ran east and west.

"I choose death."

"*No!*" screamed the woman who sat beside Eshu.

Ayodele turned and stared at the woman. There was something strange about her. She was black like Ayodele and bore a striking resemblance to her own mother, but something about her was unlike anything Ayodele had ever seen in this world. "Who is that woman?"

"She can see me? She can hear me?" the woman gasped. "But how can that be? She is in the past. Oya told me you can't change the past."

"She isn't in the past," Eshu told her. "She is in the eye of Oya and she sees you at the crossroads of time, even as you have seen her. The past isn't being changed. Her present is being created by her vision of you."

"Then you will stop her from killing herself."

The Orisha shook his head. "I cannot. It is her choice to make."

"But if she kills herself, I won't be born. You've got to stop her."

"I gave her a choice. The choice is hers to make, but the key is yours to turn."

"The key?" Chloe remembered Oyeku Meji, the Odu of death. She'd never known—the death of what?

"You have the key. You see the lock. If you want to live then you must turn the key." He turned to Ayodele. "This is Chloe. If you live, she will be your descendant. If you die . . . well, you always wanted to be an ancestor. What do you choose?"

Ayodele had not stopped walking. She was now halfway down the road running east and west, looking this way and that. "I want to be free. This road leads to freedom."

"Indeed, it does." Eshu agreed. "But it isn't the only road that leads to freedom."

"It's the road Ekundayo chose."

"She chose death, not only for herself but also for her unborn child. You can choose death. I won't stop you. I can't stop you. But what about Chloe? What about the generations of whom you are the mother?"

"I am no mother. My babies are dead."

"I'm not dead, Ayodele," Chloe pleaded. "I'm alive and I have dreams and goals."

"I had dreams and goals," Ayodele murmured. "My dreams and goals didn't matter when the beast decided he wanted to use me. And your dreams and goals don't matter either. There's nothing for Africans in the white beasts' world but endless slavery."

"Ayodele, I'm not of your world. I'm your descendant. I live in a world where black people are free."

"You live in a world with no white people?"

"Oh yes, whites are still here, but I'm not a slave. I work and get paid. I can go where I want and I don't have to call anybody Massa."

Ayodele felt confused. Nothing in her experience of the white world offered her any hope. And how could there be a future when there was no hope? This woman who claimed to be from her future sounded impossible.

"Free?"

"Yes, when I see you, I am looking at the past. I know that in a few decades there will be a great war and slaves will be set free.

You might even live to see it, if you choose to live."

Iyabo piped up, "But if you want to be an ancestor you can be one right now. Why wait?"

Ayodele walked to the center of the crossroads. She looked at Iyabo and saw the happiness on Ekundayo's face as she plunged from the ship into the womb of the sea. That was indeed a womb—a death, but also a birth.

She looked at Chloe and saw her own mother and she remembered her mother's words: "Not everyone gets to be an ancestor. You must live this life before you worry about the afterlife."

She drew in a deep breath, took one step forward and walked north.

Chapter 30

When Chloe opened her eyes, Ted and Yara weren't wearing the same clothes they'd had on before. When she looked at the clock on the wall, it was three hours later than it had been, but when she looked at the date on the big screen TV, she saw that one whole week had passed. "Hello," she said in a clear voice.

Yara jumped. Ted cocked an eyebrow. "For someone who's been out cold for a week, you woke up bright and cheerful."

"I've been out cold?"

"Yes," Yara said. "The doctors couldn't understand it. They said you weren't in a coma. You just wouldn't wake up. But we're glad you did. How do you feel?"

"Thirsty and hungry."

Ted laughed. "I'll call the nurse and tell her you're with us."

He left and Yara came close. "Chloe, where did you go? I saw the *awo* of Oya around you. Where did you go? What did you see?"

"I went to Virginia and I saw Exu. He's gorgeous."

"He is divine. You blaspheme him with such mundane ideas."

"Divine, yes. But he's been my protector all along. I don't think he'll mind if I say he's gorgeous. That's nothing but the truth."

"Well, Exu is important, but what about Xangô?"

"Xangô?" Chloe's mind raced back to that name. So much had happened.

"You still have the geas he laid upon you to build his temple."

A geas. Yes, an obligation. She had no choice. The future of Ayodele was set. Chloe's ancestor would live. And Chloe?

"This is why I'm here, Yara. I'm not on Earth to push papers around and answer phones for someone else. I'm here to build."

She'd build the theater that her community so badly needed. And that would be Xangô's temple.

Ted came in with the nurse.

"Ms. Marshall! I'm glad you're awake, but you need to take it easy," the nurse cautioned her. "You were asleep for a long time."

"I feel fine."

The nurse looked at the monitor. "Yes, well, your vital signs are looking good. The doctor will have to look at you. If all is well, we'll probably keep you for observation overnight and you can go home tomorrow."

She adjusted Chloe's pillows to accommodate her sitting position and left.

Then Chloe remembered. "My mother. What happened to my mother?"

Ted and Yara exchanged glances.

"She . . ." Yara started to speak.

"They kinda put her in jail," Ted stammered.

"Kinda in jail." Chloe let out a slow sigh. "So my mother has been in jail for a week. What about Uncle Charlie?"

Yara sighed. "Unfortunately, he lost his temper with the police, so they put him in there, too. The twelve people who were with them when they attacked my *terreiro* tried to raise money for their bail, but the Church refused to get involved."

"And Lisa?"

Here Yara brightened. "She comes to my house after school."

"The *terreiro*," Chloe sighed. She closed her eyes and fell back on her pillows. "Please don't tell me anymore. Not today. Wait 'til tomorrow."

"Don't you want to hear the good news?" Ted asked.

"I could use some, but I'm tired."

"Okay, we'll leave, but listen to this." Yara beamed. "You know all those people who signed the petition and came to the benefit? Well, when they heard about Braxbury and the city council's plot to take their money and build a casino, they all came together to have the council replaced."

Chloe's eyes popped open and she sat up." Oh, beautiful people."

Despite her fatigue, Chloe giggled.

"It's going to take time, of course," Yara continued. "The state attorney general and everybody have to approve of this. It could take a long time, but it's rolling."

"On that note, we'll leave you to your rest," Ted said.

He kissed Chloe's lips, and he and Yara left.

Chloe sat back on her pillows, exhausted but exhilarated. It would take time, but it would happen. And to think, the whole community was supporting this. This would be their theater. Now the kids would have somewhere to go. She looked back on the time when all anyone had expected from her was that she'd get a good job working for someone else. She was glad she'd never settled for that road. She was glad Oya and Exu had shown her the struggles her ancestors had suffered just so she could have a life to live that was more than just some nine-to-five shift.

The doctor soon came in and looked at her in wonderment. "Ms. Marshall, I must say, I've never seen a case like yours. I don't believe in miracles, but this is certainly inexplicable."

"Oh, I'm sure there's an explanation, doctor."

"Of course. Well, I see no reason to keep you here. You can go home in the morning."

He left and Chloe went back to sleep.

Ted came for her in the morning. As they walked to his car, he asked her how she felt.

"I feel good enough to dance."

"Then dance, baby."

She cut a few steps and jumped into his car with a laugh and a sigh. "There's nothing we can't do. And to think, this all started with dancing."

He started the engine and the radio came on. P-Funk was singing: "Here's my chance to dance my way out of my constrictions . . ."

Ted stared at Chloe, eyes wide, lower jaw in his lap. "How did you do that?"

"*Do?* I did nothing. That was just a coincidence." Then she laughed and sang, "One nation and we're on the move. Nothing can stop us now. *"*

64918334R00242

Made in the USA
Lexington, KY
25 June 2017